INVISIBLE

BOOK 3: ALEX NOZIAK FATE

MARY
USA TODAY BESTSELLING AUTHOR
BUCKHAM

INVISIBLE FATE
Copyright © 2014, Mary Arsenault Buckham
First Edition
ISBN 978-1-939210-08-1
All rights reserved.

Please Note

Cover and book design by
THE KILLION GROUP
www.thekilliongroupinc.com

DEDICATION

This book is dedicated to those readers who kept faith with me as deadlines whizzed past. While writers may live in our heads, we also live in the real world and, in spite of best intentions and for a variety of reasons, a novel can be delayed. Hearing from readers who were looking forward to this next book in the series made it possible to create it. Thank you, each and every one of you. You rock!

ACKNOWLEDGEMENTS

It takes a village to create a book and this book is no exception. A huge note of appreciation to my amazing Street Team, Mary B's ninjas, who, by being great Beta readers, helped so much in making sure the story held together. A special thanks to DA for copyediting, you are my Grammar and Comma Goddess. Also, a huge hug to Dianna Love for her support and lovely cover quote. And, of course, thank you to my husband who keeps me sane—which is a full time job—but is also willing to discuss vamps, Weres and shifters even in a public venue! Any mistakes or adjustments in detail for the purpose of fiction are entirely my own doing.

CHAPTER 1

Bran guided Jeb Noziak down a dank, murky tunnel, deep beneath the streets of Paris, trusting the shaman shifter to follow, listening for the older man's breathing, which was barely there. Jeb's son Van lay inert across Jeb's right shoulder, easy weight for Jeb's shifter self, but anyone carrying the full weight of an unconscious wolf, even in human form was going to tire.

"Far to go?" Jeb asked, his words echoing through the damp darkness.

"No." Bran kept his response short on purpose. He had his own troubles to deal with, like the blood continuing to seep from the gunshot wound on his shoulder. Unlike Jeb or Van, he didn't have a shifter's ability to recover quickly from physical wounds. And then there was Alex. Always Alex. He allowed one sharp, bitter smile and kept moving forward.

No saying what Van's mental condition would be when he woke up having been drugged and wounded in the recent fight that left several Weres dead. Bran, as well as Van in his shifter form, owned responsibility for some of those deaths. Plus Van had wounded his own sister. Was Alex dead, too?

If she wasn't, he'd be tempted to wring her neck.

How did one mule-headed witch create so much havoc in his life? Better question, how was he going to minimize the damage already done because of her rash actions and his inability to think, much less act rationally around her? He'd learned that lesson watching the destructive relationship between his parents and vowed not to follow their poisonous patterns. Only a fool let a woman drag him deeper into impossible situations and no one had called Bran a fool since he was six. Now was not the time to start.

One challenge at a time. Contain Van in a place he'd be safe until they could counter whatever drug had been pumped through his system. See to both their wounds sustained when trying to stop Van. Then discover what had happened to Alex.

It always came back to that one damnable witch.

Running his own multi-national company, which was still reeling from the recent death of its CEO, Bran's cousin, and the publicity damage associated with that death, should be occupying all his focus. But, no, there was Alex. Her and the cock-up she'd dragged them all into.

He flexed his fingers. Clench. Unclench. *Keep moving forward.*

He had learned the hard way how to approach multiple crises.

Triage. The only course of action when the alternative was to run howling at the moon in rage, even if he didn't have a drop of shifter or Were blood in his veins. Right this minute there wasn't a bloody thing he could do about the past or the immediate present. The future? Oh, yes, he planned to take care of the future. His way. The way of a warrior-trained mage and not one being led on a merry goose chase by one Alex Noziak.

He was so focused on his dark thoughts that he stumbled on the uneven rocks as he marched deeper into the stygian darkness. Somewhere, obscured in the bowels of stone and earth a roar sounded and receded. The ebb and flow of the Paris subway system snaking through parallel tunnels. The vibration echoing the clash within Bran.

He wasn't even considering the underlying issue that brought him to this, skulking around like a thief. He'd been under direct orders from the Council of Seven to report to them, several hours ago. Instead, he'd ended up in an Alex-created free for all that left a dozen preternaturals dead. Not just dead but killed in view of the entire Council.

The Council was the preternatural governing body tasked with not only maintaining order among the multiple preternatural groups inhabiting the world, but keeping those beings a secret from the humans. Seven representatives of the most populous non-humans—fae, shifters, vampires, witches, demons, shamans and druids—who were the the magic users—with each representative elected for a lifetime position, attempting the impossible with draconian control. The Council held ultimate power among the law-abiding preternaturals, and spent ninety percent of their time keeping a tight lid on the not-so law abiding ones.

They also tended to solve their issues with an all-or-nothing approach. It was easier to kill a suspected preternatural accused of exposing their world to the humans than to worry about the chance the accused might be innocent. They took the concept of ask forgiveness, not permission to the extreme. And they skipped the whole ask for forgiveness part.

Right now, Bran was the accused. Identified as being involved with supplying his cousin, and others, with a designer drug that manipulated preternaturals. The ramifications of such a drug were deadly for everyone involved, human and non-human. Create a raging Were, influence assassin vampires, give a bitter fae a suggestion that hunting humans for food was no longer frowned upon, and the murky line between the current hidden preternatural world and rampaging chaos amongst the humans could be all too easily breached.

So what did Alex do? Stage her rumble in the very public area of Versailles. No hiding dead bodies there. Dead non-human bodies.

What a cock-up.

Too bad the Were, who was Bran's best link at proving his innocence, had been killed in the same skirmish that wounded Bran and left Alex's fate unknown.

It was also too bad that Jeb, Alex's father, was following Bran, and was also the shaman representative on the Council of Seven. Talk about fraternizing with the enemy.

Earlier in the week, the Council's leader, Philippe Cheverill, had been murdered. Rumors were that Bran was the killer. Or Alex did the deed because of Bran. So now Bran had been labeled as both drug dealer and murderer in the preternatural community.

And to think he'd had a handle on his life. Being around Alex created this kind of insanity.

So why did the thought of her truly being dead gut him?

Focus. Plan a course of action to clear his name. Take the next step forward.

Jeb must have been thinking along the same lines as he paused and demanded, "Where exactly are we?"

"Abandoned line of the Paris metro system."

"You come here often?" Jeb's voice held that same sharp wryness Bran associated with Alex. No gray areas for the Noziak family. Why wasn't he surprised?

"Only when I need to go to ground," he growled, then added, "Literally."

"Fair enough," Jeb mumbled, letting Bran know he wasn't hiding how close his own temper was riding to the surface. But then this man had raised Alex and four shifter sons; being testy must be a way of life by now.

"We're here." Bran's voice reverberated from the arched ceiling of the tunnel, followed by a squeal of a metal door he wrenched open, one looking so rusted only an idiot would try moving it. "Duck your head as we step through the opening and watch out for the high threshold."

Too late, as Jeb kicked against the concrete barrier. "Thanks," he snarled, sounding more like his usual self-controlled shifter self.

Nice to know Bran wasn't the only one tether-tensed.

Inside the room, the stench of crumbling concrete, mold, and dried blood gagged him. It was his usual reaction to this space and he didn't have half the sensitivity of a shifter's sense of smell.

Bran paused, waiting for Jeb to move deeper inside as Bran reached to torch a wall sconce, handier than a kerosene lantern, though there was one of those too, on a rickety table near several metal cots. Once the light flared to life, the room looked bigger than expected. Big enough to be a dormitory more than a room. Or the cell it was often used as.

Bran could tell to the second when the older Noziak noticed the sets of chains hanging from the concrete and rock walls. Jeb paused, his body bracing. "What is this place?"

Bran glanced around, aware of exhaustion clawing at him and the kick-start of pain along his shoulder, which he'd been able to ignore as long as he'd been moving. "A Were safe house."

Since it was a group of Weres that Van had attacked, being in their territory didn't necessarily bode well for the three of them.

As if Bran's words triggered a threat, Jeb stepped farther away, planting his feet wide as if preparing for battle.

Bran nodded toward the door. "The Weres haven't used this site for some time, but the door can be barred against them. If needed, it can slow them down."

It took a moment for Jeb to digest that while Bran might not be his friend, he wasn't yet the enemy. The key word being 'yet'. Jeb gave a chin nod toward the closest wall. "You planning the chains for Van?"

"We both just saw first-hand what the drug they pumped into your son can do to a preternatural. It isn't pretty." Bran's jaw tightened, his gaze looking to the distance, thinking of his cousin Dominique and what the drug had done to her the last time he'd seen her. Not only the drug, but the lure of power the drug represented. The preternatural who could control other preternaturals would be invincible.

With an abrupt shudder, he pulled himself off that ledge. Dominique wasn't coming back. That was the past. Now he had enough challenges to deal with, one at a time. His gaze re-zeroed in on Jeb. "The restraints might be the only thing holding Van back from hurting you, or himself."

"Fair enough." Jeb eased Van from his shoulder to the nearest bed, before straightening to face Bran. "I'll be straight. You helped my son so I'll help you."

Bran nodded. It wasn't a handshake, a let's work together response, but a statement of fact. The shifter shaman owed him and neither were about to forget it.

But Jeb wasn't finished. Not by a long shot. He was just warming up. "I'll assist, but only so far. I'm still a Council member and owe loyalty to their decisions."

"Even if they're wrong?" Bran barked out the words. Mistake. Not smart to show raw emotions to another preternatural, especially to someone on the Council.

Jeb seemed to tense, his words razor-sharp. "I'll repeat, but only once. I'm a Council member, which means I'm duty bound to make sure you appear before the board."

Bran gave a quick, hard nod. "Understood."

"I don't think you do." The older man's words sounded suddenly weary.

"I know that I have to prove my innocence to the Council, which won't be easy." Understatement. Only an idiot created a public display of rebellion before approaching a governing body. For that alone, the Council could have him killed.

Jeb said nothing. Not that Bran expected less. The man had allowed his only daughter to be sent to prison when the choice was between proving her guiltless of murder or revealing the existence of preternaturals to humans. The older Noziak might be a father but he was a Council member, through and through. Best to remember that.

Bran deepened his voice. "I'm not your daughter expecting her father's help."

Jeb flinched as if struck.

Bran pushed on. "I have one goal. To prove myself to the Council." One goal that he'd reveal to this man.

Jeb raised his chin for Bran to continue.

"Someone is setting me ..." he glanced at Van. "... and your son up to take the fall for the drug that's being tested on preternaturals." It'd also been used against humans but that wasn't the Council's business.

"That's a big claim." Jeb's tone indicated a far-fetched one too. "What basis do you have to back such an accusation?"

"The individual responsible was the Were bison killed this morning."

"If that's true, the proof you might have had died with him."

Bran clenched, then slowly eased his jaw. One step at a time. Didn't have to be a full step, just a step forward. Anger wouldn't help the process. "That Were might be dead, but someone's above him on the food chain."

"And you know who this *someone* is?"

"Not yet."

The twist of his expression told Bran loud and clear what Jeb thought about Bran's chances. No proof, no case. "You'll have to take that up with the Council. "

"You *are* the Council."

Jeb shook his head. "Only one member." A granite hard glance shot Bran's way "You're not a fool. You've been accused of both manufacturing and distributing this synthetic drug."

"The same drug injected into your son. You do know that."

Jeb nodded. "I'd guessed as much, which doesn't make it any easier for me to trust you." He paused, as though choosing his words carefully.

Bran straightened, both retreating into himself, and bracing for more. "Then I'd best find the only other witness to prove that I'm innocent."

"Other?"

"Your son is one. If he remembers who shot him full of the poison."

From Jeb's shuttered expression, the older man clearly wasn't going to hold his breath on that chance. "Who's the other?"

"Alex."

Like a double kick to the solar plexus, Jeb recoiled. They'd both seen Alex attacked, bloodied, and die. Bran watched Alex's father swallow hard before speaking. "And if she's dead?"

"She'd better not be." Bran pivoted on his heel and headed toward the door.

"I can't let you leave." Jeb's voice held steel, honed by experience and saber sharp.

Bran halted, keeping his back to the shifter shaman; arrogance countering arrogance. His voice held just as much edge and banked heat as Jeb's. "You're her father. I don't want to hurt you."

"I'll repeat." It was clear Jeb wasn't about to let him walk through that door. "If Alex is dead, then—"

Bran whirled, all mage in the movement. He didn't answer Jeb's unstated question, instead spoke, his words rolling with power.

"Power of darkness and of light, I call upon you.
Make me a barrier between those here be.
Between dark and light.
Between good and evil.
Protect me as I am willing to pay the cost.

To the light, better things.
To death, watch over.
To struggle and emerge, advance as I follow.

Going on forever, light shines in the darkness.
Dispel those who seek to harm your one.
Circle round and protect. Let it be!"

Before Jeb could counter the mage-magic, it was upon him. Wrapping him until the only thing he could move was his eyelids and it didn't matter a tinker's damn how hard Jeb blinked them.

"Don't worry." The bite eased a bit from Bran's voice now that he'd gotten his way. Catching Jeb by surprise had worked, but only this once, the man's eyes promised that. "The spell will release as soon as I'm far enough away. There's food, water, and medical supplies in the cabinet over there."

Jeb didn't even glance in the direction Bran pointed. The older man's focus all on Bran, promising retribution.

He'd have to stand in line.

It wasn't likely Van could help, so finding Alex was Bran's only option. And a damn slim one at that.

"I'll return with more supplies." Bran rubbed his hand along his chin before heading back to the door. "You'd be doing the same thing in my place."

Since Jeb couldn't speak, there was no more to say. There'd be a reckoning with the shifter shaman. And soon.

But first, Bran had to find Alex.

CHAPTER 2

I didn't know where I was. Didn't care really. Only thing that mattered was holding absolutely, perfectly still. That way, the pain didn't crush me. Had someone sliced off my neck? Was that why it hurt so bad?

I was Alex Noziak, at least I was pretty sure I was. If it'd null the pain to be anyone else, I'd switch places in a heartbeat.

I could have sworn I was standing on tiptoes in the middle of a croc-infested swamp, and any movement, even as small as a breath, meant more unbearable pain: screaming, sweat-producing, please-Great-Spirits-let-me-just-die kind of pain. I had no idea what had caused it. I just wanted it to go away.

Beyond my closed eyes, a bright light blazed. Cool, recycled air kissed my skin, kicking up goose bumps, but not enough to shiver. That'd kick-start the hurt. And everything was about stopping that damn pain. A pungent scent wafted past. Sort of sour and antiseptic at the same time. The infirmary at the IR compound?

Nah, this space felt larger.

A morgue?

Could be. But if so, shouldn't I be dead?

Wouldn't that be my luck. Dead for all eternity and trapped at the same time.

Voices murmured in the background. Low, bee-humming sounds that just were. I ignored them. Ignored everything except holding back the pain.

I must have blacked out, again, because the next thing I knew, the voices had come closer, beside me.

Nothing as vulnerable as being a woman, lying flat on your back with male voices arguing near by. But even that wasn't going to make me peel open my eyes, especially when I heard a low, gravelly voice with a French accent.

"It'd be better to kill her. Now."

What?

"Killing her will be the safest for us. The most merciful."

Screw you, Frenchie.

"So she's not dead?" Another guy speaking. Younger. With an Irish lilt.

"Close."

Close only matters in horseshoes and hand grenades, French fry! I might feel like dying but there's a world of difference between the wanting and someone else pulling the plug.

"Then you must keep her alive." Colin Farrell. That's who the voice sounded like. *You go, Colin!* Death sounded like an option, relief from the burning pain, but that'd be my choice. Not some stranger's.

"Doctor. Your assignment is to keep her alive. Is that clear?"

A pause.

Listen to Colin, Doctor Frenchie. He knows best.

"I have no idea what will happen if I do," Frenchie said, his voice very low.

What was going on?

"She's a very powerful witch."

Someone else kept telling me that. Who was it? An image swam before me. Tall, dark and very, very deadly. Enemy? Yeah, that felt right. Almost.

"Save her, Doctor, or you die."

Way to go, Colin! Take that, Frenchie.

"And if she turns into an aberration?"

Me? Not going to happen. I already was one. Trust me, part witch, part shaman, all screw up.

"I need her alive and fully functioning. Make that happen."

"We have the other—"

Other what? Or who?

"I don't want to hear about the other. This is the one I've chosen."

Why didn't that make me want to cheer again? Who wouldn't want to be chosen? And by Colin Farrell, or at least a Colin Farrell voice. But there was something off. I couldn't grasp it. The pain was building again, a solid wall of fire growing hotter and hotter.

"I shall try," murmured the Frenchman.

"Don't try. Do."

"Is there no other way?" Frenchie asked.

"She's the one who will let Zaradian through. We must use her."

Who was Zaradian? And use me to do what? If my head wasn't already exploding, this conversation was igniting it!

The Colin voice was walking away. Good. *I think.* But I didn't want to stay with the French doctor. I wanted to think about the other one. The one who had called me a powerful witch. Dark blue eyes. Even behind closed lids, I remembered them. Sexy. Seductive.

Glaring at me.

"I'll check in the morning." Colin voice. "Keep her alive."

Some voice within me whispered. *Your choice, Alex. Live or die, it's your choice.*

Another tidal wave of pain spiked through me, and all I could think about was how much easier it'd be to let go. Release the human shell. Something told me that there was more than physical pain to face if I didn't.

Suddenly, I understood Scarlett O'Hara. As a child, I'd never liked her, maybe because she fell for such a lightweight guy and then screwed over everyone to get him. Puhleeze! But now I understood her. Her line, the one about tomorrow. *I'll think about where I am and how to get away from here tomorrow.*

If I was still alive.

CHAPTER 3

By the time Bran reached the warehouse he'd left less than twenty-four hours earlier with Alex, Francois and Willie, dusk muted the weathered brick facade, softening the lines of the industrial area, pulling the deep browns from the sluggish tributary of the River Seine that flowed nearby. No one was about as he pulled his vehicle near the door, but he took no chances. The warehouse turned residence worked as a safe house when he needed a space to hide out without any direct ties to him. Before Alex came along, he'd used it as a release from business pressures. Leave it to her to shatter even his sanctuary.

Though it'd been his choice to join forces with her, and much as he'd like to stay angry, it was mostly anger at himself. He was the one who'd messed things up, not protecting her, not as he'd promised.

He paused by his car and cast a quick cloaking spell before entering the building. *Mon Dieu,* it seemed like a lifetime ago since he'd left.

A noise coming from the kitchen caused him to pause. "Francois?"

"*Non, c'est moi.*" Willie, a recovering Were and friend of Francois's, popped his head from around the corner. Switching into flawless English, the Were continued, "I didn't know if we'd see you again. If you had survived."

Then he nodded toward Bran's bloodstained shoulder, his pupils contracting as his body stilled.

A Were's instinctive reaction to blood. The less control he held over his animal self, the easier to revert to basic drives.

Blood meant meat and meat meant food reaction. It said a lot that Willie was able to check himself, and he pulled back, shaking his head.

"Where's Francois?" Bran asked, keeping a reasonable amount of distance between himself and Willie, who was more Francois's friend than his. Plus, no matter that Willie had founded his own recovering Were Foundation; too much stress, hunger or emotion could easily snap any Were. Which explained why there was only one member of We're Not, the foundation's tongue in cheek name. That member being Willie.

"I expect him back any moment. He went out for more steak."

Feeding a Were and a Didi shifter, which is what Francois was, took a lot of protein, especially after the battle they'd all been in that morning.

As if Bran's thoughts hit Willie, the Were paused, scarfing down the last of the prosciutto in the fridge, and lowered his eyes. "I'm sorry about Alex. Getting, you know … you know. Killed."

"She's not dead," Bran snapped, moving to a bar stool closer to the Were but still on the other side of a concrete eating island, a barrier that could only slow, not stop, a determined Were.

Willie's eyes widened. "But I thought—"

"You thought wrong."

"Our aristocratic friend is a romantic," another voice chimed in as Francois pushed the front door open.

Bran had known Francois, easier to remember him by his undercover name than to blow his identity as an MI-6 agent, since the two of them had met at Oxford and discovered they each had secrets to hide. Francois had looked much the same then, slender, urbane, debonair, as he was getting the stuffing beat out of him by a couple of town bullies who didn't like Oxford toffs. Little did they know, that if Francois had let his Didi shifter self go, there'd have been a lot more blood and gore, and it wouldn't have been Francois's. Bran had stepped in, just before that moment, using a little warlock slight of hand to teach the thugs a lesson. The beastie blokes didn't know what'd hit them. Francois did, and a lifelong friendship was born.

Now, Francois stood just inside the doorway, one brow arched, eyeing Bran with the practiced eye of an undercover agent who'd seen too much. "You look like shite."

"Exactly how I feel," came Bran's mumbled response. He was wiped out but refused to give into the exhaustion, or the pain, riding him.

"Alex?" Francois asked as he quietly closed the door behind him.

Bran eyed him. "I was hoping you had news. You see anything after I left?"

Francois shook his head, adding a quick, "Doesn't mean she didn't walk away, just that I didn't see her."

Bran knew what his friend was doing. Giving hope. But Bran wanted more than hope. He wanted certainty and there was only one way to get it. "I'm heading back to Versailles. See if I can find some answers."

"That a smart idea?" Francois kept his voice neutral, his expression blank, as he slid a wrapped meat package towards Willie. "Isn't the Council a little too interested in you to be showing your face around there?"

Bran's barked laugh didn't fool anyone. "Interested? Nice word for looking for a scapegoat to blame their mess on."

"That's my point." Francois angled his chin toward the Were already unwrapping the meat. "Let Willie go check the place out. See if he can follow a scent trail."

Willie nodded, but Bran wasn't sure if it was because he'd just exposed the bloody, raw steak or was agreeing.

"I appreciate the help but don't want the Council to make either of you a target. This is my mess to clean up."

His and Alex's, but that was neither here nor there until he discovered what had happened to her.

He thrust one hand through his hair before he spoke again. "I think I might have a day, maybe two, before the Council comes down on me like the proverbial wrecking ball."

"I didn't know they started an enforcement arm," Willie mumbled around his first bite of raw meat, blood trickling down his chin.

"Not enforcement as much as elimination," Bran explained.

At Willie's confused look, Francois continued, "Guilty until proven innocent. The Council employs the best fae assassins."

"They'd seriously kill you?" Willie sounded as disgruntled as a Were denied food.

"In a heartbeat." Francois nodded, before turning and spearing Bran with a piercing look. "Which is why it's even more imperative that Willie heads to Versailles. Not you."

"My fight," Bran protested, hearing the weariness in his own voice as he stood, then grabbed the kitchen divider to steady himself.

"You're a right mess." Francois stepped forward, his distress revealed in his upper crust British accent. He grabbed Bran's arm and steered him to the couch.

Bran appreciated the gesture, though nurturing wasn't Francois's forte. More calm, collected and cutthroat. Sitting down helped still the dizziness washing over him. He cleared his throat before he trusted his voice. "I plan to use a cloaking spell as much as possible."

"Which takes an enormous amount of energy," Francois shot back. Willie nodding his head in the background.

Truth be told, the shoulder was bleeding again. Bran might be able to accelerate the healing process with a spell, but Francois was right. He couldn't be using two spells for opposite means. Even he wasn't that good.

"Fine." He glanced at Willie. "I'd appreciate your taking a quick run out and look around."

Willie gave a one-finger salute before jamming the last of the steak in his mouth.

Francois's shoulders eased a bit as he tucked his hands in the pockets of his tailored slacks. "I'd go myself, though Willie is a better tracker ..."

"I hear a *but*?" Bran braced himself.

"Home office called me. Some big hush-hush crisis is coming down."

"Aren't they all?" Bran leaned back against the cushions, using the movement to hide his disappointment. He'd counted on having Francois's help for at least a day or two longer.

"Sorry, mate. If there was any way—"

Bran raised his hand as he closed his eyes. "Appreciate what you've already done."

"First moment I can, I'll return."

"Thanks," Bran mouthed the word, even as he knew the MI-6 agent would be too late. What was coming down between Bran and the Council was going to happen soon. Fast and furious.

Better to say their goodbyes now. Plan for the worst. Hope for the best. Even if there was little hope.

As if following his dark train of thoughts, Francois offered, "If you can find Alex, she can back up your story."

"*Oui.*" Bran knew he was tired when he reverted to his childhood tongue. Finding Alex alive was a long shot. As long a shot as expecting her brother Van to remember enough about his captivity to convince the Council that Bran had nothing to do with drugging and using him.

A right old cock-up, as his da would have said.

"I'm heading out then," Francois's voice came from far off.

Bran cracked open one eye and raised a hand. "Thanks, mate. For everything."

It was a final farewell and they both knew it.

CHAPTER 4

"This agency is finished," M.T. Stone snarled, surprised he managed to get the words past the rage clawing through him. Ops that went FUBAR were one thing. Ops that were suicide missions were another. "I'm not sending out any more recruits until they're prepared."

The IR, for Invisible Recruit, Agency Director, Ling Mai, calmly set down her Mont Blanc pen and turned from the paper she'd been notating. She looked at home in this Parisian hotel, the *Hotel Le Meurice*. Elegant, cool, remote. The room's shades of blues and white complimented her Anglo-Asian features, highlighted the blue-black tones of her hair swept back from her face, the fineness of her bones. She could have been about his age, mid-thirties, or a very young fifty. Hell, when she was in her seventies she'd probably look the same way. If he didn't know better, he'd have guessed he was the only one controlling deep emotions. With Ling Mai, you had to look closely to see she battled her own demons, metaphorically, not physically.

"Define prepared, Mister Stone." Her voice sounded as calm as a lake. One teeming with ghost sharks and giant squid just beneath the surface.

He paced across the room. Large by hotel standards, with an obstacle course of satin-striped couches, velvet chairs, and coffee tables as well as a white grand piano. His hands curled, wanting to toss all the crap through the nearest window. To destroy something, anything. One team member dead. One near enough. Wasn't going to happen again.

His back to the director, he stilled his voice until he matched Ling Mai's, word for word. "Sending humans against preternaturals is a recipe for disaster. The fact these women are barely trained as agents compounds the problem."

"A challenge, Mister Stone, not a problem."

It was tempting to release a crude snort. He wasn't here to play semantics games. He was here to save his remaining team members. Turning to face the director, he made sure to keep the length of the room between them. "We've already lost one. Two are on the injured list." He didn't have to spell out Mandy and Vaughn's names. Ling Mai knew he'd just returned from the *Hôpital Pitié Salpêtrière*, where Vaughn was receiving the best care possible. Not that it was enough. He added, "And that's not counting what occurred to Alex."

"I too am mourning Miss Noziak's unfortunate death," Ling Mai murmured.

There were undertones beneath her words but Stone couldn't pin them down. Alex and Ling Mai had butted heads more than once, but the death, or technically the disappearance and presumed death of their only op with proven preternatural abilities, was a tactical disaster. Without her skills, they'd have to rethink their whole approach to fighting preternaturals.

Ling Mai's voice broke through to him. "I have taken several steps that will address your concerns."

She'd surprised him. Ling Mai wasn't a dense woman. Far from it, she could be cold, calculating, and ruthless. Every move she made was layered with strategic awareness. What Stone hadn't expected, though, was her easy acquiesce to the problem at hand. Finding, training and equipping more recruits would take time and money, a lot of both. Up until now, Ling Mai'd had the agency operating on a short-term mentality. Preternaturals threatening to expose their existence to humans had forced her, and through her, the Invisible Recruit Agency, into several immediate crises. A jump-first, learn how to swim later approach.

So why the sudden about face?

"What steps are you taking?" he asked, knowing he sounded wary. Screw it, he was wary.

"I'm bringing on board an additional recruit whose skills should compliment the team."

He crossed his arms. "Meaning?"

"You'll see when you meet her." Ling Mai's brow arched, as effective a communication as shouting is-that-enough?

"A start." Maybe. "A recruit strong enough to go up against the strongest preternaturals is the minimum I'd expect." Having at least one agent capable of fighting preternaturals was a step. But only a small step.

Ling Mai offered a sharp smile that would have had most people stepping back. Stone wasn't most people. "It'll be your responsibility to see that she can."

He nodded, but held his thoughts. The new woman might know how to fight, but in any animal kingdom there were stronger animals and lesser animals. Give him someone with some fighting skills or preternatural talents, a fae, one of the lesser demons, even a Nondi pixie, and he could work with her.

"What about equipment for the existing team members? You send David up against Goliath enough times and Goliath *will* win."

Ling Mai turned in her chair and punched a button on her cell phone. The knock on the hotel room door came immediately, as if someone had waited in the hall for the summons.

Stone crossed to open the door, but only after acknowledging Ling Mai's nod. Only years of compartmentalizing his emotions kept his face straight as he swung the door wide to a gangly young man who had barely hit puberty. The kid stood almost eye-to-eye with Stone, but a weak breeze could topple him. He had that whole nerd air about him, dandelion blond hair, a large Adam's apple, hunched shoulders that might someday fill out, and limbs that looked barely attached. Human? Or something else?

"Come in, Hercules," Ling Mai called, waving the newcomer forward.

Hercules? The kid had been damned from the start with that kind of moniker.

The boy-man edged closer to the door jam, squeezing himself past as if Stone had bared his teeth. On second thought, a well-developed sense of self-preservation was probably the only thing the kid had going for him.

Stone gave him a what's-up chin nod, having no idea what Ling Mai had hidden up her well-tailored sleeve. But if this was going to be the team's deep, dark secret, they were all in a worse level of hurt than he'd imagined.

"Miss Mai," the kid stammered, scuttling across the floor, putting as much distance as possible between him and the biggest predator in the room—Stone.

First mistake. Stone was a badass and was okay with that. But Ling Mai played in a league of her own, way above Stone's pay grade.

"Mr. Stone—" Ling Mai did the introductions.

"Stone?" A shit-eating grin bloomed on the kid's scrawny face. "As in Stoner?"

"No, kid, not like that. More like rock hard and not budging." Stone's expression wiped that look off the nerd's face in less than a second.

Ling Mai continued, "This is Hercules. He's—"

"Herc," the kid stammered, his gaze ping-ponging between the director and Stone. "Everybody calls me Herc. It's easier."

Was this kid for real?

Ling Mai canted her head as if being interrupted by a snot-nosed kid was an every day occurrence.

"As you wish, Herc." Ling Mai sounded like she was at the Queen of England's court, and Stone found his first glimmer of a smile since … well, since Vaughn had been hurt and Alex killed. Ling Mai continued in her formal, prissy tones. "Herc has been tasked with creating tools to help the team against preternaturals."

Stone snorted. "He makes gadgets?"

"Technically, no." Herc focused on Ling Mai. "According to design critic Reyner Banham, a gadget is a small self-contained unit of high performance in relation to its size and cost, whose function is to transform some undifferentiated set of circumstances to a condition nearer human desires. Whereas what I develop are offensive and defensive tools designed to increase the life expectancy of a weaker being against a stronger being." He ducked his head before adding, "I specialize in human-preternatural interactions."

Stone unclasped his arms. "Fine, kid, whatever. You make shit that kills the bad guys." As if this punk would know a preternatural if he tripped over one. This was the best Ling Mai could find?

"Well, technically—"

"Forget it, kid." Stone wiggled one finger between himself and Ling Mai. "The grownups have to talk. Why don't you disappear for a moment." It wasn't phrased as a question.

The kid's eyes tightened before he looked to Ling Mai. At her slight nod, he didn't cross to the door he'd come in, but turned on his heel and headed to the spare bedroom. Stone didn't know who or what this kid was, or if he could hear through walls, but it didn't matter. Protecting his team was Stone's responsibility and trusting that to a wet-behind-the-ears punk was not in the plans.

As soon as the door closed, Stone marched to where Ling Mai sat, her back straight, her expression closed. She raised one hand to halt him. "Before you make a wrong judgment, you should know he's half fae."

Didn't care. Fae were not known as fighters. Slick, sneaky bastards, yes, but not warriors. It took a soldier, with experience, to know how to stop another soldier.

Before he could spit out his objections, Ling Mai stopped him. "Give him this opportunity."

He looked at her, then at the door, snatching a second to get the frustration growling through him under control. Hot heads didn't win arguments and he meant to win this one.

"You willing to stake another team member's life on that ... that kid?"

Ling Mai nodded. "I am."

Stone stepped closer, lowering his voice, aware that anyone who knew him for more than a day, understood that the quieter he spoke, the angrier he was. "I'm not. "

"Without knowing anything about him except his age?"

"Creating a defensive weapon for someone to stop a charging Were or blood thirsty vamp was not something handed to anyone who had never faced either." Before Ling

Mai could interrupt, he continued, hammering home his point.
"That's the real world out there." He jammed a finger toward
the windows. "Not the latest role-playing fantasy game."

"What would it take for you to give him a chance?" Ling
Mai's voice was controlled. Not that he expected less. She was
a Jedi master of control. Didn't make her right though. Not in
this situation.

"Pit him against a pissed off Were or shifter," Stone
countered. She wouldn't. He was counting on the fact Ling Mai
wouldn't kill a kid. It was more suicidal than what she'd done
to the team so far, and even the director had to have a line she
wouldn't cross. "Put his life where his mouth is and then we'll
talk."

Ling Mai shrugged. "So be it. You set up the Were or shifter
and we'll see how Hercu ... how Herc's weapons work."

CHAPTER 5

Forty minutes later, Stone was still shaking his head and grinding his teeth. No way did he want to hurt the kid. Even if Ling Mai's protégé was swaggering like his namesake, Hercules.

Ling Mai had rounded up the remaining members of the IR team; those out of the hospital, which meant Jaylene; Mandy, still cradling her recently broken arm; and Kelly, looking like a loud *boo* would cause her to turn invisible and wink out. The director had also found the team a private gym called the *Centre de Danse du Maris* on *rue* Temple Street. It looked like it was used more for dance but the space was all theirs, which meant no exposure to the general public for the two shifters Stone had recruited to prove Hercules didn't have a clue how to counter fighting preternaturals.

"Go easy on him, guys," Stone murmured to Jacques, a deathstalker scorpion who Stone had met on a mission in the Empty Quarter of northeastern Yemen. The fact neither had expected to survive, gave Jacques the reason to reveal to Stone what he was when he needed to shift to heal from some nasty shrapnel embedded in his back. When Stone didn't bat an eye, their friendship was sealed. Jacques then saved Stone's life by getting the both of them the hell out of Dodge, and Stone had repaid the favor in a dark alley in Singapore a year later.

The kid probably expected a four-legged, furry creature so let him get a taste of the real nasties out there. Lisa, to Stone's left, was a shifter rhinoceros, and she looked like it even in her human form—tall, square-shaped, and all muscle. In her rhino form, she had terrible eyesight, but was wickedly fast and big enough to take out most obstacles facing her. Especially a quaking, clueless kid.

Lisa was the wife of another of Stone's ex-Special Ops buddies. Stone never had discovered what her husband was, except brave enough to take a woman on who could drink half the squad under the table, and bench press the other half afterwards. In fact, Lisa would have been a great IR asset, except her husband would never go along with the idea.

Stone hoped Hercules knew how to jump high and fast because if Lisa shifted, the contest would be over in seconds flat. Plus, Ling Mai might owe the dance studio/gym a hefty sum for repairs to their space.

He raised his arms to get everyone's attention. "Team, move to the viewing area. Now." Last thing he wanted was more injuries to his remaining squad. He nodded at Ling Mai who hadn't moved an inch. "Director, that includes you."

"I prefer to remain on the floor," she murmured.

This was the challenge working with women. They weren't always logical. Now there'd be two civilians on the floor and in harm's way.

It was her skin. But that also meant he'd be standing nearby, in order to keep the kid, and now the director, both safe. It was going to be harder having a divided focus but he'd dealt with worse.

The plan was for Jacques and Lisa to use their strength and agility to teach the boy a few lessons. They were to remain in their human forms, but even in those shapes they were warriors who possessed extraordinary strength. But Stone had learned a lot about plans in the military and the first lesson was if a plan could go wrong, it would.

If Herc pissed them off, or hurt them, not that it was likely, there was no telling what they would do. Shifters, once they morphed into their animal forms, became those animals. Only the most powerful, or well trained, could be restrained at that point, and Stone wasn't about to let anyone die because of a stupid test. Especially a kid.

"Hercules, is there—"

"Herc," the kid interrupted, tossing a hank of his fuzzy, yellow hair out of his eyes. The grin splitting his face was a telltale sign he had no idea what he was about to come up against.

Amateurs. Stone hated dealing with amateurs and now it seemed like he was surrounded by them.

"All right, kid, it's your neck. If Jacques or Lisa shifts, there's no stopping them. Is that clear?"

"C-crystal." At least the boy had enough sense to choke on the one word reply.

"Which means you high-tail it out of here," Stone added, not wanting any should-have-told-him scenarios.

"I got it." Herc shrugged and it took everything Stone had not to walk over and shake some sense into the boy.

Stone glanced at Ling Mai so she knew exactly who he was speaking to. "If at any time you want to call halt to this f … fiasco…say the word and we'll stop." If possible. Shifters, once riled, were not an easy bunch to calm down.

She gave him a slight nod. He hadn't expected more.

He turned his attention back to the kid. "You know what you're supposed to do?"

Herc, or whatever he wanted to be called, gave a solemn nod. "I'm here to prove I have created a weapon to stop them."

"I'd settle for slowing them down," Stone clarified. "No heroics."

"This ain't going to kill us, is it?" Jacques whispered out of the side of his mouth.

"I wouldn't worry about it." Stone shook his head, already braced to pick up the pieces after this FUBAR spun out. "On the count of three then."

He moved to stand near Ling Mai. Always a good idea to save the head of operations. "One."

Jacques and Lisa shook out their shoulders, widened their stances, and lowered their heads.

"Two."

Herc flapped his hands before him as if preparing for a typing test or shooing off buzzing bees.

Bloody amateur.

"Three."

As if choreographed, Jacques and Lisa split, flanking Herc from across the room. The kid blinked, hard, then bounced on the balls of his feet, his tennis shoes squeaking on the hardwood floor.

"If he dies, it's on your head," Stone reminded Ling Mai as both of them stepped back.

"He won't."

Lisa edged closer to the wall, creating more floor space between her and the boy, snagging his attention as Jacques stealthily and quietly moved closer on his side of the room. Classic misdirect.

Stone didn't realize he'd been holding his breath until one of the team in the upstairs viewing area, out of danger but still very much part of the exercise, coughed loudly. A little too loudly as the kid jumped.

But at least it broke his concentration enough to catch Jacques creeping up on his left flank.

Stone frowned and shot a quick glance toward the peanut gallery, before focusing on Lisa, who, step by step, edged closer.

Do something, kid. Anything.

But Hercules just stood there, a plucked pigeon waiting to be someone's dinner.

That's when Stone realized what the kid was planning to do. Wait until the shifters actually shifted into their animal selves to prove himself.

Idiot. Taking them out in their human forms was enough of a challenge. If he waited for them to shift, he was signing his own death warrant.

Stone decided to end the potential blood bath before it got started but Ling Mai's hand to his arm stopped him. "Give him a chance," she murmured, not looking at Stone but keeping her attention on the kid.

Fuck the monkey, a child was going to die.

Jacques must have decided the same thing as he did a flying leap, in his human form, going for a take down tackle.

Herc must have had a stronger sense of self-preservation than Stone gave him credit for as he flung himself sideways, sending Jacques slamming his shoulder into the nearest wall.

Small point to the kid, but it wasn't going to last long, especially as he hadn't used any weapons.

Lisa wasn't waiting around for her partner to brush himself off. Like a pro, she took advantage of Herc's distraction and sprinted across the short gap of gym floor, sliding into Herc's legs like a baseball All-star into home plate.

The kid flipped head over ass and landed face side down on the hard floor.

"Ouch," Stone whistled, knowing that at the very least the kid was winded, if he didn't have a few broken bones. That should smack some sense into him.

As if called, Herc turned his head, the grin wiped from his face, blood streaming down his nose, but not out. Yet.

Lisa was already scrambling to her feet, putting the kid on the defensive and crab-scrambling backwards on hands and feet until he twisted and jumped up, looking a little more scared and a lot more wary than a few moments ago.

Good. Maybe that's all they'd need to do. Stone stepped forward, assuming the kid would be raising his hands to signal a time out. But it seemed geeks named for Greek heroes were made of sturdier stuff. Or stupid, as Herc squared his shoulders, raised his chin and glared at Lisa.

A smile spread across Lisa's face. One of those now-you-die looks soldiers recognized when arrogance met experience. Greek god or not, the kid was going down.

Jacques hadn't been standing still either as he circled around, closer to Lisa now, the two of them forcing Herc into the nearest corner. Two walls would be at his back but he'd also be wedged like a block in a bung hole. Hard lesson, but then those were the kind that stuck with a man. Which Herc would be one day, if he survived.

Acting more like a predator leopard than his scorpion self, Jacques pounced first, rushing low and lethal.

Herc braced, as if he could hold against a full-body tackle, but just as Jacques reached him, the kid leaped up and forward, over Jacque's back and into a hard bounce and role on the floor.

Impressive.

Except he ended up in a squat, right in front of Lisa.

She threw herself at him, a smothering tackle that should have flattened him. Except he did the unexpected again.

Instead of curling into a ball to protect his vulnerable head and neck, he rolled backwards, thrust his hands and feet upward, using Lisa's own momentum as she hit him to rocket her over and behind him.

Someone had taught the kid a few self-defense moves.

Lisa slammed into the hardwood floor, violently enough to have cracked her noggin, if she were just human. She'd braced her fall with her hands, saving her head, but snapped her right wrist with an audible crack.

This time, Stone shrugged off Ling Mai's hand as he stepped forward, ready to call the exercise over. One shifter was already hurt. Herc hadn't stopped anyone, or showed any weapon that could halt either shifter.

"Exercise finished," he called, heading toward Lisa already cradling her wrist.

But like a red flag to a bull, pain tended to trigger an immediate response in a lot of shifters, including Lisa. Rhinos tended to be live-and-let-live animals by nature, but not if threatened or provoked. Herc had just managed to push both buttons.

From where Stone stood, he could already hear the involuntary morphing of Lisa into her Rhino form. Pain to her signaled a possible threat and that's when rhinos became volatile.

Jacques, being closer to Lisa, moved to her side, as if wanting to halt her morphing, but once started, there wasn't a lot anyone, human or non-human could do.

A shifter changing was a painful, messy business, even to watch. Bones erupting from skin, churning muscles ripping and rearranging, the tear of skin replaced by fur or shell or, in Lisa's case, by a hide several layers thick.

The horror on the kid's face was worth the price of admission, but not if he was creamed for agitating Lisa more. Stone would bet dollars to donuts Lisa wasn't going to remain stock still after she shifted. If Herc stayed splayed on the floor, remaining frozen, he might be safe, as rhinos couldn't see worth squat, but they would attack based on scent or smell.

"Freeze," Stone shouted to Herc, already moving toward Lisa to make an alternative target. "Stay right where you are."

Leave it to the kid to disregard a direct order as he scrambled to his feet.

Rhinos looked like slow, lumbering beasts but they could outrun the fastest human, especially in short bursts, which was as fast as you could get in the gym. If they were in the wild, a tree might work. Here, evade and escape were the only options.

Lisa finished her transformation and just standing still, she took up a hell of a lot of room. Single-horned head lowered for charging, she bared her sharp lower incisors, which rhinos used to slash and gore, and pawed the floor once before attacking.

This time it was Stone diving toward the floor to tackle Herc out of the way of Lisa's massive three-toed hooves, the same pads shaking the whole damn building. Together they rolled in an ungainly lump toward the nearest wall, with enough space to breathe, but just barely.

"If you have any amazing weapons, now's the time to use them," Stone huffed, keeping his eyes one hundred percent on rampaging Lisa.

The kid rose to his knees, either used to getting flattened or flaunting that damn resilience of youth. Stone followed, catching his breath at the same time.

Jacques backed away, still human, but Stone didn't think that'd last for long. Once one shifter morphed, it was like a chain reaction to other shifters in the area. Like warning signals in the wild alerted all animals to be aware of predators, Lisa's change would trigger the same response in Jacques. Their best bet for surviving was to cross the floor to the gym's closest door and get their asses out of the direct line of fire.

Stone hoped Ling Mai had already exited and the rest of the team would stay put until Lisa calmed down enough to shift back. No telling how long that might take though. Before Stone could grab the kid and run like hell, Herc moved.

Like the idiot he was, the kid strode to the center of the gym floor, placing himself smack in front of Lisa who was circling around to take another stab at what she now saw as the enemy in her territory. Weighing easily five or six thousand pounds, it was still an awesome sight to see how she could swing her size in such a tight space. It wasn't so awesome when she braced herself, lowered the deadly horn again, and charged. "Run,"

Stone screamed, lunging at Herc who sidestepped him. Instead, Geek Guy raised his arms, his fists clenched, palms down, until Lisa was almost on top of them, and threw his hands out like Moses on the mountain.

What the—

CHAPTER 6

"Pssst."

I swam up through the thick blackness, aware each inch closer to awareness, the knife-sharp pain intensified. Keep going or give up? My brothers would never know. Besides, Van had to be dead. Another kind of pain roared through me. A loss so raw it crippled me.

I'd seen him go down. Bran had killed him.

"Pssst."

Go away. Just go away and let me be.

"Pssst. Wake up."

Was it worth it to find out what that sound was?

"You! You alive?"

"Ugh, I ..."

My mumble sounded like a dead frog. Who was I kidding; I felt like a dead frog, all masticated and dried out. Road kill.

"You a real witch?" That got my attention. I cranked my head, slowly, toward the voice, a female voice. Young, and sounding determined. Underneath her words, a thread of fear echoed. The only reason I was making any effort at all. Noziak curiosity would take me so far, but someone in need sucker-grabbed me every time.

I wet my lips, which only helped so much as I croaked, "Who are you?"

"So you're alive," came the surprised-tone of a non-answer.

"Jury's still out," I spoke to myself more than her, taking stock of my body with still-closed eyes. It took way too much effort to open them. There wasn't a nerve ending that didn't

ache, or burn, or quiver. What had I done this time? Like
having the flu on top of a car accident.

So much easier to slip back into the darkness. Spirits be
damned, if I entered that spirit realm of in-Between, one of the
not-so-fun bennies of being a shaman from my father's gene
pool. I could avoid spirits. Couldn't I? "Wake up. It's
important."

Said her. Not important to me. Consciousness equaled pain.
Not a win-win in my book.

"They'll be coming back soon."

Okay, maybe I should find out who "they" were and what
they wanted with me. If the voice knew.

Peeling one eyelid open with a swallowed groan, I glanced
around. Metal bars. A jail? Weak light. A familiar stench, but I
couldn't place where, or why I should know that smell.

"Come on, witch. I ... you need help."

Wasn't that my theme song? Or maybe it was "Stormy
Weather." Or "Coldplay." That was it—"Trouble." How'd it
go? *A spider web with me in the middle.* Damn, if that wasn't
spot on.

"Where am I?" I whispered, trying to raise my head, which
was a major mistake. I let it thunk back on a flat pillow.

"The Tombs," came the girl's voice.

Maybe I wasn't awake. The voice was just another spirit
with an agenda. So why did I hurt so bad? Tears leaked around
my eyes.

Tombs? Was I dead, or near enough I'd been stashed
somewhere close to the burying grounds? Then I remembered
where I'd smelled this place before. A cell. With Van chained
to one wall, and a corpse hidden beneath some straw in a
shadowed corner.

This is where I ended up?

I had to get out of here. Now. No need to figure out the
"they" who were coming. I knew all I needed to know about
them. They had kidnapped Van. They'd caused his death. Not
directly. Bran did that, but Vaverek and his people set up Van
to die.

I curled my fingers beneath what felt like the hard lip of a
metal cot. Cold to my touch but sturdy.

One. Two. Pull.

My head and shoulders lifted as a short, raw scream escaped.

Mother of the Great Spirits, this wasn't working. Pain roiled from deep inside, molten and sharp, rushing through my veins. I bit my lip and tasted coppery blood.

But it tasted good. How sick was that?

"Come on. You can do better than that." The voice again. Easy for her to say, she wasn't dying.

That's what it felt like. Swimming against death with death winning.

"You're supposed to be this great witch. Do something."

Like what? Did she have any idea what she was demanding? "Can't," I whispered, easing down.

"You have to."

"Why?"

"If you don't, I die."

I closed my eyes again. No choice. If I could, I would have helped. The voice sounded scared, bone-deep petrified. But she was asking the wrong person. I couldn't help my brother. I couldn't help myself. No way could I help her.

"On your own," I breathed, watching the darkness creep closer. Darkness and the cold.

Yeah, she was on her own and so was I.

CHAPTER 7

As if a movie director had shouted, *Stop action!* Rhino Lisa careened to a halt, her legs locked up tight enough to cause her to topple horn-first onto the floor, peeling back the hardwood, leaving a deep gouge.

This time when Stone grabbed Herc, the kid didn't brace himself, which saved him from a nasty head-on with a rhino plow.

Damn if Lisa wasn't immobilized, flash-frozen into almost three tons of rhino flesh. The only thing moving on her was her small, beady eyes, blinking furiously.

"What the Sam hell," Stone cursed, casting a sharp glance at Herc before he warily circled around the twelve-foot long Lisa, her snorting breaths reassuring Stone she still lived. "What'd you do?"

"My weapon." Herc was standing shoulder to shoulder with Stone as they both looked down at the mound of prehistoric flesh, both of them breathing hard. "Told you it'd work."

But they'd both forgotten about Jacques, who scuttled out from behind Lisa's prone form, his scorpion tail poised high above his body in his scorpion shape.

Damn, when had that happened?

Bad question. Better question, how did they get around him? Stone and the boy were still on one side of the gym, Ling Mai on the other. If Jacques turned, the director was his nearest target.

As a deathstalker, Jacques wasn't the largest form of a scorpion but any arachnid with a deadly stinger aimed at you was scary. Especially one as super-sized as Jacques.

Stone reacted first, shoving the kid out of the way, as Jacques responded to the sudden movement. Which was good. *Keep his attention focused forward on me.* He hoped like hell Ling Mai and the kid would use the diversion to get off the floor and out of harm's way.

The scorpion reared back then thrust its tail forward, needling the poisonous barb deep into Stone's thigh as he scrambled backwards. An instant earlier and the stinger would have struck Stone's chest. The kill zone.

Stone danced one-legged away, preparing for a second attack, as scorpions could regulate the amount of venom they used, giving them more than one chance to kill.

He bit down on his lip, drawing blood while calling himself twenty kinds of a fool. His leg felt like a swarm of wasps had stung it, but Jacques was acting as his species dictated—attack when threatened. Deathstalkers were by nature aggressive, and Jacques was already scrambling for his next assault.

Then Herc skipped forward, did that hand waving ju-ju, and just like with Lisa, the smaller, cold-blooded shifter was immobilized.

What the hell was going on?

Stone leaned over, sucking a lungful of air as he fought vomiting. Damn, his leg hurt like a mother—

"You going to die?" Herc sidled closer to Stone, his gaze fixed on the two shifters.

Maybe the kid *was* learning.

Stone wasn't sure if Herc's tone sounded excited or scared. "Don't think so."

Best answer he could give. The deathstalker was among the most lethal of scorpions on the planet, but as a healthy adult, Stone shouldn't die choked by his own fluids, as the kid would have if he'd been stung. Besides, Stone wasn't a total idiot. He'd arranged for a dose of a US Armed Forces investigational drug to be on hand. He now owed his buddy Trey a bundle, but it was worth it. And no way was he going to share with Trey that Stone had been the SOB who needed the stuff.

Ling Mai eyed Stone's leg as she crossed to stand between them, handing him the venom kit before smiling at the kid. "Nice job, Hercules," she said.

Stone jabbed an elbow into the kid's side as he tried to clarify his nickname. Since it seemed whatever the geek did worked against preternaturals, at least temporarily, that also meant he was likely going to be part of the expanding team. Best to get him used to the director's ways and the fact she was in charge, and the new kid wasn't.

"Tell us what you did," Stone demanded, switching the focus back on the big issue; whatever had happened to the shifters. "And how long will it hold them?"

"A simple binding element combining adhesive properties from synthetic and natural polymers, to form a cross-linking reaction in adverse proportion to an object's molecular weight. I—"

"In English, kid," Stone growled, noticing the other three IR team members joining them from the viewing area. Last thing they needed was the shifters freed from their immobilization. Shifters were bad enough. Pissed shifters were death on steroids.

At the geek's sudden blinking and arched brow look, Ling Mai stepped in. "I think what Hercules here is trying to say is he's created a bonding net, administered in the form of an air-born substance."

The kid nodded.

"Once applied, the net has the ability to paralyze a shifter's nervous system."

"Stopping them dead in their tracks." Jaylene whistled, walking up and joining them as she looked closely at Lisa.

"How long will they be immobilized?" Stone repeated, wanting to make sure his friends didn't pay too high a price for their willingness to be today's guinea pigs.

"Based on size ratios and—"

He shot a pointed look at Herc. "How long?"

"About three minutes more for the rhino. Five for the scorpion," came the whiplash answer.

Good, the kid was learning.

"Which means if this weapon works on other shifters or Weres, then we'd stand a chance to get away?" Kelly, who was now with them, framed her statement as a question, which made sense. She, of the whole team, didn't have the street smarts, or the background, that prepped her to be a serious hand-to-hand fighter. Alex and Jaylene were the strongest in that regard. A gut instinct of when and how to fight, but Alex was gone now. Alex used to watch out for Kelly in a brawl, but here on out, the former kindergarten teacher would have to survive on her own merits. Stone would make sure she was up to the task or she'd be off the team, and her agreement with Ling Mai, broken. It'd be a tough call but that's what Stone was here to make.

"We'd stand a chance to run," Jaylene answered, then offered a knife-edged smiled. "Or we could kill them."

"A little blood thirsty, there aren't you?" a new voice spoke up.

Stone and the group all turned as one to face the newcomer. Petite. Brown shoulder length hair. Not over-the-top sex appeal like Vaughn, or attitude like Jaylene or Mandy, or country-style aw, shucks wholesomeness like Kelly, but he had no doubts this was their new recruit.

The woman, who was in her mid to late-twenties like the rest of the recruits, nodded her head to Ling Mai but addressed Stone, "Name's Nicki Yarblanski."

Mandy walked up next to Kelly and Jaylene, creating a wedge of attitude that the newcomer ignored. Instead, she kept her gaze solidly on his. "You must be the badass instructor."

"Nailed him." Jaylene laughed under her breath until Stone cut her a look and she fell silent.

"Most folks call me Stone," he said, eyeing the new addition.

"That include these guys?"

Oh yeah, Alex hadn't been gone more than two days and another smart-ass was stepping into her still warm place.

"You can call me, Sir," he shot back, turning to the rest of the team. "Enough gawking. Exercise over. These two will be moving any minute and we've had enough excitement today. We'll meet in an hour for a briefing."

He turned to Miss Yarblanski. "That includes you."

"Kelly," he nodded toward the quietest of the group, and the one grieving the loss of Alex the most. "Why don't you show our newest team member around?"

He expected a nod, or even a *yes, of course,* but what he got instead was Kelly pulling into an indignant, chin-raised ball of fury as she eyed both him and Ling Mai before dropping a bomb. "You don't even know for sure that Alex is dead and you're already replacing her."

She was breathing hard, her hands curling and uncurling at her sides.

So the kitten had claws. It was bound to happen some time, but her timing sucked. He didn't want anyone else around when the shifters woke. Plus, he needed to tend to his leg.

"What the hell is this about?" Mandy murmured to no one in particular, the first one to get her mouth in motion.

"Now's not the moment," Ling Mai stepped in, her tone laying down the law. "Miss McAllister, you are a trained agent and I expect you to act as one. Escort Miss Yarblanski to my hotel where we'll discuss anything that needs to be addressed."

For a second it looked as if Kelly would balk, but she didn't. Instead, she pulled her shoulders tight, pressed her lips into a solid line and glanced at the newest recruit. "Follow me."

Then she turned and walked out.

Something the hell was up, but Stone could only work on one crisis at a time. "The rest of you, move it. Unless you want to give our shifter friends more targets."

For once, everyone listened to him, including the new kid. Stone hoped like hell that was a good sign, but he doubted it.

CHAPTER 8

Kelly would have preferred to have stayed away from the meeting. Hide in fact, but her folks hadn't raised her that way. Good people don't disappear when the hard things need to be done, her pops would say. Her mother would have nodded, lips pressed together, sad eyes downcast.

So Kelly was here, in Ling Mai's very nice hotel room. Probably the nicest place Kelly had ever been. Well, not since she'd been an IR agent. They'd passed through a number of very nice places, hotels, the estate in Maryland, even the Kennedy Center in Washington, D.C., but passing through was different than cooling your heels, waiting to meet with the director and Stone.

She'd left the new girl in the lobby, which worked out for both of them. It wasn't like there was a lot of small talk to share.

Here Kelly was glad Jaylene was sitting shoulder to shoulder with her. That helped spunk up her backbone as Kelly's sister, Carrie, would say. She did say, quite a bit as the two of them grew up.

Buck up, spunk up, live life, Kels.

You only have one, don't squander it.

Never show your fear because the bad people will smell it and use it against you.

Sounded more like something Alex would have said, but it was Carrie who had been talking about Mary Jane Snodgross, the biggest bully in grade school. And middle school. And high school. If Kelly had stayed in Dubuque, Iowa, then no doubt,

Mary Jane Snodgross, who was now Mary Jane Fender, would still be bullying her.

"You okay?" Jaylene nudged Kelly's shoulder, yanking Kelly back to the room with a start.

"Yeah," she lied. It wasn't a real lie, more a white lie because Jaylene couldn't fix what was bothering Kelly. None of them could. She knew that from first hand experience. Grief could only be buried, deep, so it didn't bring you to your knees when you least expected it. She'd learned that when Carrie died. Now she was relearning the lessons all over again.

Rubbing her crossed arms as if she was cold, when the hotel room was a perfect temperature, Kelly reached for a shaky smile to offer Jaylene. That's what friends did, and now that Alex was gone, Jaylene felt like Kelly's only friend and ally. Mandy and Vaughn were peers but not sister-friends, not like Alex had been.

After a faint knock, the hotel room door opened and Vaughn strolled in.

Kelly jumped to her feet. "You're supposed to be in the hospital," she tsked their team leader, even as she toned down her rebuke with an ear-to-ear grin. It was so good to see Vaughn moving around again.

"You try more than two days in any hospital and tell me how well that goes." Vaughn meant the comment as a chide, but Kelly could see it took the other woman too much effort to really be light and casual.

Vaughn always looked like the former debutante she was; tall, dark auburn hair, like a fairytale princess, which is why Stone still called her that. But now it wasn't with the edge he'd once used. Not since they'd gotten together as a couple. Kelly loved happy endings. Not that their relationship was ended. Or that they were really happy, happy all the time, but she could believe in them anyway.

Vaughn crossed to one of the plush silk chairs angled on either side of the fireplace. A real fireplace only with green ferns in it now instead of a fire.

"Stone's going to be pissed with you," Jaylene remarked from her place on the huge couch, one that dwarfed even the six-foot black beauty. Kelly always felt like the plain duckling around these women.

Vaughn eased herself into the chair, trying not to wince. She failed but her voice sounded more like leader Vaughn than hurt Vaughn as she waved one hand and said, "If I listened only to Stone, I'd be spending all my time in the Maryland compound, watching computer monitors."

"Which is where you should be," Stone growled.

Kelly jumped, never hearing the door opening again. Their instructor always moved like that. Quietly, like a big, dangerous, predator cat. Not a housecat stalking mice kind of cat.

Stone moved to where Vaughn sat. He acknowledged Kelly with a raised brow, Jaylene with a nod, but when he reached Vaughn, he lifted one hand to her shoulder and let his fingers brush against her. A move so quick it should have meant nothing. But Kelly wanted to sigh.

For a man who showed so little emotion, unless it was to kick behinds in training, that subtle action spoke volumes.

Vaughn must have thought so too as her eyes softened, her lips curled in a half smile. "I'm fine. I promise."

Isn't that what they'd all been saying since they'd limped back from the brawl they'd had at the Palace of Versailles? One that wasn't even a team mission. Just helping a friend. Alex. Lot of good that did.

"Where's everyone else?" Stone asked, looking at his watch as if he didn't know to the second what time it was already. Patient was not what Kelly would call their instructor.

"They still have five minutes," Kelly said, earning an eye roll from Jaylene. "What? They're not really late. Not yet."

"I'd have thought you'd have learned by now that there's relative time and then there's Stone time. The minute he walked through that door," she jerked a thumb toward the exit leading to the hallway, "we've been running on Stone time."

Kelly shrugged as she eased back down on the couch. As far as she was concerned, she could use the extra minute or two to pull her shawl of composure around her. Better that than to have another hissy fit in public. Her folks would have been appalled.

Just as it looked like Stone was going to say something, a loud knock pounded on the door. Kelly jumped up to open it.

Mandy, the last of the original team was standing there giving a who-invited-you look to the new woman who'd been at the gym and the young man who looked like he should be a junior in high school, but had stopped the two shifters.

It was the new woman who stepped forward first, brushing past Kelly as she said, "Nice to see you again, Barbie."

Kelly had introduced herself once, even managed to get the woman to the hotel, so what was up with her tone? On the other hand, some people didn't catch names as easily.

"My name's Kelly." But Kelly was speaking to her back.

"Whatever." New Girl snagged one of the empty chairs, leaving the remainder of the couch for Mandy and the young man. Wasn't he named after a Greek warrior? Hercules, that was it. What a strange name to give a child, but after teaching kindergarten for years, Kelly shouldn't be surprised by names anymore. Some of them were actually very fun.

"Her name's Kelly. Get it right." Mandy jumped to Kelly's defense, which surprised Kelly. Except for Carrie, and Alex, she wasn't used to that, especially from the Latina beauty who had butted heads with Alex constantly. And that sharp, the pain of loss returned.

"It doesn't matter," Kelly said, wanting to soothe ruffled feathers and move beyond the grief. If this was to be their new teammate, they needed to work together. At least if they were going to continue to be a team.

She was just in the process of closing the door when Ling Mai arrived. It seemed strange that the director entered her own hotel room after everyone else. Sort of like the Queen entering the palace after all the footmen and guards. And Ling Mai was regal. Not tall, not even as tall as Kelly who was barely five feet five inches, but Ling Mai carried herself in that royal way, as if born to power and prestige.

"Good to see everyone here," the director said, after casting a smile at Kelly. A look Kelly was used to as the school principal used to have that same expression: a combination of surprised to see you but not expecting to see you around look.

Kelly closed the door, then returned to her seat beside Jaylene as Ling Mai settled into the room's remaining chair. The one facing everyone else—Kelly, Jaylene, Mandy and the boy on the couch. New Girl and Vaughn in the two chairs at an angle to the couch, directly in front of Ling Mai. Stone perched on the arm of Vaughn's chair. No doubt ready to protect, as he hadn't been able to at Versailles because he wasn't there.

"Let us get down to business, shall we?" Ling Mai said with a faint lyricism to her words, as if an accent that had never quite been lost. Kelly had noticed the director never used contractions in her speech pattern either, which made her always sound a bit formal and standoffish. But it suited her.

"Introductions first." Ling Mai nodded toward the new girl. "Please?"

"Nicki Yarblanski," came the response, followed quickly by, "like I told you all in the gym before Barbie huffed off."

Kelly had never huffed in her life. She felt Jaylene stiffen next to her and saw Vaughn raise one perfectly arched brow.

Ling Mai continued as if nothing was out of the ordinary, "Tell us where you're from, Miss Yarblanski."

Oh, oh, that wasn't a good sign. The director only called a recruit by her formal name when there was trouble. Too bad New Girl didn't know that.

"West Virginia," came the bitten-off words, as if she was daring someone to say something about them.

"I've never been there," Kelly jumped in, wanting to kick herself for being such a lightweight, but she recognized that tone, and the way the new girl sat pulled in as if hunched for a blow. Self esteem issues most likely. Or she'd been hurt in the past. Hurt badly. "What part of West Virginia?"

"Mason City, Mason County." Nicki looked at her with a what's-it-to-you twist to her lips. "Not that it matters."

"That where all the football players are able to rape underage girls and post the pictures on Facebook?" Mandy asked, her tone deceptively calm. Ouch!

"Nah." Nicki shot Mandy a smile that didn't climb all the way to her eyes. "We don't have enough computers in my town to be all that effective. If you're going to be debased we post it on telephone poles or in store windows."

This wasn't going well. Not at all. If Alex were here, she'd be able to stop this Yarblanski woman from digging herself into a deeper hole. But Alex wasn't here. And that was part of the problem.

"My name's Hercules," the young man jumped in, either knowing what it felt like to be the new kid in school, or nice enough to help diffuse the tension. "Hercules O'Brian. But everyone calls me Herc."

"O'Brian?" Jaylene snagged the lifeline the boy offered. "Why not call you Finnegan or Taranis? At least they're Celtic deities."

"Guess my old woman didn't think I looked much like a god of thunder, and my da knew all the words to the ballad."

"What ballad?" Kelly found herself asking.

"There once was a man named Finnegan.
He had some whiskers on his chinnigan.
The wind blew them off.
And they grew in again.
Poor old Finnegan."

The boy actually had quite a nice voice. Plus, Nicki Yarblanski wasn't scowling anymore, and both Jaylene and Mandy's shoulders had eased.

Nice job, Herc.

"Hercules here will be working closely with the team to create offensive and defensive weapons for us," Ling Mai said.

"You made whatever stopped those shifters?" Mandy asked, disbelief staining every word. This time it was Nicki who suddenly went still and tense, more than she had been, which is why it snagged Kelly's attention.

"Sure did." Either Herc was a natural at deflection or self-preservation, which given the way he looked had probably kept him alive on school grounds. "And I have more devices I've been working on."

"Before we get into that," Ling Mai pulled back control of the conversation again, "why don't you tell us where you're from?"

"Here and there," came the evasive reply, combined with a head duck that had his soft blond hair falling across his forehead. An effective hiding technique.

"Where were you born then?" Stone asked. More demanded, but then that was just Stone's way. Like a bulldozer.

"I was born in Ankara," the boy said, his voice low. "Lived in Italy, Germany, Hungary, Texas, North Dakota. All over really."

"Air Force?" Stone asked. Leave it to a former Special Force member to pick up on the meaning of the locations.

"Yeah. My dad was Air Force." The way he said it meant don't ask a lot of questions.

Kelly jumped in, "I thought what you did at the gym was very impressive. But I couldn't really see how you stopped those two."

Herc cast her a grateful smile. "I got the idea from Spiderman," he said, his smoky-gray eyes lighting up. Oh, he was going to be a heartbreaker this one, once he grew out of his geeky, gangly stage. *Mamma, don't let your girls off a very short leash.*

"The comic character?" Stone's question earned a hard nudge from Vaughn to which he said, "What? Just asking."

"It's how you're asking." She shook her head and turned to the boy. "Hercules ... I mean Herc."

The boy was practically drooling, which wasn't sitting too well with Stone.

Vaughn ignored the Doberman next to her to continue speaking to the puppy across from her. "Did you really mean the comic book hero?"

Oh, the *hero* word went down real well with Herc as a flush lit his cheeks. Vaughn had better watch it or he'd be trailing after her. "Yeah, you know how Spiderman could cast nets from his wrists. Well, I did something like that. Only they weren't really nets. More like a fine spray mist that could interrupt a shifter's neurological system for a short period of time."

"Why shifters?" Nicki asked. "Why not Weres or warlocks or other nasties?"

"Shifters are pretty nasty in my book," Jaylene murmured.

"Then you need a new book," Nicki snapped back.

Unsteady ground, but Kelly wasn't sure why.

"You got a reason to tap dance around shifters?" Mandy prodded.

Nicki leaned forward on her seat but it was Ling Mai who answered, "Miss Yarblonski *is* a shifter."

CHAPTER 9

Kelly glanced around the hotel room, very aware of the stunned silence greeting Ling Mai's words. New Girl was a bona fide shape shifter.

"Got a problem with that?" Nicki snarled, her gaze cutting to everyone.

Jaylene cleared her throat. "About time we get somebody with fighting power behind them," she said. What she didn't say was, now that Alex is gone. But Kelly thought everyone heard it.

Except Nicki, who'd never met Alex.

"Before you, Alex was the only member of our team with her own preternatural abilities as a fighter," Kelly said to Nicki. "She was a shaman and a witch with amazing abilities to cast a spell."

"When it suited her," came Mandy's quick response.

"That's not fair." Kelly was tired of Mandy taking snipes at Alex, especially now when Alex couldn't defend herself. "Alex was our best weapon. Much better than my stupid ability."

"Which is?" Nicki asked, sounding curious more than defensive. A first since she'd walked into the room.

Kelly sucked in a deep breath, though her answer still came out on a whisper. "I turn invisible."

"What?" Herc glanced around as if trying to figure out what Kelly had said, or if she had been speaking the truth. "Like the Invisible Man?"

"Or woman, in her case." Jaylene knocked her shoulder against Kelly to let her know she wasn't alone.

"That's awesome!" Herc whistled.

"It would be if she could control it," Mandy said, keeping her dark gaze on Kelly.

Kelly couldn't reply. Not when Mandy was speaking the truth and everyone knew it. Being able to turn invisible sounded like a great thing, but before Kelly had turned three, she'd learned that wasn't the reality. By the time she'd turned six she'd discovered just how bad invisibility could be. And that was before she'd discovered the two doors.

"Ladies," Ling Mai called the room to order. "We're not here to tear the team apart. We're here to move forward. Anyone not willing, or able to do that, may depart—now."

No one looked at Kelly but she knew this was her cue. Her put up or shut up time, as Alex would say.

So why was she such a big 'fraidy' cat? She'd already talked to Jaylene about her concerns, and it was the black woman who told her to bring the issue to the group. So why hesitate now?

"I think we need to hear what Kelly saw at Versailles," Jaylene broke the silence, keeping her eyes straight ahead but opening a door for Kelly to walk through.

"When?" Mandy demanded.

"The day Alex disappeared."

A weighted silence descended on the room. The kind when someone made such an obvious social *faux pas* that no one knew quite what to say.

Vaughn was the one who gently said, "Alex is dead, Kelly. She didn't disappear."

That's when Kelly straightened her spine and jumped off the edge. "That's not what I saw. Alex was alive when the two Weres carried her off."

She didn't expect everyone to be happy with her news, but she wasn't prepared for Stone to be the first to jump in. "And you're only telling us this now? What about the after action report? Did that mean nothing?"

If there'd been a hole, Kelly would have jumped into it and pulled the opening closed behind her. But there wasn't.

"You mean the meeting we had in the hospital? Waiting to find out how bad Vaughn was hurt?" she asked, her voice low but steady.

Stone still glared. "Yeah, that one. You were there. Why didn't you speak up then?"

Kelly glanced at her hands—held so tight—her knuckles turned white before she notched her chin and aimed it at Stone. "Because you were in such an all-fired hurry to call Alex dead and bury her that I couldn't get in a word in edgewise. That's why."

CHAPTER 10

If Kelly thought the hotel room had been quiet before she dropped her verbal bomb, it was nothing to the strain afterwards, with gazes skittering around the room, not quite meeting before they danced away.

"Well, hot damn. You can fight." Jaylene whistled, helping to ease the tension a smidge, but only a smidge if Stone's granite expression was a clue.

"Explain," he demanded. He always was the most black and white thinker of their group. "We were told she died."

"No." Kelly threaded her hands together in her lap to still their trembling. She looked directly at Vaughn, too afraid to glance toward Ling Mai who had been the one who'd officially announced Alex's death. "Remember when you, Mandy and Jaylene were fighting the Weres, and someone you couldn't see started hitting them from behind?"

"Saved our asses," Jaylene mumbled.

"That wasn't me," Kelly explained. "I'm sure you thought it was, but it wasn't."

"But you'd become invisible." Mandy sat up straighter. "If it wasn't you, who was it?"

"Alex." Kelly released the single word as a sigh.

"She hadn't ever turned invisible before." Mandy's tone said she was going to be the hardest to convince. Plus, the fact she clung to the past tense of the word. To her, Alex *was* dead. End of a difficult relationship.

"Doesn't matter," Jaylene shot down her friend. "Hear Kelly out."

All gazes cut to Kelly. After years in front of a classroom, you'd think speaking in front of a group would be easier. But it wasn't. Not with this particular group at least. She swallowed and thought about Alex, who needed their help. Which she'd never get if Kelly couldn't tell everyone what she'd seen.

"It's true. Alex was near you three, and I was farther away. Across the grass and closer to where Alex's brother was. At least I'd assumed it was her brother." She'd never met him but the man she'd watched change from human to wolf had Alex's ink black straight hair, tanned skin and stunning good looks. Or he would have if he hadn't looked so gaunt and exhausted.

Plus, three other men had him wrapped in chains. So it had to have been Van.

"Go on, Miss McAllister." Ling Mai nodded in Kelly's direction. Sort of like having an executioner giving you the go-ahead nod.

Kelly swallowed past the hard rock in her throat and continued. "As I said, Alex was alive when I saw the two Weres carry her away."

"You're sure?" Stone asked.

Kelly nodded. "The Weres said so, but ..."

"But what?" Vaughn prodded.

"Alex had been bitten by her brother and was bleeding. Badly."

"Fuck a bunny," Jaylene breathed.

"Don't think that's a good idea," Mandy shot back, but Kelly thought it was meant as a joke and not an accurate assessment. Plus, it reminded her of something Alex would say, which gave Kelly a small reason to smile.

Stone looked at Ling Mai, his expression dark and closed. "How trustworthy was the information you received about Alex's death?"

It wasn't a straight-out accusation, but close.

Ling Mai remained calm and poised, but then the room could be crumbling around them and the director would probably act the same way. "I would have said very trustworthy." She then looked at New Girl. "Tell us, Miss Yarblonski, based on your knowledge of shifters, how likely is it for someone bitten by one to survive?"

Nicki paused, a furrow lining her brow. "There have been humans bitten who've become shifters."

Kelly's smile started to increase.

"But the numbers are so rare they're the stuff of legends," Nicki said, her voice low but solid. "Weres can be created by a bite, but not shifters." Then she paused, rubbing her palms along her jeans before looking up and asking, "Didn't you all say this Alex was a witch?"

"And a shaman," Kelly offered, aware she'd been holding her breath, waiting for good news instead of only bad news layered on more bad news.

Nicki shook her head. "Then I think that'd decrease her chances of surviving." She lowered her voice, as if aware of the lethal nature of her words, before looking up and spearing Kelly with a direct look. "Sorry, wish I had better news."

"But you could be wrong?" Kelly pushed. Alex was her friend and she wasn't going to give up. Not without a fight.

"Yeah." Nicki splayed her hands before her. "There's always an unknown factor when shifter blood mingles with another being's blood. Make that being someone who is both a magic carrier and who can walk among spirits and who knows what can happen."

That weighted, strained silence returned to the room.

Mandy broke it when she raised her head. "I haven't found Alex in the spirit realm," she said.

"You've looked?" Jaylene asked what Kelly couldn't. Not without choking on the words. Mandy was the last person Kelly expected to raise a finger to find Alex. The very, very last.

As if Kelly had spoken her thoughts out loud, Mandy dared the group, "What? Alex was a teammate. Without a body, I wanted to make sure she'd passed over."

"And she hasn't?" Stone asked, his voice quieter now, more thoughtful.

"Not that I've found." Mandy paused, then continued, "But there's one person who'd know for sure."

All heads turned to Mandy, which was fine by Kelly.

"Who?" Vaughn asked what was on the tip of all their tongues.

Mandy gave a shrug. "Bran."

"Who's Bran?" Herc asked, followed closely by, "Not THE Bran? Clothing designer?"

"You don't look like someone who follows sartorial news," Stone mumbled.

"He was on the cover of *Entrepreneur Magazine* last month." Herc glanced at Stone, his gaze saying little-do-you-know. "And *Forbes* three months ago."

Vaughn placed a restraining hand on Stone's arm before the instructor clipped the young man. Kelly was impressed that Herc didn't start humming, "Nah nah na nah nah."

Instead, the new weapons guy looked around. "I'm not sure what Bran has to do with finding this missing witch shaman?"

"Bran's a mage, a powerful warlock," Jaylene explained, looking mostly at her shoes as if not sure Mandy's idea was going to lead anywhere.

"He's also combined magic with Alex before. On more than one occasion," Mandy said, her voice more insistent.

"Which means what?" Nicki asked.

Mandy released a huff of breath before saying, "It means they are connected in a way few individuals are. If anyone can find out if she's alive, he can."

Stone glanced at Ling Mai, his tone as hard as his name as he said, "We talk to him then. Act."

Kelly caught the slightest moment of hesitation before Ling Mai nodded. "By all means."

Kelly wanted to jump up right then and there, high-five everybody, and twirl around. But Ling Mai's expression put a damper on that. Then Stone dashed more cold water on the group. "I'll speak to Bran." Before Kelly could offer to come along, he added, "Alone."

It wasn't like Stone and Bran were enemies but neither were they best buddies. Kelly shot a quick glance at Jaylene before nudging her when the black woman remained quiet.

"You have something you want to add, Miss McAllister?" Ling Mai asked. "We are looking into your concerns."

Kelly understood a rap on the knuckles more than the average person. So why didn't she feel like Stone's approach was enough?

"Concerns that should have been brought to our attention immediately," Stone growled in the role of badass instructor to idiot recruit. "You don't wait nearly forty-eight hours to help a fallen comrade."

"She gets it." Vaughn nudged him hard enough he almost toppled from the chair arm. "Continuing to beat her isn't helping."

"It's helping me," he said, his jaw tight as he spoke to the room at large. "From now on, if you have something to say, the time to say it is in our after action debriefing. If in doubt, speak up."

Easy for him, but Kelly bit off her retort, remembering how wild-eyed he'd been waiting for word on Vaughn and chewing out the rest of them for going on an unsanctioned mission to help Alex.

He still was het up, which made it easier for Kelly to make her next choice.

Carrie would have been disappointed in her, though when Kelly cleared her throat. "Nothing to add. I'm sure Bran will be glad to help."

If he could.

Her last quick glimpse of him the other day wasn't a pleasant one. He'd been even bloodier than Alex, and that was saying a lot. Plus, Bran had been limping away with an older man who might have been Alex's father. Since Alex's father was a member of the Council of Seven, and Bran was in trouble with them, it was hard to say if Bran could help or not.

Once the conversation resumed with other agency business, with Stone giving orders to the team as to what they should be doing while he contacted Bran, Jaylene leaned closer to Kelly and whispered, "You should be looking happier."

"I am happy," Kelly answered, whipping out a wobbly smile.

"But?"

Kelly lowered her voice and admitted what was bothering her. "You sure Stone will *really* find Bran?"

Jaylene's eyes widened. Kelly knew why. Questioning their team instructor's honesty was like pointing a finger at the Dali Lama and asking if he was one of the good guys.

"I know, I know. I'm a worry wart," Kelly admitted, shrugging her shoulders. When Jaylene nodded and turned her attention back to the room, Kelly let the smile slide off her face.

She just wished she'd spoken the whole truth. That she wasn't really sure she trusted either their instructor or the director, after action report or not.

Which didn't bode well with remaining a team player.

CHAPTER 11

After their hotel room meeting broke up and Kelly was heading out the door, Stone caught up with her and murmured, "Meet me around the corner. Coffee shop next to the main entrance of the *Louvre*. Ten minutes. Alone"

Then he disappeared, leaving Kelly rubbing goose bumps along her arms. It wasn't that she was cold, more like wary. If she lost her position on the team, then … no, she wouldn't go there because the other alternative was just as bad. Someone had kidnapped Alex's brother. Now they might have kidnapped Alex, only she was terribly wounded. The team, or someone with more clout than Kelly alone, had to make sure Alex was okay. If she were still alive.

She told Jaylene she'd meet her back at their own hotel, the Campanile, which was nowhere near as nice as Ling Mai's place, but that was okay because Kelly felt more comfortable there. The team was moving from there into the safe house that was a fallback in case anyone was separated from the group. They should have had someone stationed there on the chance Alex hadn't been killed, but Ling Mai had been so sure there had been no question about stationing someone from their overtaxed team there. Now? If Alex *was* alive, she'd find her way to the safe house. If she could. A whole lot of ifs going on.

Maybe Stone had been right. What if Alex had made it to the safe house already and found no one there? Kelly's stomach in knots at the thought she'd already sacrificed her friend. If she had, then Stone didn't have to kick her off the team; it might be for the best if she left on her own. But then the truth would come out and it'd kill her parents, a lethal blow they'd never recover from.

Jaylene gave Kelly one of her knowing gazes, which helped the downward spiral of her thoughts, and said, "The cards speak of unexpected dangers."

"Not unexpected given what we do." Kelly tried to keep the *duh* tone out of her voice, but didn't think she was too successful. Jaylene used tarot cards to help see the future, a practice Kelly's parents would disapprove of in the extreme. The devil's work in idle hands, they'd have said.

"The dangers are to you," Jaylene shot back. "You're the one who needs to be careful."

Wonderful, as if Kelly's stomach wasn't roiling enough. She knew Jaylene meant well. Too bad most of her future visions were so vague they were less than helpful.

"I'll be careful." Kelly reassured her with a pat on the arm for extra emphasis. "I'll meet you back at the hotel, have a few things to do first."

"I can come with you." Her look was one Kelly was used to, sort of a cross between worry that Kelly couldn't take care of herself or would screw up if left on her own.

If she was going to be axed from the team, though, it was something she had to face alone. "Thanks, but not this time. I'll see you in a bit." She started walking away with a small backwards wave to take any sting out of her words.

Just to make sure that Jaylene or anyone else didn't know where she was headed, Kelly started out toward the opera house, which was in the opposite direction of the coffee house. Then she caught the *Avenue de l'Opera* that cut diagonally back toward the Louvre and jogged the last half block to reach the small bistro, which served coffee, too. Stone was already seated inside, away from prying eyes.

She was out of breath by the time she reached him.

"Someone chasing you?" he asked, looking behind her. As usual, he'd taken the seat with his back to a wall, facing the main exit and windows.

"No. Dodging Parisian traffic," she mumbled as she pulled up a chair and waved off the waiter. "*Non, merci.*"

Stone eyed her as she bought a few spare seconds catching her breath, before he jumped in. "Tell me exactly what you saw the other day. In detail."

So he wasn't going to cut her from the team. Yet. With Stone, it could mean only one thing. He'd wring every piece of intel from her before he released the guillotine.

With more calmness than she felt, she repeated what she'd shared with Jaylene earlier. Stone let her talk until she was finished.

"That's all?" he asked. "You're sure?"

Kelly nodded. "Of course I'm sure."

"Bran left with Jeb Noziak and Van?"

"Yes. Van, if that's who it was, was unconscious, and Bran was bleeding, but they all left together."

Stone leaned back in his chair, all stillness and concentration.

Kelly now wished she had ordered something to keep her hands, and mind, busy, instead of just pleating her napkin.

When Stone remained silent she asked, "You think there's something wrong?" What she wanted to ask was if she were still an IR agent or not, but that stuck in her throat.

He glanced at her as if he'd been a long ways away, then gave a quick chuckle that held no mirth. "I know there's something wrong. Can't put my finger on it, but there's certainly something wrong."

Kelly swallowed. If Stone thought there was a problem, that wasn't good news. It'd be real easy to avoid the other question pushing at her but her parents hadn't raised her to take the easy way out. She had to ask. "Does this mean we're not going to look for Alex?"

He eyed her as if she'd asked him if the team would be dancing in the streets. "We'll do more than that, we'll find her …"

"I hear a *but*," she countered, her napkin now wadded in her lap.

"It's not going to be easy." Stone never did sugarcoat the truth. "You okay with that?"

She chewed her bottom lip before giving a reply, making sure she could back up her words. Another thing her parents drilled into her. Don't lie, don't hide from the truth and if you commit to do something, then you'd better be prepared to do it.

"I didn't figure it'd be easy," she admitted, looking Stone in the eye. "That's not what I'm concerned about."

He arched a brow, which was the same as a shout from someone else.

Taking the look as a go ahead, she added, "Am I going to still be on the team?"

His forehead creased as if she'd thrown him with her question. "You want out?"

"No. No." She scooted forward, leaning her arms on the table. "I just assumed ... you know, with the way I screwed up, that you wouldn't want me around anymore."

He eased back in his chair, eyeing her. "You learn your lesson?"

Kelly nodded, hoping he didn't see that she'd crossed her fingers. That made the big lie into a more manageable gulp.

"Then you're on the team." Kelly released a breath of air, even as Stone added, "Still in the same situation though. You ready for the hard stuff?"

"I'm more worried about what we will find."

"Such as?"

"Deceit. Betrayal. Evil."

Stone canted his lips before saying. "Yet each man kills the thing he loves. Some do it with a bitter look. Some with a flattering word. The coward does it with a kiss. The brave man with a sword."

"Sounds like poetry."

"Oscar Wilde. *The Ballad of Reading Gaol.*" He nodded to the waiter to bring the check before he speared Kelly with a hard glance. "You ready to be the brave man?"

The one with the sword? She straightened her shoulders. She'd been given a second chance and she wasn't going to blow it. She might be keeping her doubts to herself, for now. "If being brave is what it's going to take, I'll do it."

"Count on it." His look matched his tone. "The only thing I can guarantee."

Kelly didn't say anything. What could she say? Oh, good? Or maybe, bring it on, as Alex would have said? That wasn't

Kelly's way. Slow, sure, and avoiding risk. That was more Kelly's style even as she knew that was all about to change.

"You heading up to meet with the team?" Stone asked a few moments later as they stood shoulder to shoulder on the busy sidewalk. An island of stillness among the swarms of tourists brushing past them.

Kelly nodded.

"Then watch your back," he murmured, moving off before Kelly could ask him what he meant.

CHAPTER 12

Bran woke with a start, not realizing he'd dozed off. He pulled himself forward on the sofa, aware of the tug of muscles irritating his shoulder, but that was better than it had been. With a tentative finger, he pressed the area surrounding the gunshot wound, glad to see the healing spell he'd cast late last night was working.

As a mage he knew magic but normally didn't use spell casting, not like a certain witch/shaman he knew. No, he preferred the human way of hard work and sweat. If he earned something, he wanted to make sure it was because of his efforts and not enchantment.

The wound wasn't completely healed but better, good enough he could gently raise and stretch his arm. Yes, a definite improvement.

A quick glance around reassured him he was the only one in the warehouse. *Willie must still be at Versailles.* Francois was gone.

What now?

First step, something to eat. It'd been a full day yesterday without food and his body wasn't happy about it. Next step, plan what to do to find Alex. Her father and brother were best kept in the tunnels for now. If Jeb Noziak needed to leave the safe house, his shifter abilities could follow his own scent, backtracking until they came topside.

Bran would have to deal with both Jeb and Van soon but his first priority was to find the other Noziak. The one who drove him crazy.

So, best way to locate Alex?

As if conjured his cell phone buzzed, the number not familiar. He answered anyway, having been away from business long enough to expect a flood of calls needing his attention.

What he didn't expect was the man called Stone on the other end, Alex's instructor from the IR Agency.

"This Bran?" came the abrupt voice.

"Oui."

"M.T. Stone here. We need to meet."

"Because?"

"Because I want your help locating Alex Noziak." Before Bran could tell him where to take his suggestion and shove it, her team had royally messed with her once, why should he trust them now, until Stone added, "And you just might need our help in avoiding the Council."

There was something to be said for blunt, straight-forwardness. The Americans took it to a new level but Bran could work with it. First, he wanted to make sure he wasn't walking into a trap. "What makes you think I know something about Alex's whereabouts?"

"We have an eye witness who said she might not be dead."

"You sure?" The words escaped before he could pull them back. That and the increase of his heart rate. Alive? But why hadn't she notified anyone? Or maybe she had, only it wasn't him, in spite of what he'd done to safeguard her brother and father.

Why wasn't he surprised? He and Alex had a few trust issues. More than a few, but now wasn't the time to linger on them.

The pause on the other end of the line told him Stone caught the mixed emotions simmering beneath Bran's words. Still, Stone was all business as he answered, "I trust my source."

"So where is Miss Noziak?" Bran demanded. Stone wasn't the only one who could be abrupt.

"Let's talk." Then before Bran could point out they were talking, the other man lowered his voice. "I don't trust the phones."

Valid point. Bran wondered if the issues were on Stone's end or Bran's. Focus on what mattered now. "Tulieres, near the *Café de Pomone*. One hour."

"I'll be there."

So would Bran, in spite of the fact he'd seen the IR Agency break faith with Alex by revealing her father's role in her imprisonment a year ago. Now they wanted to find her? Why? And why hadn't she sought them out?

Only one way to find answers. Bran had less than thirty minutes to clean up, eat and get to one of Paris' busiest parks. A location he hoped would keep him safe long enough to discover what he needed to know.

Which was where the hades was Alex? And if she was hiding, from whom? And why?

CHAPTER 13

The voices woke me, though I don't think it was intentional. Two men arguing made a rumbling sound that was enough to wake the dead. Which is what I felt like.

I was still on the flat metal gurney, but the bright lights above warned me I was in a different place. My main focus, though, was on the pain exploding from within. I swear my neck was on fire, an acid-burning blaze running from neck to head and neck to body. This wasn't a mass of bruises complaining, this was full-body screaming to shut down.

Then there was the other problem as I glanced to my left. The two men who were arguing looked back at me. One seemed familiar, as if I'd seen him somewhere before, but I wasn't sure where. The other? He was the problem. Even woozy I knew what he was if not who he was. He was Were, through and through, and pissed off to boot. At me.

What had I done to him?

I slipped my fingers against the table I was on to raise myself to a sitting position. No way did I want to face an angry Were flat on my back, even if sitting meant I wanted to puke.

"Who are you?" I squawked. I was trying for forceful but my throat was too raw for that.

Were Guy didn't seem to mind though, as he grinned, and not a nice one, more a nasty, see-my-sharp-incisors kind of grin. A lot like the Were who'd tried to kill my brother had done. The Were I'd killed in return and ended up in prison almost two years ago. Then I'd thought things couldn't get worse. As if!

"Where's Van? Where's my brother?" I asked, hope forcing the question past desert-dry lips.

The doctor shook his head. "The wolf shifter? The other killed him."

I'd known that. Known and avoided, hoping somehow I'd been wrong. But once the words confirmed what I thought I knew, I could no longer hide from the truth.

A scream welled up from within. *Not Van. Please not Van. Who killed him?* Even as I asked, my gut told me I wouldn't like the answer.

"Who?"

The doctor chuckled, one of those break-your-heart sounds. "The warlock, of course."

There was no course about it. I'd hoped I'd made up the nightmare. Bran. How could he? He'd come to help me save Van. Like flashbacks from a grainy, silent era movie, images roared against me. Fighting. Weres converging on me. Shouting at Bran to save my brother.

Instead, he'd killed him. Didn't know why. Warlocks were enemies to witches. I knew that, and yet I had trusted him.

My fault. My fault and Bran's that Van was dead.

When I got out of here, wherever here was, I'd make sure Bran paid. Tit for tat. I'd been involved in killing his cousin and now he'd killed my brother. But it wasn't going to stop there. Bran wouldn't know what hit him.

First things first. Angry Were eyeing me.

"Don't do anything foolish, Paul," the doctor-looking guy said. At last I recognized the voice. Frenchie. The one who wanted me dead last time I woke up. And he was the only one holding back an angry Were? So not my day.

Were Guy didn't seem to be listening. Then he growled, "She killed my twin."

Better and better. I had no idea who his twin was, but did remember fighting against a lot of Weres and my brother Van. And Bran. Weres died. So did my brother, but that was at Bran's hands. So I guess I couldn't call even-steven to this Were.

I slid my legs over the edge of the gurney until my toes touched the floor. Thank the Great Spirits, the gurney wasn't the kind on wheels because that was the only thing holding me upright.

Until the Were attacked. He lunged in one swift, powerful burst of speed. Out of instinct, I dropped to the floor, so my body mass hit him at his thighs, his own momentum toppling him over me and the gurney.

First round to me, but tripping a raging Were wasn't the same as winning a battle against one. At least he was still in his human form, which helped me a smidge. No telling what kind of beast he could morph into. That, and the fact his attack sent a burst of adrenaline rushing through me that gave me enough energy to scramble away. Closer to the doctor but he was human. My brothers had always taught me to keep the biggest threat front and center. That'd be the Were who was even now half-morphing into what looked like a bear.

Seriously? I had to fight a bear?

Defense or offence? It wasn't like there was a lot of room to run and even less to hide. Attack it was.

Even before I'd thought through the logic of that decision, I had rocked to my feet and sailed through the air, hitting Were-bear in his broad chest with my shoulder. I don't know who was more shocked, him or me when the blow sent him reeling backwards into the nearest wall.

Yeah, me!

Except I'd ended flat on my back on the hard floor. Not an easily defensible position.

The Were had barely dented the wall when he pivoted and shot himself forward. I tucked my knees to my chest and used my legs as a fulcrum, catching his stomach and arching him over my head and beyond me.

The shock of my bare feet hitting him ricocheted through me like an electrical jolt. I wanted to curl up and hide.

Maybe later. Now I wanted to live.

With a curse for idiots—like myself—who had death wishes, I scrambled to my hands and knees before stumbling upright. I expected to be hit before I could catch my bearings as I twisted to see where the Were was.

The Mother Goddess or Great Spirits must have heard my pleas as the Were, half-human, half-bear, lay crumpled on the concrete floor, not moving. The doctor was at his side. I could have told him it probably wasn't a smart idea because Weres, like my Shifter brothers, weren't always aware of who they were lashing out at if they'd been knocked unconscious.

My hand rose to my neck where I could feel the bandage over what happened when my brother Van had attacked me while out of his mind in pain and on drugs. Man, I must have been out of things a lot longer than I thought to have healed as well as I did. Days? Weeks?

The doctor's voice roused and focused me like cold water on heated skin. "He's dead."

"Don't be stupid," I said, not really thinking. "I can't kill a Were." At least not without calling Echo demons or using dark magic.

The doctor rose to his feet, his eyes showing way too much white. Too much for my peace of mind. The man was afraid. Terrified. I could tell because I could hear the kabooming of his heart, sense his rapid pulse rate, and even smell the taint of his sweat.

Except I couldn't do any of those things.

What was happening?

I stepped back, but the doctor was inching toward me. One hand gripping a syringe.

I had no idea what was in that thing but I didn't care. This man had wanted me dead earlier and I had no doubts that hadn't changed.

"It was an accident," I said past dry lips. "You saw him. He attacked me."

"You are too dangerous to live, Miss Noziak." the doctor breathed, a sound so low and so intense goose bumps ran down my back. Why did he know my name when I'd never met him before?

That's when I remembered where I'd seen him before. Next to the body of Philippe Cheverill, the head of the Preternatural Council, who had been murdered.

My skin went cold as I shook my head. "Did you kill Cheverill?" I asked before I could catch the words. Not a smart move.

The doc must have thought I'd never survive as he answered, "No, but I didn't stop who did."

Then he jumped toward me, syringe extended.

I didn't think, I acted and the next thing I knew my fingers were squeezed around the man's throat, his head dangling at a crooked angle as I held him a good foot off the floor.

What the—dead?

He couldn't be. I didn't have that kind of strength. And yet I held him upright, all his weight pulling at my arm, barely registering. His face blue, his neck at an impossible angle. I didn't even know what his name was. I wasn't even sure what had been in the syringe he'd held that was now rolling on the floor. Could I have killed a total stranger for no reason?

Sweet Mother Goddess, help me.

Someone screamed in the background. Followed by a barked order. All in French. A hand grabbed my free arm and before I could swivel my head to see who was tugging at me a sharp prick jabbed my arm.

What was—

"*Sacre bleu,*" another voice, male this time, called out, "Notify Byrne. Now. Now. Now!"

"Byrne?" I tried to ask but even to me the word sounded muffled. Warped.

"She's going under."

"Grab him."

The weight I held eased. Shapes of people moving in and out … the pain dulled. Not a lot, but enough that I didn't want to fight the tide tugging me under.

"*Monsieur* Byrne. He comes."

Good news? The voice sounded relieved. Less frantic. I must have tottered backwards because I could feel the gurney against me. Holding me mostly upright.

Footsteps pounded against concrete. Far away but coming closer. Slap. Slap. Slap.

Nothing made sense. Not the smell. Antiseptic, but sharper. Or the scent of fear. My own. The sweat coating my skin, warmed by an elevated heart rate, sounding like a tympani drum booming in my ears.

Another cry broke in, "By the fourth virtue …"

Why did that voice ring a bell? Like a child's rhyme once memorized.

"You two, take him away. Now."

Irish. I recognized that accent. Colin Farrell. I cracked open one eye. That didn't hurt as much as I'd expected. Another face hovered in front of me. Nice face. Boyish. Charming. Something familiar, but I was so tired I couldn't put my finger on it. Besides, last guy who looked familiar I'd just killed.

"Miss Noziak," he said. "Alex." I expected anger, because I could hear the pounding of his heart. But instead, I scented excitement. Smelled it. Which didn't track.

"Hmmmm."

"Lovely to have you back with us."

I'd just killed a man, two men if the accident with the Were counted, and Colin Farrell voice was happy to see me? How many levels of a nightmare was I in?

I found myself lying flat, squirming against a hard surface, the gurney, but now straps were holding me, binding me as my muscles fought, then eased.

Not what I needed. Time to fight.

Except I was too damn tired."Hmmmm." The only sound that I could manage. Wasn't much but I guess it kept me from getting myself into too much more trouble.

"She killed Jean Claude," cried one near-hysterical woman.

They were talking about me. But I didn't know anyone named Jean Claude.

"Broke his neck."

The snap? The weight? I didn't kill people. Okay, maybe just a few. And all bad guys. As far as I knew.

The floaty feeling intensified.

"What should we do?" the female voice shouted.

If that woman didn't shut up soon I was going to have to bitch-slap her.

"Get rid of the body," came the reply. The Irish accent. I liked the way he thought. Hadn't Jaylene told me once that you could tell your friends by the ones willing to help you hide the bodies? I wish she were here now. And the rest of the team. Even sharp-tongued Mandy.

But they weren't. I was alone. And scared.

"But—"screaming woman protested.

"Now." Irish Guy was pissed. But not at me. That was good. Usually everyone was upset with me.

Take that! And that!

Only no words would come. I was too tired.

"You rest now," Irish Guy soothed. Someone else had soothed like that once. Bran. Yeah, right, probably laughing the whole time, waiting for his chance for revenge.

A hand smoothed my hair back from my forehead. "Shhh. No worries. We'll talk soon. Very soon."

Needed to talk. Needed to understand.

My eyelids drooped closed, though I could still hear the voices around me growing more and more muted.

"We'll have to keep her restrained," Irish Voice said. "So there will be no more accidents."

He called killing a man an accident?

"She killed him," Female Voice said. Not sure I liked agreeing with her.

"These things happen." A pause. "Move her to the lower wing. Find Doctor Regore. Bring her here."

Scurried steps. A door opening and closing. A car far away. Voices whispering. Most in French. One in English. "We should kill her as Jean Claude wished. Or she will murder us all."

The woman speaking had that right. I could feel it coursing through my veins, mingling with the pain, with the fogginess. These were humans. That's all. Meat.

And I was damn hungry.

CHAPTER 14

With five minutes until Stone was to meet him Bran held his cell phone to his ear, glancing around the *Café de Pomone* from a distance, not trusting anyone. Except Willie, for now.

It was the Were who answered the phone. "Yup?"

"Can you see me?"

"Yes."

"Scent anything else?"

"Older couple to your left."

"Ones wearing wool?"

"Checkered?"

"Yes. Forty years out of date."

"Figures, they're harbingers, always one step behind."

"Anything else?"

"A cat shifter near the metro. Might be a lynx or a caracal. Two Cambion demons having lattes at the café."

Bran shook his head. That was the problem with a recovering Were, paranoid about everything. And in Paris, like most of the older cities of Europe, preternaturals tended to gather. That didn't mean they were all a threat. Most were just going about their lives, remaining under the human radar. "Anything I should be worried about?"

Willie paused, as if scenting the air. But he needn't have bothered as a waft of powerful magic pulsed over Bran.

He turned, slowly, trying not to arouse attention.

There. Near the Metro opening, where Stone should have been, four simin fae, the security guards for the Council. Simin fae might look benign but they possessed lightning fast speed and wicked tongues that could scourge a man in seconds.

Before he could even think of taking flight, one simin fae could wrap and deliver him to the Council. The fact the last time Bran had run across three of their kind, Alex managed to have them killed, would not endear him to them.

Stone had sold him out.

But Bran wasn't a master mage for nothing.

Sending a whip of magic toward the clueless Cambion demons, who jumped out of their chairs as if tazered was the first step. They knocked into the nearest tables, scattering humans who, mostly being French, were always up for a fracas. Within a minute, shouts and blows were whirling about, snapping the attention of everyone in the vicinity. Including the simin fae.

Bran waited until the fae pivoted toward the fighting, before cutting across the path and disappearing down the nearest Metro entrance.

He had seconds at most before the fae realized a diversion had been set up. That was the problem with the more warlike of the fae, smart and quick.

Which meant he had to be smarter and quicker.

And a whole lot luckier.

CHAPTER 15

Bran didn't emerge from the Metro until he reached *Gare de La Défense*. Simin fae preferred hunting in the sunlight, so the longer he remained underground the better chance he had to lose them. Since the stop was also the terminus of three converging lines, it was easier to blend among the humans surging up through the aluminum and neon lights of the nearest exit.

Once outside, he was surrounded by the city's business district, with the *Arc de Triomphe* visible in the near distance down the central esplanade. What now? He'd kept in touch with Willie by phone but didn't tell the Were where he was. Willie was still a preternatural and thus beholden to the Council for his existence. It'd be a brave man who risked death for another he barely knew.

Earlier, Willie had shared that the scent of Alex had ceased in the parking lot at Versailles. Which made sense if someone dragged her away. But there was no telling if she was alive at the time.

There had been Stone's eyewitness who'd point-blank said Alex lived, but that might have been a ploy to reel Bran in.

Should he check on Jeb and Van Noziak? See if Van had healed enough to become a reliable witness to Bran's innocence?

On the other hand, Jeb was a Council member and not too pleased to be left underground.

Maybe it was time to go back to the beginning. Check out Versailles himself. Yes, the Council had met there but how likely was it the members would still be around? Especially with the dust up after the Were attacks. Even if they left some preternaturals in the area, it was a risk Bran was willing to take as the quickest way to find a link between him and Alex.

He might not get Alex's scent trail, but he could cast a Seeking spell. How hard should it be to find one witch/shaman?

Given it was Alex, plenty hard.

Next woman he was attracted to was going to be full human. Compliant. Soft spoken, and tractable.

Only problem was, he feared it might be too late to find such a woman, especially if he remained wrapped in the spell of Alex Noziak.

CHAPTER 16

The scream roused me. A girl's scream, followed by babbling in French and English. Mostly English and curses.

I turned my head, but that was all. All I could manage.

Two big goons who smelled like Weres were dragging a girl from the cell opposite me. She was making them work at it though, kicking and biting and dragging her feet. Not that she stood a chance. They must have been told not to hurt her, though, as they hadn't yet used their full strength against her.

Until her kicking foot connected with the crotch of one of them. He doubled, shouting, "*Merde*," before he backhanded her.

She flew like crumpled paper across the tiny room, slamming into the far metal bars before sliding into a shapeless heap. One that wasn't moving.

"What the—" I wasn't even sure what I was going to say as I fought against straps holding me. With an oath my brothers used quite often, I popped the canvas and levered myself first to an elbow, then a sitting position. I didn't hurt as bad as I had been, but still felt groggy and stiff. With a quick glance down, I realized I was still in the clothes I'd worn to go to Versailles, however long ago that was. Grass stains and dried blood streaked my jeans and sleeves.

With one tentative hand, I raised fingers to my neck, expecting to feel where my brother Van in his shifter form had savaged me. Not intentionally but under the influence of whatever drugs his kidnappers had pumped into him.

But instead of a raw, oozing wound, or even a wad of bandages, all I could feel was smooth skin. No scarring at all like the last time I'd touched the same spot.

How long had I been out of it this time around? An injury like this should have taken weeks if not longer to heal. But my astonishment was short-lived as one of the goons glanced in my direction.

"Look what you've done, now." The one who could stand upright smacked his buddy with a closed fist to his chest. "Boss said not to wake her."

The other guy's response was in French but even in my fuzzy state I got the gist of it. None of it flattering to me, or women in general, with a few extra comments for either his crappy job or his crappier boss.

If he really wanted crappy he should feel like me. I raised my head to glare at him, as if that was going to do anything. But it must have as he paused, casting quick, furtive glances between his cohort and me.

Why was it always Weres? They were not only among the strongest of the preternaturals, but the stupidest too. I could deal with one but not both.

"Let's get out of here," the English-speaking one said. French Guy must have been on the same wavelength, as he scrambled over to the unconscious girl and grabbed her, slinging her over his shoulder like a sack of feed.

I eased off the metal gurney, glad when my feet smacked the concrete floor, and my legs held. "Going somewhere?" I asked, my tone saying loud and clear that it wasn't a good idea. My throat still felt sore on the inside but I could sound like a badass and not a puffball waiting to get the stuffing kicked out of me.

Small improvements but I'd grab what I could get.

"What can she do to us, anyway?" English Guy spoke to his friend, as if seeking assurance.

When he didn't see any he looked back at me, his chin nodding upward. Pure bravado. I could smell his hesitation, hear the increase of his heart rate, the blub, blub of his blood surging through his body. Something about me scared him. Didn't know how I knew, but I'd take the extra little win.

"Why don't you set her back down." I wasn't phrasing it as a question. "Nice and gentle." I spoke to the guy who could understand me but looked at the goon clutching the girl.

I must look in worse shape than I felt, which was hard to imagine, but he started doing what I asked, keeping his gaze locked on mine, every movement slow and non-threatening.

Who said negotiation never worked? Oh, yeah, that would be me.

What was really surprising me, though, was I could hold the Were's gaze. Weres, shifters and vampires didn't go for the gaze-locking or even looking eye-to-eye thing with humans. They so got their panties in a twist. Saw it as some kind of aggressive body language. Which it was and why I was doing it for as long as I could. If this Were was powerful I'd be slammed into my place any second now, but not until he realized he wasn't dealing with an equal.

Before I even had a chance to congratulate myself on a job well-done, English Idiot grew some balls. He twisted with a snarl, and lunged toward me, snapping the gunmetal bars that separated us like pretzel sticks.

I moved before I knew it. One second propped on the gurney, the next meeting Goon Guy, head-on, like a battering ram hitting a tank. I used my uninjured shoulder bone as a weapon as I barreled into him. The move had worked on another Were recently so I tried it again. Only this time I added power punches from beneath his chin. One. Two. Fist to jaw. Elbows following in quick succession. Bam. Bam. Then a step back, just enough to give me some room to raise a foot high enough to thrust him backwards.

My IR teammates would have given me a high-five. Team instructor Stone a slight chin nod. My brothers? Beers all around, and not the frou-frou craft beers, but cold draft pulled from the Iron Mule Saloon in Idaho Falls. Upscale by Mud Lake standards and one of the few bars that one or the other of my brothers hadn't been banned from in Southern Idaho.

I expected the Were to stagger, not sail through the air like a football in the winning penalty kick at a high school football game. The only thing that kept him from flying farther was the stone of the far wall.

Ouch. That had to hurt.

Score me.

I didn't know who was more surprised, him or me, or the guy still clutching the girl.

"You next?" I snarled at him as he dropped the girl.

Damn, she was going to have one nasty headache when she woke up. If she woke up.

French Goon now stood in front of me, his arms swinging loose at his sides as if he debated morphing into his animal self or fleeing. The other guy was pulling himself into a sitting position, shaking his head. Probably hearing a few bells going off inside. Served him right.

I stepped away from the open cell door, their only means of escape, and nodded toward the hallway behind me. "Be my guest."

I guess French Guy understood more English than I gave him credit for as he rabbited past me in a blink. The other guy swayed to his feet, still looking dazed, then growled before raising his hands. Should I give him a lecture on the lack of good judgment by sending mixed messages to the person who'd just clobbered him?

Nah. You couldn't un-do stupid.

"Go. Now." I meant it, and he must have heard the steel beneath the two simple words as he shuffled past, his head hung low, one leg dragging behind the other. I was tempted to shout "boo" as he passed.

Who said I couldn't be magnanimous?

Poor baby.

I waited till he was out of sight before I crossed to where the girl still lay on the floor and crouched down beside her. Two fingers on the pulse in her neck told me she was still alive, though I could hear her heartbeat, too. That scared me because it wasn't something I was used to hearing. An after-effect of my being out of commission for whatever length of time I'd been recovering?

Possibly. I didn't want to think any deeper than that. Or about the words the Colin Farrell voice had said. So did not want to go down that rabbit hole. Besides, I had hurt a girl who smelled of unwashed clothes, fear and magic.

I guessed she'd been the one who begged for help earlier. Or maybe that had been another nightmare. Hard to tell anymore. But common sense told me it was time to skedaddle.

"Here you go," I mumbled, planning to lift her up at least as far as the welded bench/bed in her cell. Guess I didn't know my own strength, though, as I almost threw her into the air. I caught her at the last second as I jumped to my feet, having her sag against me. Last thing she needed was to get banged around some more.

Speaking of last things, remaining where we were wasn't too smart. No telling how soon goons one and two would reach their boss, or reinforcements, and return. I didn't want to be here when they came back.

I had no idea who the girl was I held. Didn't care right then. In the goons against girl debate, I landed firmly on the side of helping the girl. She looked about fifteen with stringy brown hair that needed a good wash and showed bruises along her too-thin face.

Mud Lake, Idaho, where I was from, didn't have too many strays, of the human variety. It was hard to run away when most folks in the county knew you by name, as well as the names of your siblings, parents, grandparents, plus, when your truck last had an oil change.

But my gut told me this was a stray, someone with no mom or dad who gave a rat's tail where she was. And that alone made me want to make sure she made it out of here alive.

"Come on," I said, thinking walk waltzing her might be the best option. It wasn't. Reminded me of the three-legged sack race I'd lost once at the Jefferson County fair back in my stupid days. Of course choosing to be hog-tied to Jimmy Calhoun of the roaming hands as my partner earned me a smack upside the head all by itself.

We hadn't even reached the cell opening when, far down the hallway, I could hear the roar of male voices raised. That pissed-off and sharing it sound.

Running out of time.

Without wondering how the hell I was doing it I swung the

girl across my shoulder in a fireman's hold and started running.

CHAPTER 17

I jogged down two lengths of a stone and brick hallway that looked like it was old when Paris was new, straining to listen to voices up ahead. Pausing before the next turn I heard what I'd been dreading, the sounds of low-timbered tones pitched for battle. They weren't necessarily out for blood, but were that low-vibe, rah-rah thunder of bullies psyching themselves up.

Not what I wanted to meet.

I'd paused at a T in the hallway. To my left, about four-feet in, the hall dead-ended. The right led to the oncoming reinforcements. A quick glance around showed me no doors, no windows, and only one option. A half-crescent shaped arch along the base of the dead-end part of the hall, with chiseled stone blocks creating an opening that might be just large enough for me to squeeze the girl through and follow her.

First, I had to get rid of the metal grate covering the opening.

When were things going to get easy?

I eased the girl down in a heap against the far wall, the better to protect her if we were trapped, but as close to the opening as possible. Then I grabbed the bars with both hands. They were rusted in spots but unfortunately, solid through and through.

What was someone protecting? As if anyone who had any other choice wanted to head into the stink wafting from behind the bars.

It was all I could do not to scream. Instead, I pulled. I wedged one foot against the stone wall and pulled again. Then both feet. Another pull. But only a small shift.

The pounding feet were stampeding closer.

What now?

I offered a quick prayer to Saint Jude, the patron saint of bad situations then remembered what I'd been trying to avoid. I was a bloody witch. Hello? I knew magic.

Okay, most of my spells backfired, but I didn't have a lot of options.

A protection ward wasn't going to keep them away from us, not without glyphs drawn on the stone floors to back it up or enough time to round up some garlic, cedar or sage. A propulsion spell might push one of them away for a moment or so, but not for long, and not very far.

Think, Noziak, think.

Of course. Like a quick slap to the forehead, which I must have been ignoring not to immediately come up with magic 101, the basics. A cloaking spell.

It'd work better if I had a cape or jacket to hide us both, but beggars couldn't be choosers.

I quieted my pounding heart as much as possible, whispering the first words of the chant:

"Create me a barrier between man and monsters.
Between dark and light.
Between good and evil.
Hide and shadow us.

To the light, better things.
To death, watch over and guide.
To struggle and emerge, advance.
I am willing to pay the cost.

So mote it be."

It was rough and I felt like I dragged the magic from deep within me, as if I struggled to shape the words. Still shadows hovered a little deeper around us.

It wouldn't help if anyone ran up close but it'd work well

enough to let me see the length of the hallway without being clearly seen in return.

I hoped.

CHAPTER 18

The thunder of half a dozen men pounding the stone floor echoed through the hall, reminding me of the rage of a certain Werebison I'd killed recently. Probably not the best thought as I continued to mumble/whisper the chant.

"Between dark and light.
Between good and evil.
Hide and shadow us."

The first attacker, a Were, rounded the corner, his comrades packed closely behind him, all preternaturals, by their odors. They looked like angry footballers denied a touchdown. I had a feeling I'd be the pigskin they'd like to toss around if they got their hands on me.

I barely breathed as they headed toward where we huddled, then veered off like a wedge of compact anger disappearing down the hallway leading to the cells.

Once they reached there it wouldn't take them long to realize we'd escaped. Then the real search would begin.

Chewing my lip, I returned to the iron bars, wondering if a propulsion spell might work on them. I'd only used it on preternaturals and not inanimate objects but it might help. Or maybe an unlocking spell? That'd be easier.

Besides, it was one of the first spells I learned on my own. I'd wanted into my brother Jake's room. Couldn't remember why but at thirteen I knew it was important. A few minutes searching on the internet, and once I got past all the gaming spells, I actually found an unlocking spell that worked like a charm.

I glanced at the girl beside me who remained out of it, slowed my breathing and closed my eyes, raising my hands to point toward the metal grate.

"Luce. Light.
Prima luce. First light.
Umbra. Shadow
Behold that which is closed now opens.
Behold that which binds is unbound.
Behold a need greater than thou.
Release what stops us.
Free the way."

At first, there was nothing. I creaked open one eye, hearing angry shouts in the background. Goon Squad had reached the cells.

"Come on, you freakin' spell, do something. Now!"

Sometimes it's the simple things that work best. A low rumble started, followed by a squeal I'm sure they could hear two countries away, but it was working. The bars were melting for lack of a better word. Think butter on a hot August day.

"Yes!" I pumped my arm. "Thank you, Mother Goddess, and the Great Spirits, too."

And just in the nick of time, as the footsteps had roared to life again. Coming back down the hallway.

"Alley oops," I whispered to the girl as I scooped her up and slid her through the opening.

I stuck my head through to make sure I wasn't dropping her down an inky well. Just my luck. It was dark, hades dark, but I could see the faint glint of water on stone not that far below. Smelled it, too. Think cow-rendering plant on steroids on a hot summer day. Pew!

I'd say the drop was the height of a tall man but not much higher. Still, any fall when you're unconscious wasn't a good thing. Any jump that same distance when you didn't know what you were going to land in wasn't a win-win either.

Even the stench made me hesitate but needs must. I angled the girl feet first and leaned over with my hands under her armpits so she didn't have far to fall. Then I let go.

I cringed as she dropped like a bale of hay.

Now my turn.

The footsteps were so close I could feel their vibrations against the concrete floors. I had squeezed myself into the half moon opening, realizing the unconscious girl might be younger than I thought as she didn't have to be contorted like I did to slide through, too many French pastries no doubt on my part, then, as I gripped the edge of the opening I thought of what I'd forgotten.

If I just disappeared as the goons ran past, they'd see the open hole. They might be stupid but not totally dumb. Even a Were could put together an open hole and missing hostages to come up with a possible escape route.

Maybe I could buy us some time.

Clutching the rock walls on either side of the opening, I started mumbling the cloaking spell again. Easier than it sounded. Dangling like wet laundry, only heavier, my fingers cramping, while I focused on the words.

"Create me a barrier between man and monsters.
Between dark and light.
Between good and evil.
Hide and shadow us."

My fingers were slipping.

"To the light, better things.
To death, watch over and guide."

Hold on. Hold on. For love of the Spirits, hold on.

"To struggle and emerge, advance."

Footsteps neared. The first legs appeared around the corner. Not running.

"I'm willing to pay the cost."

Why couldn't they run? Whiz past me? Too focused to look in my direction?

I air-paddled my feet, seeking a purchase on anything beneath me, a wall, a pipe, something, but nothing was there. Only open space.

"They have to be near," a Were snarled.

Please. Please. Please.

Fresh blood stained my lower lip as I bit into it. More legs in my view. Standing in a huddle.

If I let go and dropped, the spell would break. As it was, it wavered, like an old black and white TV set. All it needed was one set of eyes to look too closely.

Hold on. The voice washed against me. An out-of-thin-air smack.

Bran?

No one was around. How could I hear his voice?

Hold on.

It was his voice. Deep. Resonate. Pissed. Maybe that last part was coming from me. Soul-deep anger welling from within.

Don't let go.

For love of monkeys, as if I wasn't trying to do just that. And how dare he order me around, not when all I wanted to do was find a spell that would scatter him from one end of the planet to the next. Payback.

Merge. Now.

What the—he meant magic. If I merged with him, I could use his magic as well as my own. The ability to merge was not something I flaunted, or ever used without bad consequences. Now wasn't the time to start. No way would I trust his help. I'd done so once and Van paid for it.

Go away!

I can help. Merge.

As if. Last help he gave me he killed my brother.

I sucked in a ragged breath, wiggled my arms to lessen the strain and ignored Bran's voice. *Focus on the spell.*

"Between dark and light.
Between good and evil.
Hide and shadow me."

"Harvey, you return to the cells. Take them apart. Andre, you and Beavis remain here."

My focus faltered. Someone actually called their son Beavis? Guess that meant Butthead was around here, too.

"The rest of you, come with me."

Go. Go. Go.

Alex—

Away. I almost shouted the words out loud to Bran. Only an arrogant warlock would tempt fate by approaching a witch he'd wronged, and Bran was arrogant, through and through.

Not my problem right now. My problem was escaping. Then I'd deal with Bran.

A quick glance at the two guards left, their attention divided, one looking after his departed comrades, the other scanning the route back to the cells. Now what?

I couldn't hang here indefinitely. Especially as I heard a soft moan from below. Enough of a sound to catch the Weres' fine hearing.

"What was that?" One demanded, looking around as if scenting a ghost.

Not likely, but they could scent a randy witch who hadn't bathed since a battle with other Weres.

A propulsion spell might knock them backwards, but Weres were resilient bastards. They'd be up in a heartbeat and coming after us.

I knew. A binding spell. If I could raise my arms high enough to prop against the floor. Right elbow … almost there. Just a little bit more. Whew.

Now left.

Alex!

I jerked. My right arm sliding away as my legs wind-milled beneath me.

I was going down.

CHAPTER 19

Bran knelt one knee in the rain-dampened grass of Versailles in front of the *Le Petit Trianon*, the three-story square building where the Council of Seven had met only days ago. It was here, where brown stains still marked the spot, that he'd last seen Alex.

Her blood. The only link he had left to her.

The Seeking spell was a long shot. Spell casting was not his forte, but he was powerful, and desperate enough, to give it a try.

He almost landed on his backside when he connected with Alex. Nothing as easy as getting a clear idea of where she was, or even if she still lived, but a blast of her emotions. Fear. Desperation. Determination.

It was the last that gave him the most hope. Whatever his witch was up to her glass-green eyeballs in, she was fighting back. Not that he was surprised. This was Alex.

By focusing, ignoring the tourists giving him a wide berth, he caught glimpses. Darkness. The damp smell of stone. Fingers clawing rock.

Merde, she could be anywhere in Paris. Or in another realm made of Earth elements.

When her fingers began to slip a cry broke from him. "Hold on."

But would she listen? No, of course not. Alex had to do things her way.

"Hold on," he wanted to scream out loud again, but whispered instead as out of the corner of his eye he could already see a security man approaching.

"Don't let go," he murmured, feeling Alex's resistance. When he found her, wherever she was, he'd shake some sense into her.

He could help her, but not at a distance. "Merge. Now."

Would she listen? *Non!* Witches ought to be drowned at birth, before they drove everyone around them crazy.

"Sir?" An older male cleared his throat. "Do you need assistance?"

Oui, he wanted to shout, but what the guard had to offer is not what Bran needed.

He rose to his feet, brushing his hands together as if removing dirt. "*Merci*," he replied, using every ounce of restraint he had not to thrust a mage-laced bolt on the hapless man. An action that would no doubt stop the human's heart.

Instead, he nodded toward the ground, and spoke in as strong an American accent as possible to reassure the ground's guardian that he was a clueless visitor. "I was reviewing the sprinklers. I'm into sprinklers and ... lawn ornaments. Back home. You 'all *comprehende*? The water gizmos?" he mauled the words, watching confusion crease the other man's face. "To water the grass. You understand?"

The man started to shake his head in a negative, then decided it was not worth knowing what this crazy visitor was doing. "*Non*, do not touch *l'herbe*." He shook one finger to emphasize the point. "*Comprenez-vous?*"

Bran nodded, then added, "Have a nice day," with a small wave, surprised he didn't cringe as he uttered the words.

The guard must have decided that even a little of a crazy American was enough as he backed away, shaking his head.

Bran just wanted him out of harm's way before he tried to reach Alex again. But the man marched with the speed of a snail.

At last.

A quick glance around. No one near. He willed the guard not to look over his shoulder before Bran knelt once again. Touching her blood helped the connection, fuzzy as it was.

"Alex?"

He could hear her frustration spike. *Go away.* More than frustration though—pain. She was hurting, badly enough she couldn't hide it from him.

Mule-headed, independent, that was his Alex. She'd hate knowing how much of her emotions he was tapping into.

Including her urgency. What was she doing? Why? And, most importantly, where?

There was a threat near her. Which was also Alex. How could one witch draw so much trouble?

A sudden lurch spiked her emotions and his own. If he could just reach her.

"Alex!" he actually muttered the word out loud, his hands clenched, his muscles tensed.

But instead of her opening to him, she closed down. Down then out.

She disappeared.

But how?

So focused on pushing his right hand into the grass, as if that alone would open his link with her, he didn't hear the others approaching.

Until it was too late.

Simin fae.

They'd found him.

CHAPTER 20

I spiraled through the darkness before landing with a splat against hard ground, knocking the breath out of me. The breath and a loud "Oomph!"

The only thing that helped was the girl broke part of my fall.

But what was the point of saving her if I killed her in the process?

"What're you doin'?" she grumbled beneath me. Not that I blamed her.

"Sorry about that. Bad aim."

"No kidding."

Great, I'd saved a smart-ass.

I'd barely rolled over to my knees, stumbling to my feet when I realized the other problem. The Weres.

"You see anything?" came an angry voice. Most likely Beavis. I'd be angry my whole life if I had that name.

"Too dark," came the grumbled reply.

Ha! I wanted to shout. Some Weres you are. Even I could see in the murky shadows. Which wasn't a good thing because it looked like we were in a long, barrel-vaulted chamber. By the Mother Goddess, what now? A least it looked like the chamber continued for a distance. Maybe far enough to find a way back above ground.

"It stinks," mumbled my groggy companion.

"Yeah, but so does getting nabbed by the Weres." I kept my voice to an urgent whisper. "Keep it quiet."

"But you—"

I grabbed her arm and gave a hard squeeze. She released a peep but at least she was quieter than she had been.

One challenge at a time. The two Weres above.

A binding spell? To hold them just long enough for us to hightail it out of here.

I rocked back on my heels, feeling every ache and bruise, as I thrust my hands upward. No longer worried about my voice carrying, I shouted the spell.

"Air to wind, Earth to dust.
Call forth, needs must.
By water and by fire.
Help sought most dire.
Trouble to heed and trouble to find.
Threat to cast behind.
Compel. Coerce. Constrain.
Hide away this bane.
I thee call. I thee command.
Seek thee quicksand.
Threat be gone. Power be bound."

"What the—"

Whatever Beavis was going to say stalled in his mouth as the spell took hold. Sweet! The fact the curved walls and ceiling of the tunnels helped echo the spell made for one powerful casting.

At last, something going my way.

Now to get the girl away from here before the Were woke from his bound state. I'd say we had a minute or two before his good buddy realized what was going on.

I grabbed the girl's arm again, my hold not so tight but just as insistent. "Come on, let's put some distance between them and us."

"What did you do?" she whispered, glancing back at the frozen Were still visible through the opening. At least his head was.

"Simple binding spell. Won't hold him for long." Especially if his buddy just thrust the jammed Were through the hole. Nasty but expedient. I didn't want to scare the girl with that tidbit either, as I took off running through rock and rubble. Guess fear, confusion, and a constant state of fight or flight must be giving me endorphins I didn't know I possessed.

Way to go, me.

Just wait, Bran. I could take care of myself and would take care of him. And soon!

But even as determination echoed through me, I searched for him. And found nothing.

Part of me wanted to gnaw in frustration. How like the warlock to harass me while I was hanging high and dry, but when I could actually use his help, for my own reasons, he disappears.

But a small part of me flared into worry. That gut-clenching, don't-let-anything-bad-happen-to-him kind of worry. If anyone was going to take a piece of him, it was going to be me. No avoiding what he'd set up.

With a swift kick to my mental hiney, I glanced around, wondering where in the heck I was, other than deep beneath the city. The air was suffocating and humid, the only sounds the drip of water nearby and a pulsing rush farther away. Squeaks and claws skittering against rock warned me rats were around, all around, and by the Mother Goddess, I didn't want to think about what we were stumbling through, though I was glad we hadn't actually reached the sewers. Yet.

Hadn't I read once that Paris had the largest sewer system in the world, lengthwise? I'd been looking for information on the Mammoth Cave system in the US that was the longest in the world at almost four hundred miles. In comparison, the Paris sewers stretched about three times that length.

Yeah, I focused on trivia when a panic attack threatened. Damp, stinky, dark places were not on my go-to-for-fun list.

Getting out of here in one piece, now that was topping my to-do list, especially as shouting voices sounded from where we'd just been.

Couldn't a witch get a break?

"Come on," I murmured to the girl beside me who was huffing and puffing. We'd already jogged quite a ways. I should be on my knees, but was barely winded.

What was up with that?

Leave it to me to be complaining about what was working. It just gave me a creepy feeling that I was acting more like my brothers, than myself. I mean it wasn't fair at all growing up with shifter brothers who could run, jump, endure and fight harder than I ever could. A sentiment I whined about all the time.

So maybe I was channeling them? Yeah, I could live with that. Until I had more time to focus on it. Now I had to focus on a V in the tunnel system ahead.

Crumbling stone walls in both directions. Overhead, rusty pipes to the right, a metal handrail to the left. Silence and stygian darkness in both directions. Which way to go?

Eenie. Meenie. Miney. Mo.

Left.

Why? No logical reason, just my hearing warning me the voices were coming closer. The right looked an easier route so my convoluted logic said that's the way the Weres would prefer to go. Wasn't that Occam's razor? Or was it something else? Desperation speaking?

I veered toward the left, aware the walls were closing in. Not enough to slow us, unless I was leading us into a dead end.

Deeper and deeper we trudged, noticing the slope of the tunnel seemed to be angling down, the air getting thicker, and older smelling. Like dry death.

Keep going.

I tucked my head, held my breath and hugged as close to the nearest side wall as I could, figuring the air might be better there. I used one hand along the wall to anchor me. My silent travel buddy was brushing against the walls, her foot crumbling small stones as we passed, but the sounds behind us seemed to be receding. Or my own hearing was being deafened by the closeness pressing all around us.

Didn't I remember the Teenage Ninja Turtles doing something in the Parisian sewers in one episode of the TV show? But I think they had a boat.

Lucky reptiles.

And what about the *Phantom of the Opera*? He had a boat or skiff, too.

I was catching a pattern here that wasn't helping me, being boat-less and all.

The slope was getting steeper and steeper. Maybe that was why the metal rail was in place. Something to grab, though it smelled so strongly of rusted metal I didn't think it'd hold any weight without capsizing.

My shoulders were beginning to cramp from stooping. My lungs close to exploding from the dry dust as we trudged deeper and deeper into the dim light. I think my hands were bleeding from rubbing them against the rough walls. I could smell fresh blood but couldn't see them clearly.

Good news, I hadn't stumbled on any crocodiles. Yet. Maybe those were just American urban myths.

The tunnel took another sharp turn to the right and I stumbled over rubble beneath my feet. Rubble and slime.

I think I had a nightmare that started like this once. Or maybe I was storing up material for future wake-up-in-a-cold-sweat dreams.

The walls were still narrowing. Each step forward seemed it was squeezing us closer to both sides of the tunnel. Sweat dampened my waist, slipping cold against my skin beneath my cotton shirt as the humid heat intensified.

Soon I'd be struggling to move forward. At least my companion wasn't complaining, though I could hear her breaths chugging.

Suddenly, the hand I was brushing against the wall hit an open space. Like a shelf, or pockmarks of space between crumbling walls. Then I touched it. Peered closer. Big mistake.

A skull. Lots of skulls, staring out at us.

Sweet Mercy, where were we?

The catacombs. It had to be. Good news was my companion didn't seem to notice where we were. Either that or the beejeebees had been scared out of her, leaving her struck dumb.

Swallowing a lump of fear I paused, considering going back the way we'd just come. Skulls meant death and death increased the chances of spirits and magic. And magic with death and skulls often meant dark magic. Using the resting place of people who hid in terror gave power to black magic practitioners and the last thing I wanted was to go deeper into spaces where my magic was a liability, or an attraction to someone stronger than I was. Maybe the Weres were long gone, down the right hand tunnel.

Maybe I was a delusional idiot who deserved to die in a cave-in.

Enough of the pity party. Noziaks were not quitters. End of story.

Besides, I thought there might be a small wedge of weak light not that far ahead.

Far enough. I was panting by the time we drew closer, leaving the shelves of skulls behind. I was also shaking my head to keep salt-stinging droplets from my forehead dripping into my eyes and blinding me.

One step more.

And one after that.

The light was taking shape. It glowed more red than yellow. Like a demon's eye, only square.

What?

A door. Above a series of worn steps carved from solid rock and smoothed by centuries. There, just past a pool of water where the tunnel widened.

I wanted to shout hallelujah as the walls receded. Nothing else changed, just a hint more space, wide as a kidney-shaped pool and about twice as long, between those stairs and us. That whole trivia thing keeping me sane.

This was do-able.

I stepped forward but my foot found nothing. The girl behind me plowing into me and slamming me forward, her hands clutching my shirt.

For the second time in less than an hour, the sick feeling of a free-fall engulfed me. Right before I dropped through space and my head went under.

CHAPTER 21

It all happened so fast. The splash. The girl smacking my shoulders as her weight pushed me deeper into the inky waters. A whirlpool of traction tumbling me round and round.

I didn't want to die. Not like this. Not now.

Bran! The single word roared from my thoughts.

But there was no response.

Twisting. Twisting. Scrambling.

Where was the girl? Where was I? Where was air?

It seemed like hours but must have been only seconds before I popped up, my head escaping the water long enough to chug a breath.

There. Dead ahead. A slight shelf of concrete to my right.

The girl brushed past me. I grabbed her in a macabre water ballet, groping for her neck, to pull her head up. Best I could do was clutch her hair, tug it backwards so her face would raise up as I kicked toward the slab.

I scraped against it, sure there'd be no skin left on my face as I pushed the girl out first then wrenched myself after her.

The slab was wider then I'd thought. Which was good because there were no thoughts left as I twisted to my knees and did what any partial human would do after an unexpected dousing in who-knew-what-kind-of-water. I vomited. And vomited again, retching until all I had was dry heaves. Even that wasn't enough.

I was soaked to the bone. Shivering from the unexpected cold, though the water hadn't felt chilled.

That's when the tears came. Not poor-me tears, I told myself, feeling them wash against me. But WTF, I'd-had-enough tears. Even they didn't last long enough to help.

Besides, I had to check on the girl.

I crawled on knees and hands toward her, curled in a sodden S against the concrete.

"You alive?" I hoped she could hear me. She hadn't responded since I'd pulled her out. It just felt better to hear a voice, even my own.

"What hit me?"

I'd just about reached her, my hand extended to touch her arm when her voice jerked me back.

"You alive?" I repeated, knowing I sounded like an idiot, but I was afraid I'd drowned her.

"Damn, this sucks," she mumbled, rolling onto her face and gagging.

I knew that feeling.

Like a swimmer underwater too long, she kept spitting out water, and who knew what else, until her shoulders sagged and she lay flat.

I eased myself against the rock wall, my legs straight in front of me, my feet dangling over the water. Across the way I spied that red light again. Above us and glaring. But how to get there? And would there get us out?

"Who are you?" The girl turned her head toward me.

"Name's Alex Noziak."

"You're the damn witch who wouldn't help me earlier," she shot back. Which stung, given I'd been dragging her sorry ass around for who knew how long, almost killing me in the process.

Okay, killing us both, but sometimes righteous indignation felt good. Like now.

"Where are we?" she demanded, raising her head a little and sniffing. "Damn, it stinks."

"That stink would be you," I said. Yes, snark was my second language, except in incidents like this when it was my first.

"Are we ...?" She raised herself higher, which was pretty impressive given what she'd been through lately, but I wasn't

ready to give her credit for much yet. "Are we in the freakin'
sewers?"

"No." I brushed my sopping wet hair as far away from my face
as possible, not that it was helping anything. I was beginning to
think a Sinead O'Connor look might be the way to go instead
of my waist-length braid. I'd never get it clean. "The Savoy
was booked so we're in the lower level of the Ritz."

"Asshole," she snarled, pulling herself to a sitting position.

"That would be me."

She must have decided silence was a smarter option as she
looked around. She was a mess. But then so was I. If we ever
got out of here, we'd have to find dry clothes to have a sinner's
hope in heaven of getting help.

"That a door?" she said, pointing to the rectangle of red I'd
eyed earlier.

"Looks like it."

"Then why don't we ... I dunno ... go over there?"

I looked at her then, not that it'd be easy for her to see my
glare in the murky shadows. "We'd been aiming for that. Damn
near drowned us." I turned away before I added, "That pool is
way deeper than it looks and has a hell of an undertow to boot.
You a good swimmer?"

"Don't know how to swim at all." Her voice suddenly
sounded very young.

Great. I was going to have to play nice here. As the baby of
my family, I didn't get a lot of chances to play mercy nursey
with younger siblings. Besides, the Noziak way seemed more
along the lines of suck-up, buck-up and shut-up.

I went with the latter option. Until I heard the sounds.

"You hear that?" I scrambled to my feet, looking toward the
tunnel that had spilled us out into the pool.

"No. What is it?" She stood too, inching herself up the wall,
using it to support herself. Still, she didn't complain. Which
made me feel worse for verbally beating up on her.

A PIA I could deal with easier than someone trying to act
brave when they were anything but. Which didn't say a lot
about me.

"There." The echo had come again. "Not far now."

"What's not far?"

"Whoever is coming down the tunnel."

I could hear her suck in a breath. I would have too but it'd take too much energy. Energy I needed to find a way out of here.

"Someone coming to help?" she asked, her voice ending on a high note.

"Don't think so."

She glanced my way, as if I were being a meanie on purpose. "It could be. You don't know that for certain."

"You're right. I'm not certain about anything right now." I didn't bother looking at her, preferring to keep focused on the biggest threat. The one stomping through that tunnel. "But I do know there were several—" I caught myself, aware she was human and I'd almost said too much.

"Several what?" Did her voice hold an I-dare-you tone?

Nah. Too much yucky liquids on the brain. Though I was tempted to tell her the seven dwarves might be following us. I did say I could be snarky when stressed.

"Several bad guys, the same ones who hurt you back in the cell. My best guess is some, or all of them, will be arriving at the end of that tunnel any moment."

I'd underestimated my timing as first one, then another appeared. Their shadows loomed against the walls, thicker blackness against the grayer tones, their breathing raspy as if they'd run more than we had, even the sound of them sniffing the air reverberated against the stone walls.

"What now?" the girl whispered. She didn't panic, no matter how her heartbeat picked up.

And why could I hear that? Or maybe it was my own.

Either way, it looked like we might be in luck. Well, a very thin slice of luck, but given how much I'd found recently I'd take it.

There were only two threats, neither of them had spoken yet, but remained quiet, as predators did when hunting prey. Waiting for fear to spook their quarry.

"Do exactly what I say," I mumbled in a half breath to the girl. "Exactly."

She didn't reply but did give me a hesitant nod.

I'd take it.

"Hey, assholes, come and get us," I shouted, startling my companion beside me as I began jumping up and down. "Over here!"

I'm sure the girl thought I'd lost what marbles I might have possessed, but bless her heart, she started waving her own hands, after placing two fingers in her mouth and whistling.

That was above and beyond. I doubt I'd ever put my fingers in my mouth again if we got out of here.

But it worked.

The two Weres, for that's what they were as I could smell their stench even here, growled in return.

But they didn't move.

Great! We were probably up against the only two smart Were goons in the city.

My plan was simple. Weres, like shifters, had the same type of physiology, even in their human forms. They were dense masses, which is why they were so lethal as assailants. But put them in the water and they sank like stones.

All I wanted them to do was get riled enough to step forward, fall into the pool like I did, and let the water do the rest. If there'd been a half-dozen of them the ploy might not work, but with two, it just might.

If I could get them to move.

"Come on, idiots," I called. Not too loud because I didn't want their friends to join these two. My guess was the group had split up, sending an advance recon team in this direction, the rest taking the easier route back at the V in the tunnels. Shouting too loudly might attract the attention of the rest and that would be bad. Very bad.

"Assholes, afraid of fighting two women?" the girl beside me yelled. "Cowards."

She was good. Aim for the ego if nothing else more vulnerable was available.

It seemed to work too, as one dark shadow threw off the restraint of the other and leapt forward. Just as fast, he disappeared.

The other must have edged too close to the lip of the tunnel as his arms churned, then splash, he hit the water.

Yes!

"What now?" The girl elbowed me. "Shouldn't we find someplace to hide?"

"No." The word held a finality to it that caught her attention. Snagged and held as her gaze followed mine toward the center of the pool.

Like spinning crocodiles in a death throw, the water whisked into a froth with too heavy arms beating uselessly against it. No voices cried out. Probably, because in panic a Were's first instinct was to morph. Which would only hasten what was happening to them.

I swallowed. Deeply. Death, even to the bad guys, wasn't an easy sight.

Within a few moments, all that was left was a lingering ripple across the pool's surface. And silence.

"What happened to them?"

"What almost happened to us," I snapped, hating that I stood by as two died, but knowing it'd have eventually come down to this. Survival of us, or survival of them. Besides, these two might have also been involved with my brother's death, and if so, dying quickly was too easy for them.

I turned from where the girl stared at me. Probably wondering what kind of monster she was with. Didn't blame her. I'd thought the same thing about myself more than once since joining the IR Agency.

But if we were going to get out of this hellhole, we didn't have the luxury of a long memorial over the bodies of two wanna-be killers.

I started edging myself along the lip of concrete, aiming away from the tunnel opening and toward the beckoning red light. One hand on the wall for guidance, I inched one foot at a time ahead of me into the shadows. One unexpected dunking was enough, thank you very much. Wasn't going to go ass over teakettle again, not if I could help it.

"Wait. Where are you going?" the girl cried behind me, catching the back of my shirt with her hand.

I paused but didn't turn around. "Looking for a way out."

"Is there one?" she asked.

"Yes."

"Certain?"

I knew what she was really asking. Since we'd both nearly drowned and then watched what looked like two adult males do just that, she wanted reassurances.

Somehow, I didn't think she'd like the only kind of faith I could offer her. The one that went something like we'll-get-out-or-die-trying.

So instead I lied. "Yes. I'm certain."

Another step forward.

CHAPTER 22

I stumbled against the sudden blast of Bran calling my name. At least it felt like a cry, but as fast as it pierced me, it was gone.

"What is it?" the girl behind me asked.

I shook my head. Imagining things. "Nothing. Let's keep going."

What was happening to Bran? Why should I care? It wasn't as if I didn't have enough problems to deal with, but like a lingering echo, his voice haunted me.

Later. I'd figure out what was going on with him as soon as I could catch my breath.

It seemed like we'd snailed our way across the concrete far longer than the time it actually took to reach the end of the lip. Because I'd been moving so cautiously, this time I didn't topple headfirst back into the pool. Barely.

"That's it?" the girl's voice was raising an octave a word, the pulse of her heart keeping pace. "What now?"

Like I had all the answers. I didn't. But sharing that wasn't going to help us. Instead, I squinted into the shadows around us, a little lighter here because we were nearer the red glowing door. Across from the base of the steps actually, though there was still a good dozen feet of murky liquid between the first stair and us.

It wasn't still water either. Here I was close enough I could hear the churn of the whirlpool and guess at its origin. "I'd say there's another tunnel beneath the water here, leading away and sucking anything in the pool toward it."

"You thinking we can get out that way?"

I shook my head. "Not my first choice. We have no idea if the outflow tunnel here is solid water with no headroom for air or how far it might go on."

"Or even if there is an exit," the girl added.

"Good point."

"So?"

I looked across the ten to twelve feet and weighed our odds. If I were by myself, I might make it. Maybe. I had no idea how long it'd been since I'd last eaten but could feel the fatigue weighting my limbs. Fighting exhaustion and a whirlpool were not a good mix. Then there was the whole dread of voluntarily easing back into the water. It was enough to have my stomach heaving.

And what about the girl?

She'd admitted she couldn't swim. Could I get her across? Alive?

"I think we should stay here," she said, all belligerence leeched from her voice.

"We have no food. No clean water, unless you want to drink that sludge. We're not going to get stronger by sitting around in wet clothes." Yeah, I was being intentionally brutal but I had to break through to her. It'd be hard enough helping her across with her assistance. I had no idea what would happen if she fought me.

Okay, I did know. We'd both drown.

"Look." I turned toward her. "Last thing I want to do is get back into that pool and fight my way across to the other side ... "

"But?"

I turned away, ignoring the knotting in my stomach as I straightened my shoulders. "There's no choice. You can come with me and I'll do everything in my power to get us both out alive. Or—"

"Or you'd leave me."

"I'm not going to fight you on this. Everyone should have their own choice." And I meant it. It always came down to hard choices. My going after Van on my own with only Bran and his friends. Us ending up here instead of staying in the cells. My sending Bran to help my brother, which led to Van's death.

Choices always had ramifications and they were not always happy endings.

Sucking in a deep breath and thrusting my grief about Van back into an open bleeding wound somewhere inside of me I asked, "So you coming or not?"

She released a rusty laugh. "Yeah, death by drowning or starving."

"I think the dehydration will kill you first."

"Thanks."

I eased myself down to the slab, sliding my feet and legs into the chilly liquid. Crapola, I didn't want to do this.

"You don't have any spells?" the girl asked, still standing, her back pressed so hard against the stone wall I was surprised she didn't disappear into it.

"You mean a levitation spell? Or maybe a flying monkey leap?"

She wasn't even looking at me. She was looking at the water. "I'd be happy with a stink-stink-stay-away spell."

I actually caught a rough laugh bubbling up before I tamped it down. "Sorry. Fresh out of one of those."

"Some all powerful witch you are," she grumbled, like a petulant child, but she flopped down beside me before the last word was out of her mouth so I guess she'd made her choice. "Next time I end up in a cell it's going to be with someone who has more magic than you."

"You do that," I said, turning myself to lower myself in deeper, holding on to the concrete lip like the edge of a swimming pool. When I was holding my upper body above water with my elbows, I looked at the girl. "The way I figure it, if you get in like I am, I'll get behind you to hold your head up and out of the water."

"While it's pulling me down?"

"While it's pulling both of us down," I snapped. "I'll use my left shoulder against this wall." I tapped on the stone to my left. The one with an opening down its length somewhere. "You—" Damn, this was going to be harder than I thought. "If you can keep your legs and feet raised as high as possible, you'll act like a wedge against the stone." I slapped the wall again. "We'll scrape along until we reach the steps there." A nod indicated the end goal.

"And if I can't do that?" she asked.

"We die."

Yup, I could be the queen of bitchiness when needed. And boy did we need it.

CHAPTER 23

Bran said nothing as three simin fae flanked him on each side, silent and deadly. Until one spoke in a high-pitched, scratchy whisper, "This way."

Not a lot of options. So he followed where they led, surprised when they headed toward *Le Trianon*. The building the Council of Seven met in a few days ago, and where he'd been headed when an attack by Weres on Alex derailed him.

Now he marched as if to an execution, which it very well might be. His own.

Not up the front stairs like visitors who posed to take photos, but around to a black side door. It'd always been said a black door attracted demons he recalled as he stepped from the spring freshness of outside, to the closed, stuffy air of a building created for a dead queen—Marie Antoinette.

Not that now was the time for history lessons, or any thoughts not focused on his survival.

No one knew where he was. No one expected him elsewhere, except for his business empire, whom he'd contacted earlier before he left to meet with Stone and left a message that he might be out of communication for a few days. No one who would raise an alarm if he never walked out of this building.

Knowing he was being brought before the Council, that was a very real possibility.

Time to end this charade, knowing the simin fae would slice him down before he moved far, though he was willing to take the risk. Besides, he possessed mage abilities that could take them off guard. All he needed was a moment or two.

He paused, causing the fae to halt, their gazes snapping to his.

Their leader spoke, "We're late."

"You might be," he mumbled as he braced himself to cast a spell he'd only attempted once before.

"Air to wind, Earth to dust.
By water and by fire, I call thee."

The fae started rustling, looking between one another. That was the Achilles heel of simin fae. They were warriors, through and through, but not generals.

He raised his hands ever so slightly but enough to call to the east and to the west.

"Trouble to heed and trouble to disperse.
Compel. Constrain. Conjure."

The floor started rocking beneath them, small swells of magic erupting. The nearest windows rattled. A crack appeared spidering from the ceiling.

"Halt!" The fae hissed.

It was too late. Bran notched his chin and braced himself.

"I thee call. I thee command.
Power be bound. I be gone."

A flash of orange tainted smoke was all that remained of where he'd been standing.

CHAPTER 24

It took another five minutes too long for the girl to make up her mind. We didn't have a lot of options. I was getting colder and more exhausted. "I'm not in a sauna here," I snarled at last. "Either go or stay but decide. Now."

"You're a bitch," she mumbled as she slid into the water beside me.

"I know it."

"That's okay. I'm a bitch, too," she said, gritting her teeth against the cold.

This time I did laugh. At times I could like this kid. "Hey, what's your name?" I asked.

"Why? You want it for the tombstone?"

"Something like that."

Tit for tat. Maybe I didn't want her name. But in case only one of us lived, and I was going to give everything I had to make sure both of us did, but just in case, someone should know what happened to their daughter or sister.

I glossed over my assumption that no way was I going to cash in today. It wasn't an option.

"It's Sabina," she mumbled so quietly I almost missed it.

"Like that TV teenage witch?" That'd suck.

"No. I was named for a great aunt."

"Sounds Irish."

"Well, I'm not."

If I could have lifted my hands to tell her I wasn't the enemy, I would have. Instead, I put temper in my voice. "Fine,

Sabina. Get your ass over here before I forget I wanted to save you."

The smile she gave me said, bring it on.

Good, we understood each other perfectly.

I eased myself out into the water while keeping my shoulder against the wall to my left. Almost immediately, I could feel the sucking power of the whirlpool pulling both of us down. It was stronger than I'd expected.

Damn and double damn.

The girl—Sabina—eased herself over, dodging under my right arm until she was directly in front of me.

I swallowed, willing my stomach not to start heaving from the stench and the fear.

"I'll count to three." I maneuvered my left arm along her shoulder and under her chin, sensing her panic, which I ignored. No sense both of us giving into the terror churning through us.

"When I say three I'll start swimming backwards, pulling you by your neck."

"You won't choke me?"

Might, if she didn't get her act together. But what I said was, "It could feel like that but it's only to keep your nose and mouth out of the water."

"Fine."

"You keep your body in as straight a line as possible, floating."

"Got it."

"One." *This so wasn't going to work.*

"Two." *Where was a decent power spell when you really needed one?*

"Three." I used my left foot to shove away from the wall, but even as I was pushing off, Sabina grabbed onto the concrete lip even harder.

Oh, no you don't.

I tugged with all my might, which was considerable, more than I expected and almost submerged the two of us. Luckily, most of my left side was smashed against the wall on that side so we weren't sucked under. Yet.

Like a bobbing fishing lure in the hands of an incompetent angler, we moved away from the lip, Sabina struggling and twisting, which was going to make it that much easier for the whirlpool to catch us and drag us down.

"Stop. Fighting," I ground out through clenched teeth. My head was barely above the sludge, opening my mouth to speak coherently was so not an option.

Either my anger got through, or the clutch of my arm around her neck cut off enough of her oxygen supply she couldn't struggle as much, but she slowed her gyrations.

I used my free right arm to keep us moving across the pool, my legs almost useless except for a few feeble kicks. Sabina wasn't doing that great a job back-floating on the water so last thing I wanted was our legs to entangle.

Just how far was twelve feet across anyway?

I felt I'd been dragging her dead weight for hours.

Stroke. Pull. Stroke.

I could have made it across the English Channel by now.

Only good thing was Sabina seemed as determined as I was to keep her mouth clamped shut so no complaints spewed forth.

Stroke. Pull. Stroke.

When we got out, I was going to take a shower that lasted hours, days maybe.

Stroke. Pull. Stroke.

Had to be closer. I twisted my head to check the distance, biting back a moan when I calculated we'd gone less than halfway.

Then, just when I didn't think I could be any more grossed out, my foot tangled with something beneath the water.

I jerked. My feet kicked against something solid and bulky. Yucky water splashed over both our faces.

Only my right hand kept us afloat and it wasn't doing too good a job.

I used everything I had and then some to keep pulling. Even without using my feet, whatever was down there was blocking our forward movement.

We were going to die.

No one would ever know. All my father's warnings about coming to a bad end because I was too willful roared through me.

That's when Sabina started screaming.

If I thought she'd been difficult before, it was nothing to her thrashing now.

What the Mother Goddess—

"Stop!" I gulped around the surge of liquids she caused to crest over both our faces, forcing me to squeeze both mouth and eyes closed.

When I opened my eyes I noticed her pointing fingers.

A hand bobbed above the water. Fingers curled into a grotesque fist.

Call me sick but I almost laughed out loud. Not the ha-ha kind but the relief kind.

The Loch Ness monster wasn't jamming us, only one of the dead Weres.

Only an IR agent a few weeks and I could be so callous about a dead person. But I'd take callous over fear of the unknown.

With a groan, I kicked at the submerged body, using it to push off for another foot of pool covered.

The hand disappeared. Sabina quit her banshee wailing. Only three more feet to swim.

Praise the Great Spirits, we might make it.

CHAPTER 25

I was gulping air, my heart pounding, my muscles firing with after burn by the time my right hand swung back and hit the stone base of the stairway. If I had enough energy left to shout halleluiah I would have, but it took my remaining energy dregs to pull Sabina to the slab.

We both scraped our elbows on the level, gulping air like two beached whales.

"You really are a bitch," were her first words.

I barely had the womp to turn my head and spear her with a glance. That's the thanks I got? I'd hauled her skinny ass this far and all I'd earned was another slap? "You're welcome," I snarled.

She ignored my sarcasm. Not easy to do as she asked, "What was that?" She gave a weak wave toward the pool. "You know. That thing?"

"Dead guy chasing us." No need to freak her out and admit it was a preternatural being sent to kill us.

"Oh," she released a sigh that sounded like it'd been pulled from her toes.

"What'd you think it was?"

"I dunno. A golem or an Adaro."

So maybe she knew a hint more about preternaturals than the average teen.

I shook my head. "I don't even know what an Adaro is."

"They travel in waterspouts. Come from a person's most wicked parts. Hate humans."

Fraulein Fassbinder, the IR instructor of all creatures mythical and dangerous, would love her. I knew I was impressed.

"Sounds like you know a few scary things?" The words were out of my mouth before I could snatch them back.

"Yeah, live on the streets long enough and you know there's a whole lot more scary out there than not." Her voice trailed off, as if she'd ran out of endurance, or decided even speaking about the bad things could summon them. Or maybe a little bit of both.

Since floating against the stairs wasn't getting us anywhere fast, except more exhausted, I inhaled a deep breath and pulled myself out of the sludge, first elbows then knees until I could turn on the small slab, like a cat finding the best place to sun itself. Only there wasn't any sun and as nice as a nap sounded it wasn't on the agenda. I grabbed the back of Sabina's shirt and hauled her up to land with a solid splat next to me. Not that there was a lot of room. Space for two barely and not to do more than sit or stand.

She raised her head and looked up. "We're going there?"

"Unless you have a better idea." There was no sting to my words. I didn't want to waste the effort. Though as I turned around to look at the worn rock stairs and the red glow at the top, I wanted to groan. The angle looked like the trajectory for Mt. Everest, nearest the peak, where most folks just gave up and died.

"Any idea where the door goes?" she asked, her voice puny.

"Nope." I pulled myself to my knees. "Best bet is out of here."

"Works for me," she mumbled, mimicking my moves. If I looked as all out as she did, I wondered if we'd make it to the top.

Needs must, Noziak. Get a move on it.

Then I paused. "Should wring as much water out of our clothes now, before we get topside. With as hot as it is in here they might even dry a bit."

She nodded and we wrung t-shirts and pants as much as we could. It helped, a little, till she looked at my hands, which were more visible in the red light.

"I thought you'd been bleeding earlier, from your hand, but you're not."

I followed her gaze and gave a rough shrug, searching for an explanation that would make sense. I settled for a half-truth. "I'm pretty tough."

Liar. My hands didn't look any worse for wear, which sent a chill through me that had nothing to do with wet clothes. No way was I now a shifter. If I were, I'd have drowned in the pool. Wouldn't I? So maybe the doctor had given me something to aid in healing. That had to be it.

To distract the girl, and myself, I grabbed the metal rail along one side of the stairs to haul myself hand over hand as the legs weren't fully cooperating. "First one to the door gets the first shower."

"What shower?" she wanted to know behind me.

"Somewhere. Out there. There's a shower with our names on it."

"You sure?"

I choked back a snort. We'd survived Were attacks, imprisonment, near drowning, more Were attacks, and she wanted guarantees on a shower. "We're in Paris. There's going to be a shower somewhere."

"As if anyone in their right mind would let us in to use their shower," she huffed each word and ended on a gasp.

I paused, hating the fact she was right. I'd so focused on just getting out of here I hadn't thought beyond that. That and killing Bran. So now what?

There was a silver lining. If we were picked up for wandering the Parisian streets soaking wet and looking like we did, we'd no doubt be carted off to jail. There they'd have to wash us down before they locked the cell doors. Wouldn't they? Yup, it wasn't much of a silver lining but I'd grab onto it. Plus, jail usually allowed a person one phone call. If I could connect with the IR team with that call, and if they were still talking to me, I just might get through this, whatever I was embroiled in. If I couldn't contact them I'd head to the safe house, assuming they'd let either of us out of jail.

Suddenly life was looking better.

I started pulling myself upwards again. Until I reached the last step, Sabina hot on my heels and slapping one hand on the metal door before I could catch my breath. "Me win," she huffed.

"Fine." I didn't really care. Unless there was only one shower with limited hot water. Then all bets were off.

I grabbed for the handle and pulled.

But nothing budged.

CHAPTER 26

If smacking my head against the door would've done us any good, I would have done so. Of course the bloody thing would open from the other side and it looked like it locked from there, too.

Sabina started pounding and kicking on it, tears tracking down her cheeks, visible in the red glow leaking from around the door. I pulled her back. "Only going to waste what energy you have left. We've got to come up with a plan."

"You mean like jumping back into that pool? Your great earlier plan?"

That put some starch in my backbone. "Yeah, like that. Which did get us off a useless ledge."

"So we can stand in front of a useless locked door?"

Well, if she was going to be snippy about things.

I turned my back to the door and slid down to a crouch. I was right. I knew I was, but I was also so strung out I needed a minute to come up with my get-us-the-hell-out-of-here plan.

Sabina joined me, vibrating with anger. Which wasn't going to change anything.

So I just crouched there, my hands hanging useless between my bent knees, feeling the cold press of metal against my back, wondering what now.

"And you're supposed to be this amazing witch," she muttered under her breath as if I wasn't right there, listening.

It took a few seconds for her words, and not just the tone, to register.

"Says who?" I asked, my voice having more oomph than I did right then.

She nodded her head toward the tunnel where we'd exited what seemed like a lifetime ago. "The assholes who'd wheeled you into that cell."

Which gave me a whole new shiver of creepiness. "Who were they?" I was grasping at straws to make sense of anything.

"It wasn't like they introduced themselves to me," she snipped back.

I raised my head enough to cut a sharp glance in her direction. Not that I blamed her for her nerves. Much. "So why'd they take you?"

"Duh." Now she sounded like every teen ever born. "I was plan B."

"That meant somebody had a plan A."

"You were plan A."

Okay, a few more comments like that and I'd be having a full-blown panic attack. Except Noziaks didn't do panic.

There was always a first time though.

"Any idea what plan A, or B, was?"

She shrugged.

I remembered words. The name Zaradian. And something more? But it escaped me.

There had to be a thread of logic behind whatever was going on. If I could figure that out, I might know whom I was running from and how to avoid them. Sure, leaving Paris and wanting to race home to Mud Lake was a good start, though I wasn't really escaping. I'd be returning. There was a difference.

Yeah, right.

The team would help me figure out what was going on. Maybe even help. If they hadn't already written me off as a lost cause. So the plan was still in place, if a little rough around the edges. Find the team. Tell them what I knew.

Then find and take care of Bran.

Other snippets of conversation from before came back to me. I cut a hard glance at my companion. "You're a witch, right?"

She gave a hard, tight nod. Like she wasn't used to admitting such a thing in public. I could understand that.

"So whoever is behind kidnapping you ..." Another assumption. "You were kidnapped, right?"

"Give the lady a prize."

I could get snarky. Really I could. It was my second language. My first when I was stressed, which seemed like every day since joining the IR Agency, but I was getting a little tired of getting chewed up every other sentence.

"I'm trying to find out what the hell is going on," I snarled, having a much bigger bark than the kid beside me. "So get off your high horse and start giving me some straight answers. Got it?"

It took a few pregnant minutes before she offered a jerky head nod.

"So you were snatched from where?"

"*Les Halles,*" she said. I must have looked as clueless as I felt, so she added, "Near the *Fontaine des Innocents.*" Her *duh* was unstated but loud and clear.

"That a popular place for teens to hang out?" I asked.

"Yeah. What of it?"

It was my turn to ignore her, the wheels turning in my head. "Who knew you were a witch?" At her frown I pushed, "Come on. Friends? Family?"

"My old lady kicked me out a year ago."

I held back my surprise. She couldn't have been older than fifteen or sixteen. I wanted to ask but that wasn't going to get me the intel I needed and probably just piss her off again.

"So ... friends," I muttered, mostly to myself.

"My friends would never." She shook her head. "*Non. Un acte de trahison.* Never."

"In English?"

"They wouldn't rat me out."

"Somebody did." I kept the words low-keyed, raising my hands in a half—WTF gesture. "Someone had to have shared information about you to someone else looking for a witch."

"They—" She jerked as if prodded with an electrical prod. "Aurelie." Sabina all but spat the word. "That bitch. She'd sell her soul for a few *sous.*"

"Is this—" I was going to say Aurelie, but changed my mind. "Is this bitch like you?"

"Is she a w—"

"No, I mean is she living on the streets?"

"When she chooses."

This wasn't getting me anywhere. "So how long ago were you taken?" I needed a stronger idea of what or who I was up against back in those cells.

"Four or five days. Maybe a little longer."

"How long was I out? Since they put me in the cell?"

"About two days."

No telling how much time had passed before that.

Then, like a slap against my head, an image of a man in a white coat slammed into me. The one I'd held by the throat, watching his head dangle. And another man, with an accent. Without conscious thought my fingers went to rub my neck and shoulder, where once I'd felt scar tissue. Now even that was gone.

What the Sam hell was going on?

"We going to get out of here?" Sabina nudged me. "Or you going to keep meditating."

Freaking out was more like it. So far my questions raised more questions than answers. Which wasn't getting us anywhere. But I would get answers and soon. What happened to me? Would the IR team help me? And how was I going to find Bran? And those were just for starters.

I rose to my feet, glad the door at my back helped to keep me upright.

"You got a plan now?" Sabina asked, her voice sounding wary.

"Don't have a plan," I admitted, stepping away and turning toward the door. "But I do have an idea."

If Sabina's face weren't so exhausted, I'd say her eyebrows raised, but at least she'd joined me facing the door.

"Good." I hadn't asked for her help. I could use it, but no telling what kind of state she'd be in if she pulled magic. Or even how much magic she could pull. Some witches were more focused on herbs and potions. True magic was way out of their league.

"What're you going to do?" she asked, chewing her lip.

"Try a door-opening spell."

"You mean like in Harry Potter?"

I gave her a get-real look. "No, more like this." I closed my eyes, slowed my breathing and spread my hands palm forward toward the door. My Latin was rusty but the worst I could do was blow us off the stairs and back into the pool. At least that's what I hoped was the worst.

I'd only used this spell once, years ago, to break into the boys' locker room at good ol' Terreton Jr. High. It worked like a charm then. Well, except for setting off the fire alarm, when it backfired just a smidge, and sent a tower of black smoke barreling down the hall.

Best not to think about that too much.

I took one more deep breath and started.

"Conivolus. Conivola. Conivolum.
Closed. Hidden. Covered.
Adopertus. Adoperta. Adopertum.
Veiled. Disguised. Hiding.
Clausus. Clausa. Clausum.
Impervious to feeling. Locked in. Enclosed.
Aperio. Aperire. Aperui.
Uncover. Open. Disclose.
To thine change. Through my hands.
Dissero. Disserere. Disseravi.
Unfasten. Unbar. Unlock."

I pushed everything I had at the spell. Which wasn't a lot. It took a few seconds before we heard a loud rumble, followed by a thud, then the door squeaked open.

Maybe I was getting better at this magic stuff. Or a hint more consistent. Wasn't that like life, just when you decided to chuck something because you'd never get it and return to the way you'd always been, only then did all the practicing start paying off. Maybe now I could feel like I wasn't such a loser as a witch. Being a shaman, which I'd barely touched understanding, was a whole other issue.

"Wow, you've got to teach me that." Sabina uttered a low whistle.

I was too busy scrambling to wrap my fingers around the door edge to wonder if she had learned any magic before she was kicked out of her home. First things first though.

It took the two of us to wedge the heavy-assed door open enough to squeeze through.

"Now what?" Sabina demanded as I followed her and before I got my bearings. Once I did I bit back a groan.

We'd left a wide-open area for a claustrophobic-inducing concrete shaft filled with the fire-red glow. There was a small tunnel leading off of it at about thigh height and a second tunnel, straight above us with a rusty ladder that looked taped together. It led up, way up to where the red light pulsed through some scattered holes. Manhole cover? Probably.

I craned my neck as far back as it would go to judge the length we'd have to climb and the chances of the ladder surviving two of us scrambling up it. Not good.

But we'd already survived worse and were still kicking.

"My guess is one of us at a time can give the ladder a shot."

Sabina was giving me her patented yeah-right look. "And if it crumbles?"

"Then the other one catches." I didn't say it'd be a perfect plan. With a quick glance at the cramped tunnel I added, "If the ladder breaks, we can always start crawling through the low tunnel as a fallback option."

"Why not—"

"Because anything horizontal is going to keep us down here. The streets are above us so that makes the most sense."

"Got it." I could see her weighing the odds before she asked, "Who goes first?"

"Since we don't have a coin to toss and you're lighter than I am, you head up."

"And if I can't get the grate or cover or whatever is at the top open, what then?"

"Then we deal with it."

Was I ever this pessimistic as a teen? Probably, but sheesh. I added, "If I go and break the ladder we're down to hands and knees through that." I pointed at the tunnel. "You want that for sure, be my guest."

Either my suggestion, or tone, got to her as she snarled, "I need a boost up."

I cupped my hands, bent my knees, and hoped I had it in me to lift her high enough. I had no idea how I'd do the same maneuver on my own, but one problem at a time.

"Come on," I snarled, feeling like déjà vu all over again. "The sooner you go the sooner we can get out of here."

She sucked in a deep breath and used my shoulders to steady herself as she slipped her left foot into my hands. I was as surprised as she was that we didn't both topple.

When I was sure she was as stable as she was going to get I counted to three and pushed upwards.

Must have had more in me than I expected as I thrust her high enough she easily reached the lowest rung of the ladder.

"Wish me luck," she mumbled, her words echoing in the tube surrounding her. It'd be a tight fit for my shoulders given she barely cleared an inch on any side.

I swear each rung she climbed took as much out of me as her as I stood there willing her upward. At one point she hesitated, her breathing ragged, her heart near bursting as the ladder shuddered, but didn't break.

All I could do was watch the light from the top become dimmer and dimmer as her shape blocked it.

Step. Pull. Step.

"Doing a great job," I shouted from below.

"Fuck you," came the weak response.

I didn't blame her. We were both running on fumes.

Step. Pull. Step.

"Almost there," I called out, no longer looking up to give my neck a break.

Step. Pull. Step.

I was surprised when I heard her shaky, "I'm here."

Like a shot of high-dose adrenaline, I wanted to jump up and high-five her. "What's up there?" I called when she got very quiet.

No answer.

"Sabina, talk to me."

I heard a short laugh and not the ha-ha funny kind.

"What is it?" I called out again, half-tempted to jump on that ladder and shake some spirit back into her.

"The world's heaviest manhole cover," she said, so quietly I had to strain to hear her.

"Can you move it?"

I know, I know, it was a stupid question so I wasn't surprised when she bit off a snort. "If I could, do ya think I'd just be hangin' here for the fun of it?"

Since I assumed that was a rhetorical question I didn't bother answering. So we had two options. I'd follow her up the ladder and hope it didn't break with the weight of the two of us on it or try a propulsion spell on the iron cover. Except she was between it and me, which meant I stood as good a chance of shooting her up and against the cover as I did of exploding it off.

So I guessed we were down to one option.

"Hold on, I'm coming," I shouted, taking a running leap to reach the first metal rung.

CHAPTER 27

I swear that climb was the hardest thing I'd ever done. Okay, maybe not as bad as fighting grimples, djinns, or crazy-assed Weres, but close. Each step creaked and shuddered, making my muscles tense, sweat running down my temples. I could hear Sabina's heartbeat escalating the closer I came. And I'd been wrong about it being tight, the space was impossibly close-fitting, until I was sure my shirt and skin were rubbed raw by the time I pulled myself up beside her.

"Feel like a damn sausage," she mumbled as I caught my breath.

And that was before I told her, "You're going to have to squeeze yourself as far as possible against one side."

"Why?"

"You want a propulsion spell hitting you full force from a few inches away, be my guest."

"You don't have to be snotty," she said, but at least she was now leaning as far as she could away from me.

"You so haven't seen snotty." Yet.

I had to let go of the ladder, bracing my back against the far wall to free my clammy hands, steadying myself with my wet shoes propped against the metal rungs. Only when I was sure I wasn't going to jettison down the tube I closed my eyes and inhaled a deep breath, one smelling of rain layered with gas and oil, two scents I never thought I'd be happy to guzzle in.

Focusing, I began the chant I'd used what felt like hours ago.

"Musca. Moveō. Volō."

A slight breeze frothed in the tube.

"You sure this is going to work?" Sabina asked.

"Quiet."

Concentrate.

"But what if—"

"Keep chatting and we'll never get out of here."

She sniffed in response. That I could ignore.

"Volō. Volō. Volō. Rumpō.
Musca. Volō. Rumpō.
Volō. Rumpō."

I wondered why the magic felt so sluggish? So hard to tap into? I know I hadn't used magic a lot in my life until I'd joined the team, but it'd never felt so diluted. Or maybe this was the mercurial response of a gift I'd never wanted?

"You are more than you were," a woman's voice whispered against me.

Scared the willies out of me as I jerked, glad the tube was so damn tight there wasn't a lot of room to jump out of my skin.

Mom? I said mentally, not wanting to freak out Sabina, or myself, anymore. *Where are you?*

"I've never left you," she answered. A response slicing me from the inside out. Now was not the time to tell her she sure as hell did leave me, and my brothers, and my dad. Instead I shook my head, willing myself to ignore her voice, and timing, so I could concentrate on the spell. That and getting out of this hole.

I ignored her presence, and swallowed past the deep lump in my throat, as I calmed my voice.

"Medius. Damnum. Rumpō.
Damnum. Rumpō.
Damnum absque injuria."

The manhole cover started gyrating like the lid on a boiling pot. Only then did I realize that if we were beneath a busy street I could be shooting a heavy metal disc into oncoming traffic, and given the size of some of the compact European cars on the street, that could be lethal.

Too late. Like a geyser pulled from a deep well, magic swelled up, thrusting the cover upwards, as a champagne cork released from its pressure.

"Yahoo!" Sabina shouted, pulling herself upward to suck in fresh air.

Until I grabbed her shirt and held her back.

"What the—"

"Check for cars," I warned, feeling like the fuddy-duddy parental unit, so I added, "I'm not going to pick up the pieces from a car ripping off your head."

"Fine, Mom," she shot back.

No way had I ever been that snotty as a teen. Okay, maybe once. Or twice. Or—never mind.

I watched as Sabina timidly poked the top of her head out, then shot up. She pulled herself out of the tunnel so fast I didn't even have time to hear if it was safe.

Must be.

I followed close behind her, but more judiciously, something being an IR agent taught me. But even before I reached the opening, I could feel raindrops washing against my face.

Sweet, wet, clean rain.

A low moan of pure ecstasy escaped before I caught myself and lifted my head beyond the hole's rim.

A cobblestone street, but it looked like a narrow back alley more than a main thoroughfare. There were no people about though I could make out the rustle of a cat pawing through a trashcan somewhere nearby and the scamper of rats against stone. Since when had I possessed hyper hearing?

I didn't waste a lot of thoughts on the issue as the source of the malevolent red light flashed into my eyes. A pizza joint with a neon red sign that spun and flashed stronger than any beacon warning system I'd ever seen. That was it? I'd been following the SOS siren-call of a pizza light? How sad was that?

"You coming?" Sabina was already melding into the shadows of the nearest buildings.

"Yeah." I heaved myself out, wondering if I should try to find the manhole cover and replace it before some person or car fell into the opening. But as I glanced around, I couldn't see the disc. Garbage cans and one huge dumpster, cardboard piles, windows with bars across them and scarred metal doors. It could have been any dive area of any major city.

"What are you doing now?" Sabina was gaining a lot more attitude now that she wasn't dependent on my saving her scrawny ass.

"Leaving the hole open is an accident waiting to happen."

I swear she groaned, then ran around the corner and disappeared. No good bye, no nothing. Of all the ungrateful, self-absorbed witches ...

"Here." She crept up behind me as I was pulling myself to my feet. I swore she did it just to see me jump.

"What—" Then I saw what was in her hand. A traffic cone. Two actually. "Where'd you get those?"

"It takes about three seconds to find someplace falling apart in this city. You find one in the process of being fixed and voila, warning cones."

"But doesn't that leave another place for innocents to get hurt if these cones aren't there?"

"Duh! I only took two. The French always use six times more than they need. As if the more cones the more they must be working, when the exact opposite is true."

Since I wasn't here to get into a discussion of the pros and cons of the French work ethic, I grabbed the cones, positioned them and went to wipe my hands on my jeans only to realize they'd get dirtier not cleaner. The rain was helping a little in rinsing some muck off us, but not enough.

First things first though. "You have any idea where we are?"

"I'm thinking *Montmarte* but can't be sure. Around on the street you can tell we're looking down on the city and we're not that far away so that's my best guess."

"Wouldn't it be busier?" I looked around at the backs of what might be closed bakeries and small mom and pop shops.

"Not if it's early or late enough. Most places shut down by two a.m., and the bakeries don't start until closer to four so it's probably between two-thirty and four."

"I'm impressed." And I was. I liked her logic.

"So what now?" She cocked her head to the side like a bird waiting for crumbs.

"Now you go your way and I go mine." Yeah, it was brutal but to the point. The longer this kid hung out with me, the more chance she had of getting in the middle of more than she could handle.

"That's it? Kicking me to the curb?"

"For your own good." Damn, now I sounded like my dad right before he grounded me for months on end.

Exhaustion. That was part of it. Feeling lost and disconnected didn't help. I had no phone. No money. No way of even knowing if my team was still at the safe house in Paris. My dad was, or had been here, but where?

One problem at a time.

First problem—Sabina. What about her?

"Don't even think of ditching me now," she growled as if she could read my mind.

"You'd be safer far away from me." That was the truth. Until I could figure out who had nabbed me and why, I was putting anyone around me at risk. It was one thing to ask a fellow IR team member for help. Another to bring a civilian into the mix, even if she was a witch, or wanna-be witch. On the other hand, if I kept her close, at least for a short period of time, I might find out more about who took her and that could lead to who took me. Convoluted, I know, but it made sense to me.

Besides, I hated the thought of her being alone with a target painted on her. If they had nabbed her once, what was going to keep them from grabbing her again?

"Come on, then," I said. "But I'm making no promises. I know some people staying at a place that shouldn't be far from here. If they are still there, and it's a big if, at the least we could get some grub, change our clothes and find a place to catch up on sleep. Then you're on your own." I meant that last part. The team, or Ling Mai, was in a better position to keep her safe.

"Sounds great," she said with more enthusiasm then she'd showed about anything so far.

I decided to use the rambling walk through cobblestone streets while Paris woke up around us as a chance to ask a few more questions. Hadn't someone said knowledge was power?

"So how much do you know about witchcraft?" I asked, obviously more wiped out than I realized as I jumped right to the sixty-four thousand dollar question instead of leading up to it.

Sabina actually stopped and cut me a withering look. "What kind of stupid question is that?"

I scrubbed my face with my hands, forgetting they were not that clean. Yuck! "Look, I'm not trying to pry. I'm trying to figure out what the bad guys might have wanted from you that I also have. If we can figure that out, we might know who they are or what they want."

It was a long shot. It wasn't like there was a Witches-R-Us hierarchy to consult. Some witches followed certain practices or beliefs and others crossed the lines. You could be witch-born, like I was, a Celtic witch, a kitchen witch, a Dianic witch, a Strega witch, a hedge witch and that was the tip of the iceberg.

"Makes sense," Sabina admitted, chewing her lower lip. It wasn't a rousing endorsement. More a grudging acceptance, followed by her starting to walk again, though she kept her gaze averted. I was reminding myself to go slow, though it wasn't my way, at all, when she started talking, "I don't know what kind of witch I am."

Okay, maybe we did have something in common. If there were a category of screwed-up witch, I'd be head of the class. But what I said was, "Did someone teach you magic or did the magic manifest itself without study of the craft?"

"You mean like when I made Damion Brown get warts in first grade?"

"Without knowing a spell?" I would not laugh. Of course it wasn't warts I'd created in grade school, it was a bloody nose. Stevie Urbanik deserved it though. Who knew that would cause so much trouble?

She nodded her head. "My mom didn't believe I'd done it, but she was pissed about it."

Now this sounded familiar. Do something that came natural, like being athletic or super smart in math, and you got gold stars and way-to-go's from everybody. Cast a few rudimentary spells and you were either a liar making things up, or needing to see a therapist.

"Do you know if your mom was a witch?" I asked, looking straight ahead.

"Nah, she didn't hang around that long." Sabina creaked her neck as if a physical movement could release the kind of tension riding her. I could tell her it wouldn't, but some lessons we had to learn for ourselves. She continued, her voice lower, "My mom came and went when I was little. Then after my dad died, she stuck around just long enough to get tired of the mom-gig and disappeared. The landlady technically kicked me out because mom *forgot*." She used air quotes. "To pay the rent for three months before she took off."

I was not going to get all mushy and teary-eyed, no matter how easy it would have been. Noziaks were more the kick-butt and take-prisoners type than the warm and fuzzy kind, though the kid'd had it rough. At least I still had my dad, even if I wasn't on speaking terms with him, and three out of four brothers since Van's death. I tamped down the grief long enough to admit that I wasn't totally alone. "You sound American," I said out loud. "Not that it matters."

"Was born in Minneapolis." She shrugged. "Dad was a musician. We followed him around a lot."

"Must have been hard."

She jerked to a stop, her chin cocked up. "I'm not asking for sympathy. Dad was a great guy. Mom ... well, some folks just aren't meant to be parents."

I held my hands up in surrender. "Got it." Time to get back on track. "So we'll assume you're a hereditary witch."

"Which means?"

"You're born to the craft."

"Oh. Okay."

"I am too. Through my mom." The mom who'd tried to contact me not that long ago and I'd ignored. Not that turnabout wasn't fair. She'd ignored me for twenty plus years, was my turn. As long as she didn't disappear entirely, a small voice within me whispered.

"So what's so special about being born a witch?" Sabina asked, jerking me back to the present.

"It's like any other gift. Some people can practice for years to be a musician or baseball player, and they can be very, very good. But if you're born with those talents, it usually means you can tap into your own magic easier and deeper. If you have the proper training."

Sabina snorted. "Which I don't." She made it sound like I'd just opened a door and slammed it in her face at the same time.

"Neither did I," I admitted.

"But you did all those spells. Back there." She drove home her point with her thumb pointing behind us. "Can't tell me you don't know anything."

"Now I do but I wasn't trained as a child. Except for three months that ended abruptly when I did a bad thing."

Sabina's brows arched. "How bad?"

"Bad enough my witch mentor sent me packing." Okay, maybe I was still a little sensitive. Or wary.

"Okay, okay, you don't need to get yourself all riled up."

We moved on, as the streets were getting more and more populated with Parisians going about their early morning routines, small zippy cars and mopeds already chugging down the main streets. Sabina and I had to have more in common than being witch born and ill trained.

"What about lately?" I asked, sidestepping a matron with three poodles decked in rhinestones. I thought of Franco, a Didi shifter who could become any kind of dog. He'd have loved the look of these three and probably worn the stones with the same élan.

Back on task, Alex.

"Did anything happen recently that might have brought attention to your abilities?"

By the way Sabina became very quiet, I knew I'd hit the nail on the head. But before I backtracked I smelled something that I'd been ignoring for a bit. Wafting between the scents of bakeries, dark coffee brewing and petrol exhaust, there was something deeper and darker.

Weres.

I sidled closer to Sabina. "Don't look around but I think we're being followed."

Her shoulders tightened but Lord love a duck she didn't panic even if her voice sounded a little breathless. "By the bad guys?"

What she meant was the ones who held us captive. I nodded, not telling her these weren't guys at all. Sometimes too much information only scared the crap out of you. "If they attack." Not really if, but when was more like it. "I want you to run, as fast and hard as you can."

"Leave you?"

Wouldn't be the first time. What I said though was, "Yes. No questions. Get yourself safe and then—"

There was no more time as two burly guys stepped out of an alleyway half a block ahead. To our left a trio emerged from a doorway. A quick glance over my shoulder showed me a half dozen behind us.

How had they found us so easily?

Better yet, how could I have been so stupid? Yeah, it was broad daylight but we were on a side street that was all but deserted, except for the threats moving in. Why hadn't I paid more attention to the fact some smelled preternatural?

Too late for recriminations now.

I grabbed Sabina's arm and tugged her against the closest building. That left me facing almost a dozen Weres who, judging by their expressions, were out for blood.

"Remember what I said," I huffed, pushing Sabina behind me as I stepped forward, rocking on the balls of my feet. As if I stood a chance. I was running on adrenaline but not much else.

Not the best odds but that's what juiced a Noziak. Sick, yes, but I could feel the blood pumping through me, my skin cold as steel, ready to rock and rumble.

"You jerks want something?" I asked, my voice saccharine sweet and taunting.

"You're coming with us," one Were thundered. I glanced in his direction. One look told me this was only a spokesman, and not the biggest threat.

"Think again, doggie breath."

Oh, big bad Were didn't like that. His eyes darkened, his face tightened. All Weres had anger management issues. Some were easier to prod into rash action than others.

"Come on, big guy," I whispered under my breath, but loud enough that even a deaf Were would get the message. "Or you afraid to fight an unarmed woman?"

His face started elongating. Yup, easy peasey to stir up this one. And one Were changing tended to kick-start others. One thing about Weres was they were most vulnerable when changing. I was counting on that. If I could take out a few, I'd stand a better chance. Not that his fellow thugs were going to wait around and twiddle their thumbs.

Best defense was an offense. New Noziak rule.

I launched myself forward, head down, a bowling ball of pissed off witch, hitting him against his shoulder, hard enough to hear bone crack.

Damn, that hurt!

A voice shouted, "Take them."

Free time was over.

CHAPTER 28

Bran landed hard on his feet, bent in two, blood-red smoke billowing around him.

"C'est des conneries!" he cursed, waiting for his gut to spew. When it didn't he glanced up, looking around.

The tunnels. More specifically the one where he'd left Jeb Noziak and his son.

If he had any sense of irony left he'd laugh. Right now, all he could manage was to make sure the simin fae hadn't followed.

They hadn't. Which gave him some breathing room, but not for long.

May as well check to see if the Noziaks had remained in the Were house or left. Out of the fire, looking for the frying pan.

It took a few steps to make sure his legs held before he headed deeper into the tunnel. Last time he'd tried that particular spell he'd been seventeen and avoiding his mother. It'd worked then but hadn't felt like he'd been put through a wringer. Good thing he hadn't appeared someplace where the fae could find him quickly. He didn't have enough resources left to try that stunt again. Like any energy, magic had its own price. Right now, leaving him turned inside out.

Sort of like Alex.

Now the laugh came, but it sounded more bitter than anything.

Oh yeah, when he found his witch there'd be some reckoning.

CHAPTER 29

It took a few seconds to realize the Weres meant to take me alive and not outright kill me. That was the good news. The bad news? Weres didn't fight like humans, even when holding back. Think wolves, bears, or pumas playing rough with your family pet and you'll get the idea.

What surprised me is I was getting a few good licks in. *Go, team Noziak!* An oomph here, a squeal there, had me grinning, even as my energy seeped though every pore. All I could think was, *run, Sabina, run.*

As if calling her I could suddenly smell her near. Damn, she hadn't left.

Throwing punches in any direction I could I tasted my own sweat and blood. All the kid-witch had to do was escape. One little thing.

I was so pissed I didn't realize it was her tugging at my arm, holding it in a death grip.

Like I could fight one handed. Whose side was she on?

With a growl that was mostly a curse I spied her between arms and bodies, her expression one hundred and ten percent determined. I recognized that look, having seen it in my own mirror more than once. But what did she want?

"Come," she snarled, tugging me closer to her.

Trust whatever the hell she was doing? Or get us both killed?

Did I have a lot to lose? Not really. I was flagging. The stuffing would be pummeled out of me soon.

So I followed my gut and threw myself toward her, tripping a few Weres in the process. Enough to give us a foot or two of breathing room.

That's when she did it. Grabbed my arm with two of hers, looked to the sky and I don't know, jumped or blasted off, or who knew what. Next thing I knew, the Weres were lunging toward my feet dangling above their heads as Sabina and I rose in the air. Not like a helium balloon either. More as in jerky bursts of flight that spun us around until I wanted to hurl. We kept moving like that, as if a strong wind caught crumpled paper in its grasp and was beating the snot out of us.

Before I could scream Sabina smacked us against a stone ledge, causing us both to cry out.

Clawing my hands against the gritty rock, I closed my eyes. We were a hell of a long way up and the ledge wasn't all that big.

"You okay?" she whispered next to me.

I shook my head negative, trying to figure out what I needed to know first. Finally I mumbled, "Where are we?"

"On *Sacré-Cœur*."

That had my lids popping open to glare at her, not at the distance to the ground, or the little stick figures running around on the plaza below.

"You mean the big church on *Montmarte*?" My mouth was so dry I was surprised I could say anything. Especially with a WTH attitude.

"It's a basilica, not a church, and yeah. That one."

Whatever!

"So what just happened? You can fly?" I tried to keep the anger out of my voice but not the awe. Flying? Now that would be a cool skill to have. Then I remembered. "If you were able to fly, why did you make me drag you across the water pool? You damn near drowned the two of us."

"I didn't say I was good at flying."

Understatement.

"Oh." There were too many spells I'd bombed lately not to immediately understand.

"Yeah, we were lucky we made it this far. Almost—"

"It's okay. Got it." I was already focusing on the ramifications of what she'd said. "Flying is a pretty damn rare and powerful ability, in spite of what all the movies and TV shows indicate. It means you've got some serious magic mojo."

"Really?"

Now she sounded like she was about ten. I could recognize the sound of hope. That spark of wanting so bad it clawed a hole deep in your stomach just by thinking you might be able to do something well, something right, instead of being a freak.

No way was I going to burst Sabina's bubble by telling her that fragile belief would burst and sooner rather than later.

"I think if you found a witch mentor, one strong enough and experienced enough to handle your gifts, you might make something of your ... well, what you can already do."

I was focusing on the mundane until my stomach stopped twisting and I could deal with what had just happened. And not just the flying. But how the Weres had found us so easily. And how the Sam hell we were going to get off this damn ledge.

Besides, it wasn't like I was being untruthful. If Sabina could get a little witch mentoring she might survive, but who wants to hear that? Especially at her age.

"How old are you?" I asked, as the breeze picked up, chilling me to the bone. Not even the pigeons were flying this high.

"Sixteen," she mumbled, looking away from me.

"You're lying."

She snapped her gaze to mine and I thrust out my arm, an automatic reflex to sudden movements in high places. I was playing the mom card again. Lucky me.

"How could you tell I was fibbing?" Her voice sounded like she didn't want to believe I could tell, but didn't want to risk if I really could suss out a lie. Convoluted, but I understood.

"One of my abilities," I lied. But if she thought I really was a human truth detector, it'd be more likely she'd be straight with me the first time. Yeah, I could be devious with the best of them.

"Fine. I'm fifteen."

I raised a brow.

"Next week I'll be fifteen."

"That's better." Damn, she was young. And vulnerable.

"You going to teach me to be a witch?" she asked in a tone that said when's-my-first-lesson.

Talk about a spew-your-coffee moment. Not something you want to be doing on a high ledge. "No way." Then I lowered my voice, but not the intensity behind my tone. "You need someone who has lots of experience." I raised one finger. "Can consistently use magic." Another finger. "And will be sticking around." Third finger popped up until I curled my hand into a fist.

"You're not staying?"

I could actually like this kid. Go for the easiest problem to solve first. Ignore the rest until they bit you on the ass.

"Not likely."

Nothing more for me here. I didn't know if I was still an IR agent. My brother had been killed by Bran. Who knew when I could face my dad again or even if he was around? And bad guys wanted me for something. Once I took care of Bran, I was so out of here. Unless my team had other plans.

"But—"

"No buts." My tone squashed any question about whether I was serious or not. "Besides, we've got to get off here." I waved one palm to include the church and the sky before us. If heights didn't give you the heebie-jeebies it really was an awesome sight, Paris spread out for miles, looking like a fairytale kingdom.

I caught myself. Noziaks so did not do wistful thinking. So I looked at Sabina. "Can you get us down or only up?"

By the way she glanced away, I had my answer. Sweet Goddesses, just my luck. I was stuck, even temporarily, with a one-way flying witch.

I slowly stood, my back against cool stone, swallowing the wedge of vertigo jamming my throat and making my knees shake. "Guess we have to find another way down."

"Like stairs?" Sabina scurried to her feet, obviously not having an issue with heights like I did.

"Unless you have a better idea. Or a mini-helicopter handy." Yeah, my snark factor was back in full force. But I was also worried. And exhausted. And wondering who in the Universe I'd pissed off so badly. Nah, I knew the answer to the last one.

Everyone!

CHAPTER 30

"Thanks for meeting me," Bran said to Willie, while scanning the street for threats. He trusted the Were, but only so far. After a lifetime of betrayals better to be wary than disappointed.

Willie grabbed the chair opposite, waving off the waiter hustling over. The café was small, shabby and out of the way. Perfect for a meeting spot where they wouldn't be overheard, or recognized.

"You're looking drained," the Were remarked. "But you're alive and here so I'll assume the fae didn't find you."

"They did." At the Were's raised brow look, Bran chuckled, though it wasn't a happy sound. "Finding me and taking me before the Council are two different issues."

"I see." The Were leaned back in his chair, but carefully. Even recovering Weres still possessed a lot of strength. "What do you need?"

"Info," Bran said, leaning forward so his voice wouldn't carry. The Were had been right, he was running on adrenaline and determination. Mostly the latter. The Noziaks had not been in the tunnel safe house so he assumed they were both mobile and able to take care of themselves. His most pressing concern was what had happened to Alex. "Any word on the street about our witch?"

The Were shook his head, and Bran's stomach took a dive. Then Willie leaned forward, his expression intense. "I wouldn't take that as bad news."

What Bran wanted to scream was, *why the hell not*, but

years of business negotiations had taught him that the first man who let emotions rule him, lost the deal. Right now Alex was the deal and he wanted her. "Why?"

"The absence of any intel is in itself revealing."

"Look, Willie, I don't need obtuse here I need facts."

The Were spread his hands before him and toned down his voice. "Weres tend to boast a bit."

Bran gave him an and-that-means-what look.

"Okay, we brag. A lot."

"Get to the point."

Willie leaned both arms across the table. "No word on Alex but someone's throwing a lot of cash around for several small snatch-and-grab operations. The word is they want Weres who can keep their mouths shut and follow orders."

"And this means?"

"The targets are two women. One a girl. The other wounded. Easy pickings."

"Alex?" If so, she wasn't alone. He tamped down the image of her injured even as he knew Van had attacked her. First he had to find her.

"No names have been mentioned." Willie must have sensed Bran urging him on as he rushed his words. "Key point is there have been two attempts and both have failed."

Now that sounded more like his Alex.

"Any idea where these attacks happened?" he asked.

"No, but I know something better." Willie grinned.

"Not the time to play coy." Shaking his only remaining ally was not a good idea but sometimes the Were tempted him. Like now.

"Okay. Got it." Willie jerked himself about like a dog shedding water before leaning across the table. "I signed up to be part of the next attack."

It took everything Bran had not to lunge and grab the Were by his throat.

Willie reared back. "Not for real, man. Just so I can tell you what's going on. If these guys are involved in ... you know ... in doing something to Alex."

Bran scrubbed his face with his hands. He should have known better. If the Were had meant to hurt Alex he would have done it when they were all together. "Go ahead," he mumbled.

Willie nodded, though his expression was still wary. Bran didn't blame him. "We're meeting at a café in the 18th arrondissement," he said.

"Near *Montmarte*?"

"*Oui.*"

"I'll follow you."

Willie shook his head, then looked as if he thought something. "You able to do a cloaking spell?"

"*Oui.*" Bran didn't clarify that he'd depleted most of his magic escaping the fae. By the time he needed to cloak himself he'd do so.

"You'll have to disguise your smell too. Weres can pick you up that way."

"Don't worry," Bran bit the words out. "Just get me close and I'll manage the rest."

Willie didn't look convinced. That was his problem. This was the first solid lead Bran had on Alex since Versailles and he wasn't going to lose it.

As they stood to leave, Bran waited for the waiter to scurry off before turning to Willie. "If this works out, I'll owe you, my friend."

Willie gave a Gallic shrug. "I've asked the saints to watch over us."

Bran barked a short laugh before lowering his voice. "I don't know that there are any saints looking out for mages." Or witch/shamans either. But Alex had him, that'd be enough. He'd make sure of it.

"Let's go," he said, leading Willie, though the Were was the only one who knew where they were going.

Bran didn't need to know where yet. He had the why. To save Alex. That's all he needed to know.

CHAPTER 31

Don't ask me how we got down from the cathedral or basilica or whatever kind of church it was. By the time we scooted from one ledge to another, and found an access door on the roof leading to the smallest, tightest stairwell made of stone and age, I'd started praying to any beings willing to listen if only they'd let us get to the ground safely.

We did, but literally on our last legs. It was one step at a time from there to the safe house, no energy left even for talking.

What felt like a lifetime later, I walked right up to the door of the small, single dwelling apartment as if I owned the place, Sabina dogging my heels. It must've been just beyond noon as the spring sun made the building look older and in more need of repair than I'd remembered.

My luck. I'd led us to the wrong place.

Only one way to find out. Last thing I wanted was some snoopy neighbors sticking their noses in where they didn't belong and start asking some prying questions so I squared my shoulders and acted like I belonged. I didn't have any ID, and really wasn't sure I had a place inside either.

Sabina held her tongue as I marched up and knocked, a rabble of butterflies kamikaze flying in my stomach. I might refuse to show the nerves but that didn't mean I didn't have them.

I knocked again. Louder this time. Was everyone gone? Had they left the country already? Both questions made me want to growl.

"Don't think anyone's here," Sabina said at my side. As if I couldn't figure that out. "What now?"

Ling Mai at her hotel if she were still there? Since our last conversation hadn't ended on the nicest of terms, I'd rather face charging Weres. Oh wait, I'd already done that not so long ago.

"We move on to our second option." I hadn't figured out what that was yet but I wasn't going to stand around like the poor, pitiful red-haired stepchild not wanted.

I shrugged rock-hard shoulders and turned to leave when the door cracked open.

Part of me was relieved, part of me braced myself for facing my teammates.

Except it wasn't an IR agent opening the door. It was some gangly blonde kid who mumbled, "Y-yes?"

He actually managed to have his voice crack halfway through the single word, but at least it'd been in English.

"Who are you?" I demanded, then realized that was beyond rude. It was just that I really hadn't expected a stranger. Which meant my team really had left Paris. Without me.

It took a second or two for me to get my act together. Okay, maybe a minute as Sabina cleared her throat next to me. "Sorry," I sighed. "I was expecting someone else."

I turned to leave, my limbs as stiff and wooden as my shoulders had been. Shock. It must be. One too many blows. They'd really left me? Sabina grabbed my elbow to steer me down the sidewalk. No doubt I looked like I'd been on a three-day drinking binge as I shuffled away, taking everything I had to put one foot in front of the other.

Mandy I could see being happy to wipe her boots of me and our short acquaintance, but I expected more from Vaughn and Kelly. Especially Kelly. She'd been the sister I'd never had. Did she really leave? Without even a message?

If the team moved on then she'd have to go. Right?

We were about four doors away when the young man's voice called out. "Your friend. What's her name?"

Sabina pulled me to a stop. "What's your friend's name?" she prodded, her voice gentler than I'd heard from her so far.

"Doesn't matter." It was a lie, but I was salvaging what pride I had left. I knew when I'd become an IR member that if I didn't cut the job I could be returned to where I'd started from at any time. The fact that it was the Pocatello Women's Correction Center, aka jail, gave me a reason to stay with the job until my year of service was complete. Then I'd be free.

I wasn't looking forward to being cut adrift so easily. What now? The jail was still in Idaho and that's where, if the truth was told, I belonged. Not gallivanting around the world screwing things up.

Still, I couldn't leave Sabina at risk because my Noziak pride made asking for help stick in my craw.

I pulled my shoulders and chin up and turned to answer the kid's question. "Kelly. My friend is … was Kelly."

Both his brows raised. "Anyone else?"

How many friends did a person need to pass his muster?

"What is this, fifty questions?" I snapped.

He opened the door wider as he said, "Maybe we should talk inside."

That's when it hit me. That damn hope. That sense that maybe everything wasn't lost. That I hadn't been abandoned. Again.

I swallowed, hard, and kept my chin high as I walked back and entered the house.

CHAPTER 32

I didn't expect a big neon sign that shouted "We Haven't Left You Behind" the moment I walked inside the safe house. Okay, maybe I did, but it'd been a rough few days.

The place looked like someone had just cleaned it, without a telltale sign of anything anywhere. Not a lot of intel I was going to get by a quick look. Guess I'd have to resort to the interrogation technique. One that wouldn't give too much away to Sabina standing by my side, checking out the guy closing the door.

Or maybe I could blab all I wanted and she'd still be clueless.

"Who are you?" I asked the guy as a place to start. I thought I'd kept my voice non-combative but the look Sabina shot me said otherwise.

"Name's Hercules," he said with a blush as he jammed his hands in his pockets, his gaze ping-ponging between Sabina and me as if trying to figure out whom to talk to—the cute chick his age, or the scowling woman who clearly wanted answers. "But everyone calls me Herc."

I just bet they did.

"And you know Kelly? Kelly McAllister?"

"Ah." He ducked his head as a hank of hair curled across his forehead. I could swear I heard Sabina sigh. "I didn't catch Kelly's last name."

Not helping here. "Was Kelly with any of her other friends?"

"Yeah." He jumped on that, then pulled back as if realizing how little he could or should reveal to a total stranger. Good.

He had some common sense at least. Especially when he added, "You got some photo ID?"

I shook my head, nice and slow, keeping my gaze locked on his. *What now, kid?*

He surprised me and pulled out a phone, snapping a photo of me before I could protest. Then punched in a few clicks before looking back up. "There."

"There what?" I asked, wondering if I'd just led us into another ambush. I grabbed Sabina's arm and started dragging her toward the door.

"Where are we going?" she protested, obviously recovered from the last battle way too quickly.

"No idea who he sent that photo to," I said, easing toward the door even with the kid blocking it. Only the closer I got to him the more he didn't look as much a kid, height or strength wise. "Out of our way, buster," I snarled, hoping that was enough.

But it wasn't, as the confusion that had been on his face, mirroring Sabina's look, cleared. He raised his hands. He was smart enough not to show fists or I'd have to clock him rather than take the risk he meant either of us harm. No telling how soon whoever was on the other end of the phone might be showing up.

"Wait, you've got it all wrong." His voice sounded sincere but his heart rate had picked up. Why?

"We're out of here." I went to push him aside, assuming he was only human, when Sabina changed position, aligning herself with him.

The idiot.

"Can't you give him a chance?" she said. "Just hear him out?"

Oh, brother. Did the girl have no sense of self-preservation?

My tone became more growl than we're-all-BFFs-here as I looked at him and ignored her. "I'll give you to the count of three to move it."

"Or?"

"Or I'll turn you into a Hercules toad."

He actually smiled. A big ol-boy smile. Not quite the response I was aiming for. "You can do that?"

Did he know what I was? Did I dare wait around to find out? Maybe to the first and no, to the last.

"One," I said, taking a step closer, my hands curling.

"They should be here any minute," he shot back. Like that was good news.

It wasn't. Not to me.

"Two. Three," I jumbled the words together, nudging him aside as I grabbed Sabina. Only my nudge sent him careening into an armoire across the room and Sabina squawked, like I was the bad guy in the room just as the room's door clicked open.

CHAPTER 33

"You're supposed to be dead."

Leave it to Mandy to verbally bitch- slap me before she entered the room. Fortunately, behind her I heard a shout.

"OMG!" And that quick, Kelly pushed Mandy aside. Not an easy feat, as Kelly launched herself into the room and wrapped me in a rib bruising hug.

That made me feel better. Even if Noziaks as a rule were not the huggy kind. A back slap maybe. Or slug to the shoulder, definitely. But ... not hugs.

"I knew you weren't dead. I just knew it." I could actually feel my shoulders relax, accepting that at least one of my teammates hadn't abandoned me.

"So where the hell have you been?" Mandy demanded as she marched past Kelly then eyed Sabina. "And who the hell are you?"

I gave Kelly a quick back pat then stepped back, in part because I knew I still smelled like eau de catacombs.

"This is Sabina. She and I have been held hostage by unknowns until we could escape." There, that about summed things up. A little. More details could wait.

"Unknown what?" Mandy gave me the stink eye.

"Unknown implies I don't know." Yeah, there was enough smarm in my tone to drown a bull elephant. Then, to make sure no one said anything they shouldn't say in front of civilians, I added, "Right now I could eat a half a cow. I need a shower, clean clothes and sleep." I nodded to my cohort who was still drooling over Herc. Wait till she saw Stone. Or Bran. Now they were drool worthy males. Nix Bran. Not the way I wanted to get my hands around his throat and squeeze. My voice was a little deeper and a lot more ragged as I said, "Sabina here needs food, new clothes and a break."

"Of course." Kelly grabbed the hint and started hustling Sabina from the room. "Shower's in here. I've got some clothes that might fit you. And I'll run next door and grab some food."

Man, Kelly was good. And efficient. Before I could blink she hustled Sabina out of the room and reappeared.

"So spill," she said, sitting on the edge of the nearest chair like it was a sleep over. Not that I attended many, once I discovered I was usually invited on the off chance one of my brothers might show up at sometime during the night.

I arched a brow at the remaining civilian in the room, which Kelly waved off by saying, "New team member. He's making some awesome weapons we can use against preternaturals."

About time, I wanted to shout, even I was surprised that life had gone on so quickly without me. "How long have I been away?" I asked, sinking down beside Kelly, the exhaustion catching up with me.

"Five days," Mandy snapped, still standing by the door, her legs braced as if for battle, her arms crossed in a badass attitude. Only with her, it was her normal approach. "And why aren't you dead?"

"Nice," I snipped back.

Herc kept me from telling Mandy just where she could shove it as he interrupted, "You mean you really are Alex Noziak?" His eyes were saucer-wide.

"Yes. Unless there have been more teammates missing."

"No, no, not that." He cast an anxious look at Kelly then Mandy before continuing, his voice shakier, "It's just that I thought ... I mean ... didn't you say—"

As my energy took a nose-dive so did my patience. "What's he babbling about?"

It was Mandy who answered. "We were told you were bitten by a shifter. Your brother. If that was true why no wounds? You should be dead."

"Well I'm not." I jumped to my feet before I realized the ramifications of Mandy's words. She was right. I should be dead.

Unless ... I sank back on the chair, fast-forwarding through the last day or more. The pain. The ability to throw and lift more than I'd even been able to before. My sense of scent and hearing amplified. Even now, I listened to four heartbeats in the room, Mandy and Herc's elevated, Kelly's slower, and Sabina behind closed doors muffled.

But I shouldn't have heard any of them.

I glanced at Kelly who must have seen some of what I felt as she took my hand. "What's important is that you're back."

As if. I raised my head, shaking it because the words jammed somewhere south of my breastbone. *No way, no way, no way.*

I could *not* be a shifter.

CHAPTER 34

A hard knock at the door took the focus off me, which was just as well. I hated falling apart; to do so publicly was beyond the pale.

Mandy looked out the side window next to the door then yanked it open.

Stone marched in like he commanded the place, Vaughn right behind him. It was she who caught my attention more. Her and the bandages and bruises she sported. A look I should be wearing if I was still mostly human.

"You're supposed to be dead," Stone growled, glaring at me.

"Yeah, I've been getting that a lot lately."

"What the hell happened?" he snapped.

I gave a short, sweet summation that skipped over the amount of pain, the fear, the more fear, and the off chance the Weres were able to track me. I'd get to that in a minute, but not while everyone was looking at me like a circus freak. A look I'd be shooting at myself if there were a mirror handy.

"So you don't know who's behind snatching you or what they wanted?" Vaughn asked, focusing in on the salient issues. Which is why she was the team leader.

I shook my head. "All I know is the name Zaradian. Needing me to find some demon and two guys with accents. One French. One Irish. And the Weres. Except you don't need to worry about the French dude."

"Why not?" Kelly said beside me.

"I killed him." Guessing by her wide-eyed expression I forgot to mention that small point. And the way the new kid was looking, we might need to find a paper bag for him to hyperventilate in.

"Were you trying to kill him?" Kelly asked.

"Technically he was trying to kill me first, so yes." Since everyone seemed to have gone quiet I added, "The Irish guy didn't seem to be bothered by the death."

"And you never saw this Irish guy before?" Vaughn asked.

"No, but there was something that seemed familiar about him. Other than he sounded like Colin Farrell."

Stone rolled his eyes as Vaughn placed a gentle restraining hand on his arm. At least it looked gentle until I noticed her white knuckles.

"Damn, you're riling a lot of folks," Jaylene offered, having joined the group about halfway through my after-action report. "And you're sure the girl in the other room doesn't know anything more?"

"She might, but it wasn't like I had a lot of time to question her." I shook my head. "I wasn't even sure where to start."

"Kelly, you might be the best to take the girl and talk with her. See if she might know more than she's shared or even that she's seen," Vaughn suggested, realizing that of the team Kelly would be the least threatening to Sabina.

Kelly looked wary for a second, then nodded, giving me a half-smile before she rose and headed to the back bedroom where from the sounds of the shower being turned off meant Sabina could be joining us any moment.

"I think we should have a physician look you over," Vaughn continued, looking at me, but it was teammate to teammate and not leader to freak. "See what they can tell us about your ..."

I didn't blame her. I didn't even know what to call me now. Witch/shaman/shifter? I'd never heard of such a screwed-up genetic make up. "I'd need a doctor used to working with—" I waved my hand around.

"Ling Mai will know of someone," Stone said, his tone less badass than usual. "You didn't mention Bran or your father. You've been in contact with either of them?"

"No." I wouldn't call hearing Bran's voice as contact. It wasn't like we communicated. Then I looked at Stone's face. "Why? What's happened?"

Bran wasn't hurt. He wouldn't be. No way. Which left my dad. And as mad as I was about what had happened between us, that didn't mean I wanted him in any danger.

"I was to meet with Bran but some simin fae interrupted us," Stone said, earning raised brows from everyone in the group who knew who the fae were and who they worked for. "Last I saw of him they were trailing him."

Mandy whistled. "Doesn't sound good for your boyfriend."

"He's not—"

But I never finished the sentence as another knock on the door had Jaylene heading to answer it. But before she could, the door burst inward and a swarm of Weres came stampeding in.

What was it with these guys?

CHAPTER 35

There was no time to think, just act.

Jaylene went flying against the nearest wall. Stone stepped in to stem the tide pushing aside Vaughn who didn't look in good enough shape to go after Weres or even kitty cats. Mandy grabbed a floor lamp and swung it like a baseball bat. I'd expected the blonde kid to scamper to safety but he surprised me. He stepped forward rather than ran though I could see it took every ounce of courage he had. Then he started flapping his hands.

What the—?

I ignored exhaustion as I waded into the thick of things, swinging fists as fast as I could. If I was going to be a freak shifter, at least I should get something out of the mess. And initially it looked like I could. Weres were flying backwards like confetti at a wedding but we were seriously outmanned.

Four Weres were dog-piling on Stone. Mandy was still recovering from a broken arm and her swings started flagging. Vaughn was sidestepping out of the way which was the best thing she could be doing then. Looked like she might be heading for the kitchen. Good idea. Knives in kitchens when there wasn't much else that would slow a rampaging Were.

Jaylene lunged toward Stone to save his ass. Which left me and Greek-god-named kid to keep the onslaught from getting to the backroom where I hoped like Hades that Kelly was getting Sabina to safety. I just kept butting heads and tasting blood from a split lip or gash along my eye. Damn, it stung.

Then I noticed Hercules. What was he doing? He waved his hand like an apprentice sorcerer, and a Were would freeze mid-attack.

"New weapon," he huffed, between ducking a flying Were and wrist-zapping another.

"Cool!" Taking out a flash-frozen killer was a heck of a lot easier than stopping a full-fighting force Were. That's where I started putting my attention. Grabbing an incapacitated Were and swinging him with all my might. If the house had anything less than stone walls, it'd have been in rubble by now.

I spotted a frying pan whipping through the air. Just enough to connect with a head or exposed body part before it pulled back and whapped again.

Kelly. It had to be.

It took a long, drawn out few minutes before the tide of the fight changed, from us zero, to attackers scrambling for the gaping doorway. Those who could, grabbed their buddies and hustled outside, with Herc following them, yelling, "Take that. And that. And don't come back!"

I didn't know if I wanted to hug him or take him aside and teach him a few facts of life—Noziak style.

Instead I limped over to where Jaylene was pulling Stone to his feet, blood streaming down his face. Vaughn walked over to the frying plan suspended in air and murmured in a low voice, "It's okay, Kelly. They're gone now."

Kels winked back into existence, but with that scared look she got when she did. Only because turning invisible like she could meant she she'd be blinded for twice as much time when she reappeared.

Herc re-entered the room and set the door at an angle over the doorway. It wouldn't stop anyone but might not draw as much attention as a wide-open hole either. Mandy sank into the nearest chair as Jaylene shuffled to her side.

"Sabina?" I shouted, earning the sight of her poking her head around the corner.

"All clear?" she asked.

"For now."

"Wow!" She summed things up succinctly as she stepped over broken furniture and tossed cushions.

I slipped into the only remaining chair near me, one with a big gash releasing stuffing in small clumps. It wasn't home decorating I was thinking about though, as I gingerly touched a slash above my eye. One already healing though still tender.

"You brought them here." Mandy glared at me. "No one else knew about this place."

"New Girl did," Jaylene said, her voice a cross between back-off and not-another fight.

"New Girl?" The words escaped before I meant them to. In for a penny, in for a buck. "You mean you replaced me already?"

There's a fine line between sounding whiny, hurt, and pissed off and I was straddling it.

It was Vaughn who took the stuffing out of me. "She's a shifter."

"And where the hell is she when we could have used her?" Mandy demanded, obviously scenting a new bone to chew on.

Vaughn glanced her way. "With Ling Mai." Vaughn cut her glance at me. "Stone was tired of us getting hurt so easily. We needed some fresh bodies that could fight ..." She glanced around the room, not needing to say more.

"Makes sense," I mumbled, though I still couldn't process how easy everyone had moved along.

"Think the issue we need to be dealing with now is finding out who wants Alex so badly they'd attack us all to get her." I shook my head, the same question racing like a squirrel on crack around my head. Who? Why? Out loud I said, "We've got to figure out who or what Zaradian is."

"I know," a familiar voice spoke from the doorway, the cantilevered doors not masking him.

Bran.

The son of a bitch was back.

CHAPTER 36

I didn't think. I rocketed forward. Not to embrace but to pummel the crap out of him. Standing there. Tall. Dark and arrogant from the tip of his designer shoes to the lock of midnight hair that had grown a shade too long.

Murderer!

Whatever Bran was though, he wasn't a lightweight. He used the shield of the door to counter my launch and sent me spinning backwards.

His one hundred percent focus was on me. Fear rippled in the back of my throat. He wasn't the kind, considerate lover here. Or even the ally. I didn't know who or what he was anymore but I did know he killed Van and I wanted to rip his head off.

"We need to talk," he said, stepping warily into the room as my fellow teammates backed off.

Didn't blame them. I'd be leaving by the back door if I could. But this was *my* fight. And talk wasn't on the agenda.

"You killed him," I snarled, anger shaking my voice, firing my determination as I crab walked backwards on my hands until I could find protection at my back or enough space to scramble to my feet.

"Now wait just a minute." He was using that calm and reasonable voice. That alone was enough to have me screaming.

Instead, I felt wetness dampening my cheeks. What the—? Noziaks did *not* cry. Never. Ever.

We got even. Eye for an eye. Death for a death.

Something bitter, deeper than sorrow exploded within me. Bran cared for me once. I cared for him. More than cared. Which was why his betrayal clawed at me all the more.

Right now he was making a bad thing worse. Softening his voice, extending one hand like one did to a frightened dog. *Come here puppy, all will be well.*

Only it wouldn't. Not ever again. Van would never be coming back and Bran was the reason why.

With a snarl of rage dragged from deep within I scrambled to my hands and knees, never letting my intention waver. "You killed him," I whispered, my voice so ragged it tore at my throat. "I asked ... you said you'd ..."

He actually frowned. Like I was the crazy one. His glance shifted then, for a split second as he looked toward Vaughn and Stone as if asking what I was babbling about.

As if he didn't know.

I took his distraction for permission and kick-started myself across the room at a speed that took us both by surprise. My shoulder cracked into his legs as he flew up and over my head.

Not so urbane sophisticated now as Mister Big Shot landed with an exploding crack.

I was just getting started. A death for a death. It was only fair. Only just.

Blood pumping through me so loud I couldn't hear beyond it even as I caught Jaylene and Kelly shouting something from their corners in the room.

This time I made it to my feet as Bran's head still shuddered, looking dazed. I raised one hand, a spell dancing on the end of my tongue. I brushed against the blood from the earlier battle still staining my skin, added it to blood I drew from savaging my lip.

"By darkest night. By deepest hole.
Debt be owed. Debt be paid."

This was black magic. The kind I swore I'd never use. The kind that took my mother from me. That needed blood to activate.

I bit down harder. Fresh blood fueled the strongest black magic. Mine worked.

"Debt be owed. Debt be paid.
A life for a death.
Black for white. Go—"

Bran had raised his own hand, pointing one finger at me. His Celtic blue eyes ages older than when he'd walked through the door, his words even older, spoken in a harsh, garbled tongue I didn't recognize.

"ἄβυσσος
κυβερνάω
ἄγγελος
ἱερός, ἱερός, ἱερός
ἔργον
δράσις."

What? In the heartbeat between one second and the next I went rigid.

His words wrapped around me, heavier than chains, thicker than steel. Like whatever Hercules had done to the Weres. I froze; body, voice, action.

But not my mind. My thoughts screamed for release.

Whatever he'd just done he'd have to undo. And when he did, he was mine.

CHAPTER 37

"What just happened?" Sabina was the one to break the terrible silence in the room, the one broken only by heavy breathing until now.

"Lovers spat taken to a whole new level," came Mandy's snarky comment, though even her words sounded wary.

Bran dragged himself to his feet. Slow like. Acting hurt. As if. He'd not begun to hurt. Just wait.

"You kill somebody Alex knew?" Stone stepped to the fore, ice in his tone.

Go, Stone!

Bran shook his head, that unruly lock of hair tumbling across his forehead. "Not anyone who wasn't trying to kill me. Or her." He actually glared at me. Me? The one frozen!

"Can you undo what you just did?" Kelly asked, walking right up to the warlock, her fists clenched, her eyes still sightless. How she knew what had gone on was beyond me but the Great Spirits love her, she had my back.

"Yes." Bran looked at Kelly as if he meant the word. He might, in his own Machiavellian way, but he had no idea of the payback I was going to unleash his way the second he freed my voice. That's all I needed. Just a few words.

"Were you speaking the truth when you said you knew who or what Zaradian is?" Vaughn asked, all business, as if I wasn't standing here, a wedge of fury.

"Yes." Bran said again, straightening his shoulders, looking pained. Not that I was noticing. He deserved everything he got. What you sow so you reap.

"And?" Stone's tone said get-on-with-it.

"Zaradian is the name of a demon cast out of Earth three thousand years ago. A follower of Satanail."

"So he was cast out before Christ came?" Herc asked, doing the math.

"Yes. Or so the legends say. Many were lost in the battle between good and evil and it was a near miss that Zaradian was banished from Earth." Kelly's voice hitched as her hand went to her mouth. I knew the thought of dealing with demons pushed her buttons, given her background. But who knew if Bran was even telling the truth? What had I done to anger a demon? One gone for three-thousand years? Seriously? Was anyone really listening to this crap?

As if answering my thoughts, Bran looked at me as he continued, "Zaradian was not only one of the followers of Satanail, a fallen angel, Zaradian chose his destiny when he joined with Satanail."

"And Satanail was who exactly?" pragmatic Jaylene asked.

"The older of the two sons of God."

Hercules whistled, looking down at something in his hand. A phone? The kid was interrupting a warlock with info from a phone? Oh, this babe had a lot to learn. Kelly looked paler than before and Mandy was casting Jaylene a WTH look. I was with her.

Hercules nodded his head. "He's right. Christ was the second son. Zaradian the first."

I must not have been the only one wondering how the kid knew what he was talking about as he looked up and said, "What?"

"How would you know anything?" Leave it to Mandy to verbally bitch-slap him. Once again I was on her side. This was beginning to worry me. Not that I needed more to occupy me. My mind was razor focused. Get unfrozen. Kill Bran. Everything else was on hold until those two steps were done.

"It explains about Zaradian on Wikipedia," came Herc's reply as he raised his phone. "It doesn't have a lot but does say in spite of the esteem God held his son in it wasn't enough for Satanail. He rebelled and promised his followers relief from devotion. God cast him and his followers out and Satanail wandered in the void with several other fallen angels."

He glanced back at his phone and continued, "He wandered until he decided to make a second heaven which he called the universe. Then he created the physical world filled with misery and suffering."

"Fraulein Fassbinder isn't going to be happy you're getting all your intel from Wikipedia," Jaylene snorted, looking back at Bran. "Any of this true?"

"Most of it." Bran straightened his cufflinks as if talking to a Rotary club meeting, or whoever passed as high-ranking mucky mucks in his world. And he must have used up a heck of a lot of his magic by chilling me out. By the intentional way he moved, as if he had to think through every action, he was either in pain or exhausted. Either would work for me the second I got unstuck.

Bran finished, "Zaradian became one of Satanail's main Watchers."

"And a Watcher does what?" Jaylene asked.

Probably didn't freeze witches, that's for sure.

"Watchers prepare the way for Satanail to return. When Christ came to this plane, he cast out Satanail and many of his Watchers. But not all. Those who remained continued to stir up trouble on Earth and in the universe until they were routed and banished, one by one."

Nice fairytale, warlock. Doesn't mean you're not going down!

"So what does this Zaradian Watcher want with Alex?" Vaughn asked. At least she hadn't forgotten I was in the room, listening to all this poppycock.

Bran looked at me then. Really looked at me and if I wasn't hurting so bad at the thought of Van's death I might have caved right then and there by that look. Sorrow. Resignation. Regret.

I'd have toppled if I wasn't a solid mass of pissed-off witch.

"My guess is someone wants Alex, or her abilities, to free Zaradian."

No way would I release a demon. No freakin' way!

My whole team looked at me as if I was Hitler personified. Thank the Great Spirits for Kelly who stepped to my side, her sight now restored, as she bumped up against me, hip to hip. Not hard enough to topple me but just enough to make it very clear whose side she was on. "Alex would never do that. Never. And I can't believe even one of you would even consider that she would."

She said the last bit directly to Mandy. *You tell her, Kels!* The kitten had some wicked-ass claws and wasn't afraid to use them.

"No one said she would," Stone grumbled.

"There's choice and then there's no choice," Bran said, earning all eyes once again on him.

"What'd you mean?" Kelly asked.

"Every one of us, Alex included, have trigger points. Push them hard enough and we'd do whatever it'd take."

"You mean like pain?" Kelly prodded.

"That's the tip of the iceberg." Each word Bran dropped was like ice shards in the room. "A lot of people can withstand pain. To themselves. But what if the threat was directed at someone they loved? A lot easier to make an impossible choice if it meant a loved one lives or dies."

CHAPTER 38

If I weren't as frozen as a turkey the week before Thanksgiving, I'd have jerked at Bran's words. I hated it, but he was right. I'd done everything in my power to save Van. We all had loved ones, except maybe Mandy, who I'm sure was devil spawn, but that was beside the point.

But what about the rest of us? What would I do to save my family?

Wait, what was I thinking? Van was already dead. My own dad had abandoned me to prison— for life. My other three brothers were so far away from here I doubted they'd be brought into this mess. I was pretty safe.

Except.

Because it was the only thing I could move, my gaze skip-jumped around the room, landing one by one on my fellow teammates. What if someone threatened Kelly? Or Vaughn? Or Jaylene? Stone might be the biggest badass on the planet but he was still human, or mostly human, as far as I knew. And what about the teens in the room? Sabina was vulnerable and while I didn't know Herc well, he had his whole life before him. Would I be willing to see him sacrificed?

No way. Even Mandy. I might grouse and grumble about her but I wouldn't let her die if I could save her. Suffer maybe, but only a little.

And Bran?

It was one thing for me to want payback for Van's death by taking Bran's life but would I let someone else do the same? If I could shake my head, I would have. If I could have let the tears acid-etching my eyes escape, I would have. Instead, I held myself still enough that even my breaths were minimized.

Bran's words had slammed the whole room into emotional reactive mode, which could get a person killed faster than lighting the tail of a polder duck demon. And that was fast!

It was Vaughn who jump-started clear-headed thinking. "One step at a time. Before we start worrying about what Alex might or might not do, we need her back with the team. Bran, can you do that?"

He quirked one arrogant brow as if wondering why she'd bothered to ask.

But there's a world of difference between can and would.

Vaughn didn't waste any more breath on him. "Good. Next is to create a plan of action. Standing around here is inviting more Weres to attack. Kelly, I need you to make sure Sabina is safe. Can you take her to Ling Mai's?"

It wasn't a suggestion, it was an order. Ling Mai might be a PIA but she could protect her people. When she chose to. There was that damn word again. Everything kept coming down to choices.

Vaughn turned to look at the other teen in the room. "Herc, can you get us up to speed with using your weapons?"

"Ah, yeah, maybe one or two, but probably not everyone," the young man replied. "I don't have enough ingredients to keep the whole team supplied."

"One or two is better than none. I'll volunteer and Mandy— that'll help us as fighters be on par with the others." She turned to Stone. "You know of another place safer than this one?"

He nodded, a funny cant to his smile like he couldn't get enough of his sweetie kicking butt and giving orders.

Vaughn gave him a quick, just-wait smile in return before she turned back to the group. "Jaylene, I want you to update Ling Mai on what's gone down here and what intel we have on this Zaradian demon."

"Soon as I figure it out myself," Jaylene murmured, already heading for the door.

"Mandy, I want you to contact Fraulein Fassbinder, and the librarian if you have to, we need as much intel on Zaradian as possible."

"Will do." Mandy followed Jaylene out the door. If Kelly

took Sabina and Herc away, there'd be fewer targets here to attack if the Weres decided to try again.

"And me?" Bran asked, as if he accepted directions from others all the time. Not! He was more the giving orders and then giving more kind.

"You? I want you to unfreeze Alex, or whatever you did to her."

I owe you, Vaughn.

Bran must have translated my second thought, which was I owed him first, in a whole different way as he asked, "You sure?"

Oh, I'd make him pay for that.

"Yes, I'm positive."

"Then everyone stand back," he said, stepping back himself.

"Why?" Sabina asked. I'd almost forgotten she was still here. She'd been so quiet except for her eyes getting bigger and bigger. "Will it hurt her?"

Not as much as it was going to hurt Bran.

"No," he replied, looking me eye to eye. "But I can't say the same about anyone else in the room."

And in a blink three things happened at once.

Bran raised his voice, speaking that bizarre language and the spell broke.

I shouted,

"Abeo. Abeo. Abeo."

Depart. Die. Depart.

And Sabina threw her body between me and Bran, receiving the full jolt of my spell head- on.

CHAPTER 39

"No." My scream sliced through the room as both Bran and I reached the girl crumpled on the floor. Bran, a split second ahead of me, pulling her into his arms. He didn't even waste a breath berating me. He didn't have to, I was doing enough of that myself.

"Did I kill her?" I whispered, past the lump of misery in my throat.

Bran didn't pay any attention to me, his aristocratic fingers seeking for a pulse. One I could have told him wasn't there. I couldn't hear it. Not her blood, not the beat of her heart.

I hadn't meant for this to happen. I hadn't really meant to even kill Bran, just give him one hell of a jolt, one a full-fledged warlock could take. It'd have knocked him on his ass, but wouldn't have executed him.

This was all my fault. My choice that backfired in my face. What now?

Wait, there was something. A long shot, getting longer each second that ticked past.

"Please." I clutched Bran's wrist, leaving nail bites in his skin, earning the heat of his stare piercing through me. "Can you do it? What you did for me?"

He knew what I was talking about. Once, when a Were killed me, Bran brought me back to life. A gift only the most powerful mages could use. I'd never told anyone about it. Using it now would expose his secrets to everyone in the room. But it also was Sabina's only chance.

"Please," I repeated. "She's just a kid."

His gaze shifted away from mine, as he shook his head. "I

can't."

"Can't?"

My heart shuddered.

Did he really say that? He could save her but was choosing not to? I stiffened, hope replaced by anger surging through me. My voice roughened, razor-edged and caustic. "Can't or won't?"

He grabbed my other hand, the one I had started beating against his chest. I didn't even realize I was doing it. "Can't," he said, his voice just as saber-sharp and lethal as mine had been. "I used up too much magic finding you. Stopping you. There's nothing left."

How like a warlock. Way to gut a person.

It was my fault. All my fault. I brought Sabina here instead of sending her away. I messed up the magic of the only person in the room who could save her. I cast the destruction spell. Called upon the black magic.

Magic always had a price, but it was Sabina paying my price.

"Noooooo," the word wrenched from deep inside. "Nooooo."

Kelly knelt beside me. "Don't give up," she whispered, hugging me like I wasn't a cold bastard of a killer.

I looked at her, aware of how blurry she was. Tears? Nah, Noziaks didn't do tears. We specialized in pain. Mostly to ourselves and others. Me more than most.

But wait. There was a small something that might work.

"Bran." I shook him. Hard. "If we join ... Can I channel your magic?"

"You mean like when you usurped it before?"

Usurped? Sabina's skin was growing cold. We didn't have time for semantics. "I don't care what you call it. Can it work?"

He looked wary, but then he often did around me. It was amazing how easy it was to ignore that, too. "Hurry. We're running out of time."

"We can try," he said, his voice sounding years older than seconds ago. "But it'll be dangerous. For all of us but mostly you."

Who cared? He'd said yes. That's all I needed.

Brushing the wetness staining my cheeks I stood, towering over Bran and Sabina as I started pulling from Bran's magic. Making it my own.

"Adeo. Adeo. Agero. Adepto.
Come. Come. Increase. Acquire. *"*

"Careful, Alex," Bran whispered. "It's dangerous. You've used too much of your own magic. You don't have a lot to draw from."

What did he know? He didn't care about me. If I just repeated that enough times, I might believe it, too.

Listen to yourself. I'm here with you. You're not alone. The woman's voice again. Mom. Who else could it be? Why did she only come when I couldn't connect with her?

Because you need me.

No, I'd needed her as a child. Now Sabina, barely older than a child needed me. No more distractions.

I steeled my voice as I continued,

"Suscipio. Solvo.
Receive. Break free. *"*

I pulled words I'd used before, each time causing more problems and misery than before I cast. But I'd run out of choices.

"Singluaris. Praesentia presencia.
Free the power."

Bran glanced at me, a frown knitted between his brows. Neither of us could speak. It was taking everything we had to weave the magic. I could feel his exhaustion. Or was it my own? His pain. And mine.

He'd told the truth, he really had little to offer. Between us, we might make one okay spell. If that's all we had then that's what we had.

A slow rush washed against me. Not like before when I'd have to brace myself against it as I pulled not only from Bran and any other non-human abilities around us. But an eddy was an eddy, it could still pull you under and drown you whether it was hurricane whipped or a lazy-lying pool beckoning the unwary.

I stood statue-still in the nexus of a power vortex that built and built. I didn't revel in the potency as much as call it to me. Begging and pleading. Promising and cajoling. Save Sabina.

This is who you are. What you're meant to do.

This time it wasn't the woman's voice. It was Bran's. Unlocking the last ounce of magic rising within me.

I nodded, accepting, biting my lip till I drew blood. I tasted the copper tang and zeroed in. Thrice called, thrice to contain.

"As thou were, so now be.
Thought to image gone.
Image to bind present.
Present to blood let and be."

I raised my hands skyward, aware of the sound of Kelly inhaling beside me, bracing herself.

Like the psychic vampire I was, I tapped into her power, too.

"Vita. Anima. Fides.
Live. Breath of life. Trust. *"*

But I needed more. I glanced at Bran. Knew what I was asking. Draw enough magic from a magical being and you risked killing it.

He nodded, glancing back at the still girl in his arms.

"Vita. Anima. Fides."

My arms and legs quivered with the strain, as did my voice.

"Abduco. Abeo. Abstergo."

Light motes danced before my eyes.

"Undo what I have wrought. Change the unchangeable.
Ash to life. Life to breath.
So mote it be."

I pulled from Bran's magic and made it my own, amplifying
like a tornado funnel amplified wind until I was the still spot in
the center, dangerous to everyone around.

Time careened to a halt. My head roared, blood pounding
behind my eyes, nerve endings jangling.

Then the room went dark.

CHAPTER 40

I had no idea where I was, who I was when the male voice broke against me.

"Alex, *merde*, wake up."

Bran. Angry. At me. Again.

I didn't want to open my eyes. Didn't want to feel anymore. Didn't want to always be fighting him.

One time it'd seemed easy. He wanted me. I wanted him. That was enough.

Not anymore.

"Please," he whispered, so close to me his breath fanned my face.

That wasn't the Bran I knew.

A groan escaped before I could lasso it back, but it helped me open one eye. Then close it just as fast.

He was too close. Cradling me in his arms. Holding me tight enough I felt safe. When was the last time that had happened?

Then I remembered. Sabina. The spell.

I opened both eyes this time, tried to raise my head, my voice hoarse and raw as I asked, "Sabina?"

"I'm okay," the teen said, crawling into my vision near Bran's right shoulder.

"I killed you," was all that would come.

"And brought me back. So awesome. You've got to teach me that spell."

Not in this lifetime. Or the next one.

I glanced at Bran. Those blue eyes that could suck a woman's soul dry. My soul. Willingly. "I was trying to kill you," I mumbled, the truth rustling on my tongue.

"You're going to have to try harder." He knocked me for another loop when he released a rusty laugh.

How could you hate a person who knew how to coax a smile from you when you were sure you'd never smile again?

"Next time," I offered, feeling what little energy I had left ebbing. My eyes closed. I couldn't keep them open a second longer.

"Will she be okay?" Sabina asked, her voice a decade younger than her years.

"For now," came Bran's response as his arms tightened.

"And then what?"

"Then we face battle. Again."

Why wasn't I surprised by that answer?

CHAPTER 41

Next time I woke up, I was in a luxurious bed, filled with pillows and silken textures. Alone.

I could feel my own frown.

Where was I?

Kelly popped into view. She must have been nearby as she smoothed the blankets and tucked me in like I was one of her former kindergarten charges. "You're safe. Bran found us this place. He's gone now but he's been here for hours, watching over you."

I didn't know what part of her comment threw me the most. The vulnerability of being defenseless with Bran nearby? The lie that all was now safe? Or the fact Kelly seemed to trust that if Bran found wherever we were all was well?

My head ached trying to sort out the Gordian knots racing through me. I finally latched on to the easiest question first. "How long?"

Kelly's brows dipped then cleared, making her look as young as Sabina. "You mean since you've been out? A good twenty-four hours."

I lurched upwards, looking no doubt like a rusty robot. Before I could smash two words together, Kelly spoke again. "I know, I know. The Weres still seem to be after you, according to some friend of Bran's who's named William or something."

"Willie," I mouthed.

"That's it!" She made it sound like I'd earned a gold star on a test. "Anyway, they don't know where you are now."

"Because?" They'd found me before, more than once, so why not now? But those words wouldn't come either.

"You appeared to have some kind of magic tracking device on you. Bran disabled it or watered it down or something, so you're not as easy to find."

I noticed she didn't say impossible to find. They would just have to try harder. Given the number of attacks already I'd say someone wasn't afraid of a little hard work to get me back. Which reminded me.

"Sabina?"

"Oh, she's safe. Out in the other room. Bran's been teaching her a few basic magic spells."

I guess I groaned out loud as Kelly was quick to add, "Nothing dangerous. Just some stuff to keep her mind off of, you know ..." She waved one hand in a nervous gesture, unlike her. "... you know, the whole demon, kidnapping, locked in a dungeon thing."

Oh yeah. Kelly made it sound like a cheap movie with bad graphics, which minimized all the fear and terror. As if.

"So, are you feeling better?" Kels asked, her eyes wide, her hands pleating one another.

Better than what? Death-warmed over? Road kill? Or a weeklong flu binge?

But this was see-the-sunny-side-of-things Kelly so I gave her a stiff nod. Little white lies never hurt anyone. Did they?

"Good. You're probably starved as who knows how long it's been since you've had anything to eat."

As if on cue my stomach rumbled like thunder in the distance. But there were more pressing matters. For one, I was buck naked under these fancy sheets. Two, bad guys were still after me even if they were not currently attacking. Key words being *current* and *attack*, but that could change any minute. Sabina was still at risk being anywhere near me and Van was still dead.

That quick it slammed against me. I'd forgotten the weight of that grief. That loss. The sheer darkness of it swallowing me.

Kelly sat on the edge of the bed, taking one of my hands that I hadn't even realized was strangling the duvet cover. "It'll be all right," she murmured, doing that kindergarten thing again even as I wanted to scream, which part of this would be better? Van's death? Bran's killing him? Someone out to use me to unleash a demon on the world?

But before I could get past the stranglehold the anger had on me, Bran strolled into the room.

Why was it some men owned a room whenever they entered? Just once, I wished he would look like a mere mortal. But he wasn't. He was a mage master who could reverse death.

I eased back on my pillow. Not giving up as much as regrouping. Yeah, man it sucked when I started lying to myself.

Kels slid to her feet, talking to Bran instead of me. "I'll go get her some soup or something. Leave you two alone. You probably have a few things to talk over."

Traitor!

I thought she'd had my back. But face one gorgeous, domineering, warlock with a determined glint in his eye and Kelly caved.

She disappeared before I could call her back.

Just as well. If I weren't up to fighting Bran, even after being raised with four brothers, no way would Kelly survive.

"Feeling better?" he asked in that low sexy, make-goose-bumps-along-your-skin voice of his that I didn't trust for a second. He stood less than three steps away from the edge of the bed. Way too close for comfort. Hell, down the street would be way too close, but no way was I going to let him know he rattled me. He was arrogant enough as it was.

When no words would come I nodded.

"Good." Some words meant the exact opposite and this was one of those times.

He stepped closer.

My skin went cold then heated. If I wasn't naked and he wasn't within a hand's breath I'd have been fanning myself with the sheets.

Instead all I could do was swallow. Deeply.

"We have unfinished business," he purred, stepping so close he bumped up against the bed.

Oh, oh.

Why did I know he didn't mean a simple chat among colleagues? Or even a hair-raising peel-the-skin-off-my-hide tirade like Stone or my dad could do? No, this man was more diabolical, craftier, a master at scaring the willies out of you before he ever did a thing.

But I was a Noziak. Offense was the best defense. Witches trumped warlocks. End of story.

I popped into a sitting position, grabbing for the bedding before it slipped too far. For the space of a wickedly erratic heartbeat I noticed Bran's gaze slipped too.

So maybe I wasn't the only one unnerved here and trying my damnedest to hide it.

That gave a little oomph to my backbone, and by the Great Spirits, I needed it, Noziak blood or not.

"You want to talk," I started out, sounding a whole lot more in control than I felt. "Let's talk." I pointed to a chair. Not the one closest to the bed, but the one across the room. "You, there, and we'll talk."

I thought that sounded reasonable. Two intelligent, mostly rational adults. At least I was rational. With Bran it was always a thirty-seventy chance.

Like now. Did he nod? Walk across the room? Agree?

No. This was Bran.

He grinned a wicked, wicked smile that curled my toes and made my breath back up before he pressed one knee on the bed and leaned forward, space disappearing between us inch by inch until I had to bend my head back until all I could see was him.

I went to shake my head, but his hand was there, caught in my hair, tugging my head even farther back, playing his own cat and mouse game. Him, the biggest, baddest, predator cat. Me, the trapped mouse.

Then his lips eased toward mine.

I told myself I should fight. Scramble away. Toss away dignity for escape. But I didn't.

Instead, I leaned toward him, not away.

CHAPTER 42

Some kisses you ease into. Some you dive. This was shouting halleluiah as I plunged over Niagara Falls with a smile on my face!

The rush started somewhere near the tips of my toes then exploded my brain cells.

Hot. Wet. Deep. And we'd only started.

One of us moaned. Maybe it was both of us as he pressed me back onto the pillows and I held on to him every inch of the way.

His hands were in my hair, cupping my face, heating my bare skin, and I couldn't get enough. I didn't want to come up for air long enough to get him naked but there was too much bedding, too many clothes between us.

I pulled back. My lips only, frantically demanding, "Here. Now."

He snarled, which was the sexiest sound in the Universe when made by a frustrated man who wants you as much as you want him.

Then someone coughed.

We froze. His expression promised pain to someone. Skin drawn tight, nostrils flared, the blue of his eyes swallowed by the black of his pupils.

"I didn't mean to interrupt. I can come back later."

Kelly's voice and the scent of chicken soup reached me at the same time.

I couldn't help it. This time I was the one who laughed. It started as a small snort, waltzed into giggles, then became a full body chuckle I tried to muffle by pulling the duvet up to stuff in my mouth. It didn't help.

Bran, ever the aristocrat, narrowed his heavy-lidded gaze at me, promising retribution for my enjoying his discomfort a little too much, stood with that slow, pompous dignity only mastered by Brits and male movie stars from the forties, and tugged his clothes into a semblance of neatness.

I could have told him it wasn't working, he still looked like a frustrated, aroused Alpha male who was being thwarted.

I could see Kelly standing near the door, a tray acting as a flimsy barrier between her and Bran should she need one. She raised one brow at me, girl talk for should-I-stay-or-should-I go?

I smiled at her in return. What are good friends for except to save you from your own rash and potentially stupid mistakes. Yes, I wanted Bran. Would that have complicated things? Enormously and that wasn't even touching the heartbreak still splintering me at the thought of what Bran had done to my brother. That alone sobered me. Sobered and reminded me.

Thank you Kels, and your sense of timing.

Kelly held her ground. I owed her.

Bran gave me one last we're-not-done-by-a-long- shot look, which whooshed the giggles right out of me, nodded at Kelly and marched from the room.

"Oh my," Kelly released one hand from the tray to wave in front of her face. "Oh my, oh my, oh my."

I scrubbed my hands over my face even as I mumbled through my fingers. "Yeah, Bran has that impact on a lot of women."

"You lucky girl," she smiled, adding, "You know you might be sending him mixed messages."

"Seriously?" I meant it as a snide comment, mostly to myself, but leave it to Kels to take it as a serious question.

"One minute you're trying to kill him. The next—" She actually blushed as she set the tray down beside me. "Just saying."

"I know." And boy did I. I hadn't meant things to get out of hand, but the road to Hades was paved with good intentions, or weak will, or both. "This soup smells great."

Yes, I was trying to change the conversation and Lord love her, Kelly let me. "Ling Mai has called for a team meeting in about," she glanced at her watch. Did anybody really wear a watch anymore? Now that I thought about it, Kelly always did. An old-fashioned one that looked like it belonged to someone she cared for some time ago. "In about twenty minutes," she finished.

I choked on my sip of chicken noodle soup. "Twenty minutes?"

"You've got plenty of time to get ready."

"I don't think there's enough time in the world to get ready for facing Ling Mai."

"Good point." Not what I expected Kelly to say. "But on the bright side the fact she's coming here to see and talk with you means you're still on the team."

Miss Sally Sunshine had a point. I refused to consider the word—yet—at the end of her comment.

I slurped my meal like an Olympic racer, ever so thankful that Kelly had tracked down my suitcase and brought me a change of clothes. I even took a shower, though I braided my wet hair before I quieted my nerves and braced my shoulders when the knock on the door came.

I'd joined Sabina, Bran and Kelly in the front room of what looked like a hotel to rival Ling Mai's. Only Bran would expect comfort and class from a safe house. Kelly went to answer the door but I stopped her. "I'll get it."

Movement gave some release from the ants crawling along my skin. Of course some of those ants were because of Bran who had been looking at me like a snack ever since I had walked into the room.

I know Kelly told me team meeting but I hadn't really expected eight people marching into the room one after the other. Ling Mai led the procession, followed by Stone and Vaughn together, Jaylene, Mandy then Herc, and a new woman I'd never seen before.

"Who are you?" I asked, glancing back at Kelly.

"Your replacement," came the whip-fast reply as her coal brown gaze locked with mine. Attitude in spades. But she was messing with the wrong Anglo-Native American chick, especially after she added, "You smell like a shifter."

Suddenly Bran was at my side, one hand pressing against my shoulder hard enough to weld me to the floor. But that didn't stop my tongue. "I might smell like a shifter but I sure don't *act* like one."

Whatever was going on with my being a shifter or not was my nightmare to untangle, not her business to agitate.

I offered a take-no-prisoners smile, leaned a smidge closer to her with a small whisper meant only for her ears, "Meow."

I thought she was going to start swinging right then, but either she had smarts she was hiding, or a stronger sense of self preservation than she'd shown so far. Of course, Ling Mai interceded with a quick, "Alex, this is Nicki Yarblonski, our newest team member. Nicki, Alex Noziak."

"Play nice, ladies," Stone said, then when we both cut as-if looks his way he added. "If you're going to draw blood do it on your own time. Not now."

Got the message. I grabbed the only remaining spot in the room, one Kelly saved me, that also put me right next to Bran. Beginning to wonder what side Kels was on.

Ling Mai cleared her throat. "Nice to see you alive and well, Miss Noziak."

No she wasn't. Dead I was no longer a pain in her ass. Alive? Alive, I caused complications.

Bran nudged me, which was his subtle way to tell me to play the game. I gave a tight smile and nod. There. That was mostly polite.

"After contacting the librarian for some more information on this Zaradian demon, it appears this threat should be taken seriously."

As if I hadn't already? Oh, yeah, she hadn't had gangs of angry Weres attacking her regularly for the past few days, so maybe that explained why she was a little slow on the threat assessment issue.

"Miss Sabina, I notice you're still with us," Ling Mai continued, doing a total about face and making every gaze whip to Sabina's.

Oh, no you don't. No throwing the teen witch to the wolves, metaphorically.

"She's here because whoever wants me also wants her. If I'm not available, they're going to go after her and the demon will be released." Sabina would probably die, too, and I made sure my tone said just that.

Ling Mai's expression was a cross between how droll, the screw-up-speaks and not-our-problem.

Stone was the one who stepped in to avoid a second dust up. "Alex has some valid points. We've agreed the primary goal is to stop the release of this demon."

"And all we know about the process is that a witch is needed to make that happen. Sabina and I have been targeted as witches who possess whatever talents they want."

"How do we know other witches aren't also being held?" New Girl said, slurring the word *witches* just enough to indicate what she really meant.

"Because they keep coming after us," I replied, glancing at the rest of the room, a duh tone in my voice.

Ling Mai interceded, "If the demon is successfully called—"

"Holy shit, humans are screwed," Herc blurted out, earning an eye roll from Stone.

Sabina leaned toward me to whisper, "Is that what she meant?"

I nodded. "Yup. We're all about to get screwed if Z-demon dude gets here."

"Then why didn't she just say that?"

"She's speaking Ling Mai speak. You'll get used to it."

Not that she'd be hanging around that long. If the demon came, none of us might be around for long.

Ling Mai continued, "Which leads me to believe we should inform the Council of Seven about what's happening."

It made sense. So why did goose bumps crawl up my skin?

Bran spoke up. "There's another key element we've been missing and haven't discussed. Something that needs attention before the Council is notified."

Leave it to a warlock to add more fuel to the conflagration.

"Such as?" Ling Mai asked.

"Who is behind wanting this demon unleashed? We have to stop him—"

"Or her," I mumbled, thinking about Bran's cousin Dominique, who had been one nasty villain that got her comeuppance when I killed her. A fact Bran still held against me, just as I held his killing my brother against him. Had I mentioned Bran and I had a complicated relationship?

"Or her." he didn't miss a beat. "We also have one additional piece of intel that can give us a clue to who is behind this scheme."

I had no doubt I looked as confused as my teammates, as Bran looked at me. "The Irish male voice you heard while you were being held captive. He seemed in charge?"

I nodded, remembering I'd actually rooted for that guy. He seemed like my protector then. And now? Colin Farrell voice was behind using and destroying me as well as the bigge r point of unleashing horror and havoc on the world.

My taste in men obviously needed some work.

Bran continued, "I say if we can find this man, we'll be that much closer to stopping the demon."

"What then?" Mandy demanded. "We accost every Irish-accented guy in this city on the off chance Alex will recognize his voice?"

She didn't have to say it that way. I had no doubts I'd recognize his voice again. But she was right about the needle in a haystack mission. Paris was a ginormous city and who knew if he was even still here? Bad guys could fly in and out just like ordinary tourists.

I caught Bran watching me, waiting for me to reach some conclusion he already understood. When I realized I was shaking my head, he glanced around the room. "We need to go further back than the attack on Alex."

Now he was really losing me. I was used to being Johnnie-on-the-spot. Or Jane-on-the-spot, but I was in a fog here.

Bran was using his CEO voice, the one that sounded like it was okay to be clueless, just trust him and he'd lead the way.

I felt a rather heated flashback on where I'd like him to lead me but he was already explaining. Thank the Spirits, as I subtly fanned myself.

Bran gave me a wicked, I-know-what-you're-thinking look before prodding. "Before someone kidnapped you, they kidnapped your brother."

That fast the ice-cold tsunami of reality hit me. I knew what happened next. Van died. And here I was lusting after his killer. How screwed up shallow could I get?

"Someone has been manipulating all of us, not caring who was killed."

I tried to pay attention, though my emotions were locked in on Van's death. He so did not deserve that. He was one of the good guys.

"What's the common thread among what's been happening?" Bran asked the room at large.

"Alex," Kelly piped up.

But Bran wasn't finished. "And?"

I think we were all at a loss until I started thinking a few things through. The drug dealer, Vaverek, used Bran's cousin Dominique to test a nasty designer drug. Van's capture by Vaverek led to my enlisting Bran's aid to find Van. But Bran had his own reasons to help, as he wanted the ones who embroiled his cousin in a plot that led directly to her death. Van led to Vaverek, and Vaverek led to someone higher. Someone with connections to the Council of Seven.

I glanced at Bran, suddenly seeing fine details in the puzzle pieces. "The Council," I murmured, still working through the gray areas. "Which could explain Philippe Cheverill's murder."

"And your father being in Paris," Bran added.

That pulled me up short. "You think my dad's behind all this?"

He so had the wrong end of the stick. I might still be PO'd at my dad but no way was he this Machiavellian. I could see him killing someone, but it'd be a fair fight, not a knife to the back and then going after all the person's relatives.

"Not your dad. Think!" Bran prodded.

"The Council." I could hear the *kerching* of the key piece sliding into place. "You think the Council is behind this?"

Even Ling Mai raised her brows at that, but it was Kelly who spoke first, "But that doesn't make any sense? They work to keep humans from being aware of preternaturals. Wouldn't unleashing a dangerous fallen- angel -demon guy on the world be counterintuitive?"

"It would." Bran nodded his head with a calculated precision, before he went in for the zing. "But what if it's not the Council itself but one person on the Council working for his … or her," he cut me a glance while continuing,"… for their own gains with the Council's mandate."

"Or it could be someone associated with the Council," Sabina spoke up, earning a few what-do-you-know-about-it looks. So she added, "You're right, I don't know anything at all about this Council but aren't there assistants or people or beings or whatever that help?"

"She has a point," Vaughn conceded, offering an atta-girl smile.

"So notifying the Council—" Jaylene started and Mandy finished, "—means we'd be tipping off the very individual we're looking for."

"They'd go to ground," Stone, the strategist said. "Postponing their plans until they could eliminate those who know too much."

"Us." Kelly cleared her throat and said again. "We'd all be at risk, not just Alex and Sabina."

Stone nodded. "And then the master-mind would unleash the demon without fear of being stopped."

"But if the Council or someone near it is involved how does that get us closer to the master-mind?" Kelly asked, which saved me the trouble.

Bran looked at her. "Alex will."

"What?" Like hell I would! Ever feel like the downhill terminus of a dunghill? "Why's it keep coming back to me?"

I sounded whiny, but for love of the Great Spirits, the world did not revolve around me. In spite of what I'd told my brothers for years.

"You're the only one with a contact on the Council," Bran said, making my heart skitter and my skin chill. "Your dad may be our best lead to who is acting against all our interests."

"You want me to track down my dad?"

"If you want to stop a demon," he said in a voice so calm I wanted to slap him. It wasn't like he was suggesting I give Dad a ring, ask him if he knew any colleagues of his who might want to destroy the world then ask about the weather. He was pushing me to face my father who sacrificed me for his beloved Council and hid that tidbit from me until I found out on my own.

Not going to happen.

I closed my mouth, clenched my jaw and crossed my arms.

So not going to happen.

"Intriguing supposition," Ling Mai said. "You may have twenty-four hours to discover if there's any validity to your hypothesis. After that, I shall speak to my Council contact. This is too big of a potential catastrophe not to keep them informed."

Not a rousing endorsement of Bran's plan, which was fine with me. I would rather have a triple root canal than find my dad for a little *tête-à-tête*.

Just plain not going to happen.

Kelly reached over and laid her hand over mine. She alone seemed to understand what was being asked here. What was being asked of me. Then she turned to Bran. "What's going to happen if Alex doesn't talk to her father? Isn't there another way?"

"Yes." Bran gave her his steely-eyed glint. "We wait until this unknown threat attacks her again."

Okay, I could live with that. Wasn't looking forward to it but I'd take that choice over begging my dad for help. Again.

But Bran wasn't finished. "Or the master-mind tries for Sabina because she's an easier target. Or takes out some of the team because he's not going to keep holding back."

My stomach plummeted, a long, slow, painful dive off a very high cliff.

I was going to have to do exactly what I didn't want to do.

So much for choices.

CHAPTER 43

Bran went with me. Lucky me. I'm sure it was because he thought I'd bolt without a warlock escort.

I hated that he could read my mind.

Afternoon was seeping into early evening as we exited a town car that Bran had hired. How he could keep a low profile at his level was beyond me, and yes, I was focusing on inconsequential details instead of the sweat pooling on my lower back and the quivering of my knees.

"How did you know where my father is?" I asked, my voice barely squeaky.

"I knew where Philippe Cheverill lived and assumed your father would stay with him when in town."

How civilized. Logical actually, but I wasn't feeling generous enough to give Bran any brownie points. It was because of him I was here, and there wasn't enough time in the world for him to pay me back for that fact.

We stood outside an old stone building with a million-dollar view of the Eiffel Tower. Bran probably owned a similar swanky place nearby.

Snark was also something I could manage well when nervous. Okay, all the time, but I so didn't want to go up and ring that doorbell.

The building looked old, but with that elegance that a beautifully crafted home carried. Mud Lake, Idaho, didn't run with any buildings that looked like this, which was only one of the reasons I couldn't see my father staying here. Man, when he lived a double life, he did a dandy job of keeping it quiet.

"You ready?" Bran whispered in my ear, startling me out of my thoughts and making me aware I was standing frozen on the sidewalk as if he had bespelled me again.

"Sure." If my shoulders tightened any more they were going to snap. It'd be a cold day in Hades before I let Bran or anyone else know how bad my nerves were misbehaving. "Let's go."

I didn't know what I expected as I hit a hard rat-a-tat on the gray-painted doorway. *Hi, Dad, how are you? Hi, Dad, why'd you abandon me? Hi, Dad, I hate you but I still need you.*

Whatever I expected it wasn't to see Van open the door.

CHAPTER 44

Time jerked to a stop. My hand had been raised to strike the door again. The half-open door. Van standing there, his face thinner, lines etched near his eyes, a slow grin growing on his face.

He reached for me first and only when he touched me did I believe it was really him and not an illusion or wraith.

"You're alive," I blubbered into his knit sweater, squeezing him so hard I could hear his breath catch. "I thought you were dead."

Damn. Damn. Damn. Relief warred with anger. All this time when I'd thought the worst. Here he was. And no one told me.

He pulled back enough to look over my shoulder then back at me. "How could you know? Your friend here saved my skin."

I glanced back at Bran. Okay, it was more a hard, payback's-coming kind of glare. "You knew I thought he was dead. Why didn't you—"

"She was too busy trying to kill me to listen," he said to Van, like they were BFFs.

"That sounds familiar." Van chuckled, a sound I never thought I'd hear again as he pulled me into the house, my fingers tangled in his sweater as I was too afraid to let him go again. He waved Bran in too. "You'll never change," he laughed at me.

I smacked him on the shoulder, hard enough it staggered him. He rubbed his side as if it'd really stung. "Ow. When did you get muscles?"

Since he'd bitten me.

So did not want to go there, which was clear in the look I shot Bran. He grabbed the ball and said, "We actually came to see your father. If he's here."

There were undercurrents here, something that happened between Bran and my father, or Bran and Van. I didn't know which but could feel the swirls and eddies.

"You sure?" Van asked. That's when it hit me. Bran was still wanted by the Council. My father being a Council member would be required to restrain him and produce him in front of the governing body. Bran was a strong warlock but my dad was a shaman powerful enough to be on the Council so no telling how this could play out.

I'd just walked Bran into a trap.

I'd been so focused on why I didn't want to be here that I'd buried the threat to Bran.

I jerked to a stop, barely noticing the frou-frou antiques and soothing color tones of the small room we'd walked into as I turned back toward the door, grabbing Bran's arm in the process. "On second thought, this can wait."

"Alex? Is that you?" The voice came from closer to the front door. "And what can wait?"

Dad. Between us and escape.

"Mr. Noziak," Bran said as my dad's eyes narrowed. I don't know if Dad even noticed I was in the room as Bran and Van made a very effective wall in front of me. But I could see my dad from the small gap between them. My dad who looked as if he'd aged as much as Van had recently. More gray in his sable black hair, deeper grooves in his face, an air around him I hadn't seen since my mom had disappeared.

"I didn't expect to see you here." My dad was focused on Bran, the comment so cold it sliced.

"We need your assistance," Bran replied.

Much braver person than I was.

"We?" my dad asked.

Oh. Oh.

Good thing I was a Noziak, and digging a hole was not an option. No matter how good it sounded.

I muscled my way past Bran and Van, and trust me, it wasn't easy, which explained why I was out of breath as I came face to face with my dad.

"Yes, us." My tone held mostly bravado as did my stance, legs apart, arms folded across my chest, chin raised high enough it dared him to take his best shot.

But he didn't. Instead, he inhaled sharply as if one of us had rammed him with a stout stick then stepped forward and wrapped me in a hug as if I were five and not twenty plus years older than that.

"I thought—" he started then choked and started again. "I looked for you. On the other side. But couldn't find you."

He released me enough to look down at me, tears glittering in his eyes.

I looked twice because my dad did not cry. Ever. Not when Mom left. Not when Van and two of my other brothers chose lives fraught with danger. Not when I'd been sent to prison. Not ever.

And just like that, I felt like I was five all over again. Trusting my dad to know everything, fix everything, including a little girl's broken heart. Only now I was the one who'd broke his heart.

I hadn't thought what he must have felt, how he could have been worrying, playing the what-if-I'd-done-something-different game. The same bitter, pointless, painful game that had been scouring me when thinking Van had been killed.

And yet. My body stiffened, my strangled emotions roiling as I cleared my throat. "I'm here because I need your help."

Less than a dozen rock-hard words built a wall between us. No warm and fuzzy reunion here. He'd hurt me. I'd hurt him. We'd go on hurting each other. I didn't know for how long. Betrayal burned deep. Understanding could take a lifetime to repair the damage. We only had twenty-four hours with the minutes ticking past.

Dad angled his head as if listening to what I wasn't saying, but even I couldn't get clear what was screaming from within me. *Why? Why your Council instead of me? Why not once explain to me what you did?*

Too much rage, too little time.

Bran stepped forward, brushing his shoulder against mine, allying himself with me against my father even as we both needed my dad's help to save lives. A whole lot of lives.

The warlock at my side broke the tinsel-fragile silence. "We're looking for someone with an Irish accent who works closely with the Council."

Like a lightning bug flaring and dying in the same heartbeat, my father stepped back. A rough jagged movement, quickly replaced by a whipcord savagery. "You expect me to speak of the Council."

The words were more accusation than question.

"Someone within or close to the Council who speaks with an Irish accent is seeking to use your daughter, or another powerful witch, a very young one, to unleash Zaradian."

That sucked out all the air in the room, even as I noticed something flash in my father's gaze.

"You know something," I whispered my words hoarse and dry. "Or suspect someone."

My father spared me a half-second deadly glance. This was not the dad of my childhood, my knight in shining armor. This was one of seven of the most powerful preternaturals existing on the planet. It took everything in me not to step back.

"We don't ask you to betray anyone," Bran said.

Like you did me.

"We need your help. We can't stop the threat to both preternaturals and humans without it."

A pause before my dad said, "A worthy cause." I started breathing again, but it was too soon as he added, "But what proof do you have?"

Bran glanced at me and waited until I gave a barely perceptible nod.

"Alex can identify the voice of the individual who held her hostage." Before Dad could rear back, Bran kept pushing. Nothing like a tightly leashed, if pissed off, warlock determined to find justice. "The same person who's behind a plan to release **Satanaial**'s right hand." As Dad opened his mouth Bran raised one hand. "We're not asking you to call him out. We're only asking for help in identifying him."

"And then?" my father asked, his tone lethal.

"Then we find a way to help the Council stop his actions."

My father's lips turned in a mockery of a smile. "So says a man who refuses to appear before the Council. Is in fact fleeing from them?"

Once again my father was choosing the Council. Why was I not surprised. I stepped forward. If it'd been another I might have jammed my finger, hard, against his chest to get him to listen, but I did have a small smidgen of self-preservation still in me. My tone, though didn't hold back. "Bran's here because I'm here. Trying to stop a cataclysm. Trying to save lives. He's putting his life, his freedom on the line and all we're asking is for you to listen. For you to accept that there may be something rotten within your precious Council."

"Enough," my father roared, shocking all of us, Van in particular, who grabbed my shoulder and thrust me behind him. "You have no idea what you're talking about," Dad bit each word out as if chipped from granite. "You are calling to account the only institution that has allowed humans to survive for the past thousand years. An institution you know nothing about."

I leaned around Van's arm, so angry I'm surprised my touch didn't burn him. "I know Philippe Cheverill is dead. Murdered by someone close to your beloved Council. Why can't you see what's right in front of you?"

"You have no idea of the danger you seek to unleash," Dad murmured, his tone almost sorrowful now. "Go home. Away from here."

"It's too late," Bran said, stepping closer to Van, which effectively backed me up. Damn warlocks and shifters for treating me like a fragile human.

But then I felt Van still beside me and heard the sound from outside. The tramp of heavy footsteps marching up to the front door.

"You expecting company, Dad?" Van asked, knowing our dad could hear what we were hearing.

Dad shook his head, his expression suddenly tight. He didn't look at me but spoke to Bran. "You brought her here. Can you hide her?"

A knock rattled the door.

Bran whipped around to me, speaking Latin, the words of a simple cloaking spell.

I glanced at my hands, which I could no longer see. "What the—"

"Stay quiet, I beg you," Bran murmured. "No matter what."

What was he talking about? Who was on the other side of that door?

Van looked at Dad who gave a stiff, jerky nod. My brother glanced around, walking toward the front door only when he was assured he couldn't see me. Maybe he could smell me, he was a shifter, but it was harder to cover a scent than sight.

I still wasn't sure what was happening until the door opened and I could hear the voice speaking. "I must come in."

And then he was there. Colin Farrell voice. The man we were looking for had come to us. Not only come to us but was giving my father a hug.

CHAPTER 45

Even before Colin Farrell voice finished embracing my father he noticed Bran. Emotions raced across the stranger's boyish face: surprise, anger and, what sacred me most, calculation. If I'd only seen this face I would have thought him charming, handsome even. But I recognized him, from the night of Philippe Cheverill's death and later in a stark and sterile laboratory.

Now? Now all I could do was rage. Could this be the man who'd caused so much pain? Was planning to cause infinitely more? The man behind Dominique's betrayal of Bran, behind Van's kidnapping, behind the attacks on me?

I thought my feral growl was silent until Bran stepped back, knowing full well he'd smacked right into me. But his action had the desired effect. I stopped being a ninny and snapped to attention.

Who was this Padraig? What did he want with my dad? And why was he here?

My dad glanced over at Van. "Padraig, I don't believe you've met my son Van."

The sociopathic bastard smoothed his features to a surprise that was all subterfuge: I could smell the deceit from where I stood shaking. But Irish Guy stepped forward, extending his hand as if he really cared. "I've heard about you."

"Sorry, I can't say the same." Van met the shake, dropping his hand as soon as possible. Only one of the reasons I adored my brother.

The creases around Padraig's eyes deepened before he turned to my father and said, "I didn't know that your son was freed."

Yeah, I bet.

"Congratulations are in order for both of you."

He actually had enough balls to make it sound like he had helped in Van's release. The sheer gall.

Then he cast a hard look toward Bran before addressing his next comment to my dad. "I didn't realize you'd also captured one of the Council's most wanted fugitives." He lowered his head without losing eye contact as if he was giving my dad his due, then negated his action with his next words, "It is what you've done, is it not?"

Slimy rat bastard.

Even I could read between the lines. If Dad said no he'd be hauled before the Council, too. If he said yes ... my heart flip-flopped. If he said yes, Bran would be taken prisoner, dragged before the Council and sentenced for involvement in Dominique's drug dealing. Which he didn't do. Plus he was involved in Vaverek's death in front of the Council. That itself was bad but not as bad as being caught fighting Weres in full view of humans. It didn't matter that the Weres attacked and Bran was only trying to save his life and mine. Little details like that meant squat to the high and mighty Council.

Please. Please. Please. Don't throw Bran to this man, Dad!

"I'm curious why you came, Padraig," my dad said, neatly diverting the conversation. "Especially with an armed escort."

He meant the dozen Weres ranged behind the Irishman. They might not be carrying weapons, at least none that were visible, but their numbers and strength meant resistance was futile.

"My friends?" Padraig laughed and I clenched my hands. "These gentlemen are accompanying me because the Council felt this one." He nodded toward Bran, "might be a danger to the board members."

Dad's brow arched. "And I was not informed? Or had a say in the matter?"

My dad's voice might be low and even but he was pissed. "I am still Council, am I not?"

Direct thrust and twist to the kill zone for anyone who knew my dad. I could see Van inhale a breath as deep as I had.

"I brought your guards." Padraig's tone actually sounded surprised. "And here you astonish me by apprehending Bran before he could do more harm."

Seriously? Who was this guy acting for? No one in this room believed him for a second, so why was he working so hard to be congenial and hale-and fare-thee-well hearty mates? I was going to gag.

Bran said nothing through all this posturing, these lies. I couldn't smell what this Padraig was but he had a taint of dark magic about him. Powerful dark magic. Could Bran still take him? Would he?

I could only see Bran's profile from where I stood but even that glimpse warned me that I wasn't going to like what was going to happen next.

"I came willingly to Mr. Noziak," Bran said, as if he had no idea of the cost of each word.

No! No! No! You fool! You're giving up. Not even trying.

"Did you surrender?" Padraig's tone made a lie to Bran's words.

I moved, meaning to step forward, call out this Irish coward for the pile of crap he was, when I heard Bran's voice in my head. "Don't, Alex," he whispered, the words torn from him and slamming into me.

Like back in the tunnels when I was escaping from the Weres. I didn't know how Bran could connect to me. Strong emotions probably. By the Goddess, I knew that's what was whipping through me.

I stared at Bran's wide back, an empty spot growing into a deep dark hole inside of me. "We can take him." Even mind to mind I could hear the pleading in my own voice. "Van will help us."

"Can't."

Won't, I wanted to scream, but already the Weres surrounded him.

"You're not planning to fight us are you?" Padraig made the question sound like a dare, then added, "The simin fae owe you for their disgrace."

Bran had managed to outfox the simin fae? No way was anyone going to be caught off guard again. Unless?

"I hope this doesn't mean you plan to have a prisoner abused before he faces the Council," my father said in such a reasonable tone that I missed the subtext. The one saying hurt-him-and-pay.

Go, Dad!

What happened next happened so fast I almost missed it. Padraig pointed a finger at Bran that brought him to his knees, writhing.

Van flung his hand out as if to go to the warlock but in reality to keep me from him. Dad speared one look at the Irishman, lowering his voice before saying, "I realize your power, Padraig. So who is your show for?"

"No show, Jebediah. A promise. For our prisoner here. If he resists, in any way, he'll suffer the consequences."

One, no one called my father Jebediah. Two, creating pain to prove you can create pain was overkill. Three, stopping Padraig just became very real and very personal.

"You understand, don't you?" Padraig spoke to Bran, but the words were meant for everyone in the room. Bran couldn't speak, he was in too much pain, so my father answered. "We all understand. Now take your prisoner and leave."

He was going to let this psychotic sociopath waltz out of here with Bran?

"Tell the team," Bran murmured through my thoughts, each word wrung from him.

Tell them what? The trap I'd led Bran into worked? One of our strongest allies was in the hands of the enemy? The enemy that now had a name and face, not that it was going to help us at all.

Whatever Padraig had been doing to Bran, he paused it with another small flick of his finger.

That gave me an inkling of hope.

"Bran, link with me," I spoke directly to his mind. "Now. Between us we can take them out."

"And expose you," came his determined response as he straightened, still clutching his stomach. "Remain hidden or die."

That was it? He was sacrificing himself for me? This was my crappy choice?

I looked at Dad who was shaking his head in my direction, his expression shuttered. He couldn't see me but he had no doubts how I was reacting. And why not, this was betrayal, clear and simple. And betrayal pushed all my hot buttons. Dad, of anyone should know.

Van moved in front of me, my scent betraying where I was, his action blocking me even more.

Padraig twisted his head to smile at Dad, a smug, self-satisfied grin I wanted to wipe off his face. The words of a spell jammed in my throat when Padraig looked in my general direction but spoke to Dad, "Have you heard anything about your daughter?"

I froze, my blood stilling. If Van as a shifter could scent me the Weres should be able to, especially if I moved or my heartbeat alerted them. So far, they hadn't seemed to notice me but that could change at any second.

"Why do you ask?" Dad replied.

"Just interested," came Padraig's lie.

"Do you need her?" Van ratcheted up the tension in the room with his four simple words. This is why he was a warrior and not a diplomat. Take the direct approach rather than tap dance around the situation.

"Not really," Padraig murmured, then added in an undertone, "Not anymore."

And that's when my legs buckled. Padraig needed a powerful witch for whatever he had planned. Now he'd found an even more powerful warlock.

Would anyone in the Council question if Bran quietly disappeared? Not likely.

Would they even know about an accidental death, no doubt preceded by torture and pain? Problem solved. Humans would miss Bran more than preternaturals, but not as much as I would.

In the sound of heavy thuds and a slamming door they all disappeared. Bran's spell broke, showing me a quivering pile kneeling on the floor. Van and Dad both stepped forward.

I waved them off.

"He's going to do it, isn't he?" I looked at Dad, not seeing him through the mist obscuring my sight. "This *friend* of yours." I made such a strong emphasis on the word *friend* I was surprised it didn't snap. "He's going to release this demon. Use Bran to do so. And no one can stop him."

"We can," Van said.

I cast a disbelieving gaze at him, shaking my head though even that took effort. "You're not even up to full fighting potential. No way."

"I didn't raise quitters," my dad snarled, whipping titanium through my backbone.

My glance toward him contained pure venom. "No, you didn't." I staggered to my feet, keeping my distance, protecting myself. I'd fought myself, my abilities for so long that now when I needed them, when they could save Bran, I couldn't trust them. But there was a reason for this. One burning deep within me, molten anger laced with fear. "What you did raise was an ineffectual witch who, because you feared my kind of magic, has been stumbling around doing as much bad as good."

He looked like I'd slapped him. That was the problem with truth. It hurt like a banshee's backside when you weren't ready for it.

"Alex," Van whispered beside me, "Dad's not the enemy."

"You sure about that?" I glanced at Van before meeting my dad's gaze head-on. "Then ask him why he let me go to prison."

With that, I walked out of the house.

Bran was right. I needed to get back to the team, and fast. Now that Padraig had Bran, he also possessed all the power he needed to release the Zaradian demon. Nothing holding him back now.

CHAPTER 46

Like a heat-seeking missile I focused, wending my way through the Parisian night traffic, pedestrian and vehicular, whipped by anger and desperation, driven by the need to find Ling Mai. She and the team were my only hope.

When the front desk staff glanced in my direction I expected resistance. What they didn't expect was this intruder could wave a quick and easy cloaking spell. One minute, a wild-eyed desperate woman, the next, nothing.

One spell that always worked for me. Sometimes I wished I could use it all the time. The easy-way out of past mistakes catching up with me.

But Noziaks didn't do easy.

Lucky me.

I knocked on Ling Mai's door with an urgent thud, thud, thud, desperation driving me, fluttering through my system, thrusting my chin up as she opened the door.

"Miss Noziak?" She stepped back, not looking surprised or wary.

Her first mistake. I was in the room between one heartbeat and the next, and I was gunning for bear.

No words would come though. Probably a first for me as they tumbled over and over inside, fighting for release. So many questions. So little trust.

"Why didn't you look for me when you'd heard I died?" I asked at last, not because I was abandoning Bran but because I needed to have a damn good reason to fully trust this woman again.

Ling Mai didn't answer directly. Instead, she waved one hand toward a chair.

"I'd rather stand." So many emotions pulsed through me standing was my only option.

"As you wish." She crossed to a far window, folding her arms across herself. Defense or offense? With her you couldn't always tell.

I waited, but when the seconds ticked by I pushed. Yeah, go figure, me being impatient. "Why?"

"I needed to," she said at last, turning to look at me, letting me weigh the truth of her words. "I needed to trust my source."

"That source wouldn't happen to have an Irish accent?" I asked, striking out blindly.

She offered a partial smile. "Does it matter?"

"It does to me." I stepped closer to her, hands wedged at my side into tight fists. When she remained mute, I egged her on. "I could have died in that cell. I could have already unleashed a nightmare before anyone had a chance to stop it."

"But you didn't."

My voice shook as I chewed a response. "Don't you try that I-did-it-for-your-own- good crap on me."

"And yet did you not survive? On your own merits?"

"What happened to being a part of a team? When you threw one of your team members away without a backwards glance?"

"Is that what you think happened?"

"Damn straight I do." Hello? Where had she been? What else could I think?

"Your challenge, Miss Noziak, is you lead with your heart before having the whole picture."

I know my brow crept high on my forehead. How could it not while playing semantic games with this woman? "And what exactly has been the whole picture?"

She turned to face me head-on, and for a second, I glimpsed what might be the real Ling Mai. Driven. Determined. Holding so many threads in the palm of her hand at any moment it scared the willies out of me. As if the room suddenly couldn't contain both of us, each with our own agendas, each holding thinly to too-volatile emotions. If either of us let loose there wouldn't be much of the other, or the hotel, left standing. I had no doubts.

I took a step back, away from the edge, as she started to speak.

"If you're asking did I use you then yes, I did."

Talk about a hard, fast blow to the solar plexus.

"And I'd do so again given the stakes. You are a soldier. Soldiers at times are expendable."

I inhaled to steady wired nerves but didn't have to ask a thing as she continued, "The one we've been seeking is capable of such evil it's hard to comprehend or to stop him."

As if I hadn't just been in the company of Padraig and still wanting a shower.

Ling Mai turned back to the window. "I was asked by a Council member to uncover what he feared."

"Who?"

"When you need to know I shall share."

I could so easily hate her. But one battle at a time. "So what did you need to find?"

She looked at me like dealing with a young child, so I answered my own question. "Betrayal." The emptiness twisted within me. Of course. Why wasn't I surprised?

She nodded. "At the highest levels."

"So you used me to what?"

"To force him to act."

"And you couldn't tell me? Warn me? Ask me?" I didn't scream the words. Though it was tempting. I spoke slowly and evenly, each one more deadly than the last.

"No."

Like a face slap I staggered back. "Just no? I had no choice?"

"Sometimes we have no choices. No good choices." She remained staring out the window as if answers lay behind the darkness of the Parisian skyline, lit by twinkling lights, a fairytale, unreal world. "Don't mistake me, Miss Noziak, if I had to make the same decisions now, I would."

I swallowed. Hard. But Ling Mai wasn't finished. "Sometimes we act on behalf of the Council, our goals mutually compatible."

Bully for us.

"But not always. This was one of the times we were assisting factions within the Council against themselves."

Talk about circles within squares. My mind was about to explode.

"The one we sought was not to be drawn out easily. He had been laying his plans for years, decade upon decade, slowly, painstakingly woven until even those closest to him were blindsided."

A realization whispered through me. "He was the one who killed Philippe Cheverill?"

An unclear expression flittered over her face, her voice low as she answered, "Yes. An unforeseen consequence."

"So what have I been? The staked goat?" By now, my voice rose with each word.

"Yes. He wanted you and didn't care who he killed to get what he wanted."

"And now?" That was the big question. Followed closely by, "Am I still expendable?"

She had the balls to smile. "You've proven time and again that you are not that easy to eliminate."

"No thanks to you," I mumbled beneath my breath, not really caring if she heard me or not.

"I admit, I have taken certain risks with you." Ling Mai smiled. Not an apology by any means. "But have I not said since we first met that I have always had greater trust in your untapped abilities than you have had in yourself?"

That had me straightening my spine. "Saying 'you can do better ...'" I used my fingers in an air quote so she received my message loud and clear,"... is a world of difference from throwing me into the hands of someone like Padraig."

She inclined her head. Probably as close as I was going to get to an atta-girl, especially when she added, "Actions always speak more clearly than words."

As if a switch flipped, I heard her words and found myself pausing. Damn if she wasn't right.

Still didn't mean I liked her underhanded manipulations. Or being used. "So what now?" I asked. "You flushed out Padraig. I'm assuming that was your goal?"

"Yes. We've identified him as the threat, both to the Council and the humans."

I repeated my earlier question. "And now?"

"Now we eliminate him."

Now she was talking Noziak language. Maybe Ling Mai and I had more in common than I realized.

I still didn't trust her, and might never be able to, but I could work with her to mutually compatible goals.

Bring it on!

CHAPTER 47

It took a little over ten minutes for Ling Mai to contact all the team members and what sounded like a few more allies to assemble in her room. When she ended her last conversation I asked, "Aren't you a little concerned about my attracting Weres? After all I should still be marked."

She shook her head. "Bran informed me that when he was unable to remove the tracking device on you he did the next best thing."

"Which was?" I was getting mighty tired of folks conspiring to take care of me like I was some fragile, conservatory flower. I was more a weed, through and through. Hack me down again and again, but don't expect me to stay down.

"He covered your scent with his own."

I thought of those moments in the bedroom, feeling my face heat. "I don't understand."

"The Weres could no longer track you because they couldn't use your scent."

"Instead they'd find Bran's?"

She nodded.

I slid into the nearest chair, my knees no longer solid. No wonder Padraig was fishing at my father's. Maybe he'd expected if he found Bran he would have found me. Or one of us in hand was better than continue to seek me.

I was still shaking my head at what Bran had done for me when the first knock hit the door. He'd sacrificed himself for me more than once and that was just in the last twenty-four hours.

When would he stop twisting me in knots? Just when I thought I had a handle on how I felt about him everything changed. Hating him for killing Van was easier than caring for him, and I feared caring might be easier than what was roiling through me now. I feared for him. Didn't want to face a world without him in it and didn't know if we stood a chance finding and freeing him.

Focus on saving his sorry ass. Then deal with ... whatever ... later.

Too bad my emotions wouldn't fall in line so easily.

"Alex?"

I glanced up, not aware Sabina had been standing in front of me. Some hotshot agent I was.

"Hey." It didn't have a lot of oomph to it, and then I realized who I was seeing. "Why are you here?"

"Ling Mai seemed to think I could help." She smiled over at the Director. More wheels within spinning wheels. Sabina waved Herc over. "In fact, the director asked if I'd be interested in being trained."

"For what?" That wiped the smile off her face. Way to go Alex. Way to kick the stuffing out of a kitten, but she had no idea how devious Ling Mai could be with her "offers of help".

Sabina squared her shoulders in a move I recognized only too well. She was growing her attitude. "I'm going to be a real witch." She glanced at Herc. "And we're going to be trained as agents."

I stood up, towering over her. "You're a kid. And this sure isn't a game for kids." Hell, it wasn't a game for adults either but no point in sharing that because it didn't take any witchy magic to see she wasn't going to listen to a single thing I said.

Oh yeah, attitude in spades.

"Look, Sabina." I tried a different approach, though back-pedaling wasn't my style. "You should be doing teen things."

"Such as?"

Oh crap. "I dunno, like proms and football games. First dates. First kisses. Girlfriends. That kind of stuff."

"You seem to forget I've been living on the streets. There are no proms, football games, girlfriends where I've been." Bitterness etched her words, cutting into me too as she glanced at a silent Ling Mai. "This is the first chance I've been offered in a pretty crappy life." She turned back to me, determination steeling each word. "I'm grabbing my chance with both hands, with or without your help. Or your permission."

"Okay." I held my hands in front of me. "I deserve that. You're right and I'm wrong." At her hesitant smile I added, "But don't expect to hear me say that again. Got it?"

She jumped forward and wrapped me in a hug. I could see Herc's grin over her shoulder as I wondered how to protect her without her knowing I was protecting her. I hadn't done anything so far, except embroil her in a boatload of trouble.

I pulled back, bracing both her shoulders with my hands. "You've got to promise me one thing."

"What?" Wariness slipped back in her voice and in her eyes. If she could just hold on to those hard won lessons she'd already learned, she just might survive.

"Don't go taking any chances, any risks until you're fully trained. You got me?"

She gave me a two-handed salute. "Yes, Momma."

I gave her a one-finger salute in return. "I soooooo am not your momma."

"Oh, Lord have mercy, who's claiming you?" Jaylene laughed as she walked through the door.

"Love you too." I smiled back, aware how the tension eased from my shoulders.

Then Mandy and New Girl walked in.

Well some moments lasted only a few seconds.

Stone was the last person arriving, or so I thought, until one more tap sounded on the door.

I looked at Kelly who shrugged, then her eyes widened as she faced the door and saw who was entering.

I turned in my seat, not sure who I expected.

It sure as hell wasn't my brother and father.

CHAPTER 48

Oh, no Ling Mai wasn't. She so wasn't going to pull my family deeper into this mess. Not until we had a chance to sort out a few things amongst ourselves. Which wasn't going to be happening anytime soon. Not until I lost the huge lump of anger choking me.

Ling Mai played gracious hostess, looking at the group as she announced, "This is Jeb Noziak, and his son, Van."

There were a few hellos and head nods even as all eyes snapped from my family to me like a stinging rubber band.

"You know about this?" Kelly leaned forward to ask as Mandy gave a small snicker. Obviously her family had no skeletons in their closets.

I stood, answering Kelly's question, as well as the unspoken ones from the group in the same breath. "I don't think this is such a good idea." I looked at Ling Mai. A look that screamed—oh, no, you don't. Fat lot of good it did.

Van waltzed up to me and slung his arm around my shoulder. "Nice to see you again too, little sis. You ran off in such a snit earlier you didn't get to hear a few things you needed to hear."

That took the cake. All the cake as I glared up at him. Not an easy feat as my head was smooched in the crook of his arm. "I don't do snits and you, or more specifically, dear Dad here, are responsible for Bran being taken prisoner by a crazy slime ball who wants to gut him in the process of unleashing terror on the world. That's all I needed to hear."

"Bran knew what he was walking into," my father said smoothly, as he walked away from the door and stood amongst the circle of us sitting on chairs and the room's single gigantean couch.

His words stopped me in my tracks. "What do you mean, he knew?"

Dad didn't answer me directly but instead glanced at Ling Mai. Why was I feeling more and more like I was the last person in on the must-know crap swirling around? Maybe because I was.

I pushed Van's arm off me. Was it only hours ago I was so very happy to see him alive? I'd forgotten what a pain in the backside he could be.

He smiled as if he knew exactly what I was thinking, leaned in and gave me a hug, whispering, "Love ya too, Alex."

Then he skipped backwards and grabbed a seat next to Kelly who scooted over to make room for him.

In my next life, I was going to be nice like Kelly because I sure wasn't feeling the love right now. I turned back to my dad. "I asked what you meant about Bran knowing."

"He knew there was a good chance he'd be apprehended by the Council if he contacted me, and he still chose to do so."

I was beginning to hate that word. Choose. Chose. Choices. Bull-puckey! As if any of us chose anything. Crap happens and then you shovel as fast as you can.

"So you're saying Bran walked eyes open into an ambush?" I knew the warlock was smarter than that.

"To save you, yes."

Oh, fuddelbuckets. He so didn't say that.

But when I heard Kelly's sigh I knew he had. She was a dyed-in-the-fluffy-cotton romantic.

"I didn't ask him to," I said with a high breathless sound to my voice I couldn't control.

"Bran knew that unless Padraig found an alternative to using you he'd keep coming after you," Van added, like this whole mess made perfect sense.

It didn't.

"And he let himself be taken?" New Girl asked. I was with her. Go figure.

"Part of a larger plan," my father said, stepping near Ling Mai who inclined her head, adding, "We need every resource we can get to outwit Padraig."

"What exactly is this Padraig?" Kelly asked, saving me the trouble.

"A druid." Van was the one who answered, looking directly at her with a smile I hadn't seen on his face since high school and his first over-his head crush.

"I thought druids were tree huggers," New Girl piped in, turning everyone's attention to her, except mine as Van leaned in to ask Kelly a question. I saw her blush, dip her head and whisper something back that had Van's brows arch. He said something else that had Kelly pausing then giving him an I-dare-you smile, so unlike her I wanted to jump up and pull them apart. Van was way too experienced for sweet Kels. She didn't realize there was a place inside him that might never heal.

A cough dragged my attention back to the group and my dad looking at me like he'd just asked a question.

Obviously he had by everyone's expectant glances as I said, "Sorry. You said something?"

"I asked if you wanted to add anything about druids," he repeated, his look saying he too had been watching Van interacting with Kelly. Which Dad probably took as a good sign. Sort of like watching someone awake from a dormant state.

"Druids?" I'd only met one once before who'd tried to rape me when I was thirteen. "Nasty, arrogant pricks who think the world still deserves to bow down and kiss their feet. Egos a million miles wide, dominant personalities, sneaky rat-bastards." I looked around at the stunned expressions. "I think that about covers what I know."

"Jeez." Jaylene whistled. "Tell us what you really think girlfriend."

"I'm sure Fraulein Fassbinder will love to add your insights to her grimoire," Ling Mai interceded, a small smile dancing around her mouth before shifting to her all-business-all-the-time mode. "Now that we have an idea of who we're facing let's get back on target here."

"Is this when the rest of us expendable pawns are going to be let in on this almighty plan?" I asked, and yes, you could've cut my snark with an axe.

Dad gave me that stink-eye I recognized from childhood. But I wasn't a kid anymore and my cutting glance at him said as much.

So instead of answering me directly he glanced to Ling Mai. At her nod, he pulled up a chair and sat down. "Looks like we're all ready to hear the plan now."

Why did that not make me feel much better?

CHAPTER 49

There were okay plans, might-work plans, and then oh-hell-no plans. After   thirty minutes of my father's patient laying out of each step of our let's-save-Bran-while-stopping-a-determined demon plan, a demon who'd been looking for a way back to Earth, for three thousand years, we were way deep into the oh-hell-no plan.

I hadn't said a word. Not because I didn't have a few doubts, more than a few, but because I didn't want another public smack down. I was still reeling from the last one. But when Dad described Sabina's assistance in this cockamamie scheme I rose to my feet.

"Oh, no you don't," I said, spearing both Ling Mai and him with my gaze. "Sabina's too young and too inexperienced to be involved today. End of story."

"Not your choice," Sabina jumped to her own feet.

Choice. If I heard that phrase one more time, I was going to take off heads.

"You said you would wait until you were properly and fully trained." I stabbed a finger in her direction, not caring if she sassed me by calling me momma, g-ma or great g-ma. "You are not going to get hurt because of me."

Kelly reached up to touch Sabina's hand, then looked at me, before speaking, "Alex, it's going to take all of our abilities and all of our help to stop this de … this really bad guy. Sabina wants to help. How can you deny her that?"

Et-tu, Kelly?

So much for thinking my best friend had my back. Kelly of all people, I expected to understand. I saw the look Van cast her, a quizzical glance that at least reassured me I wasn't the only one caught broadsided by Kelly's comments.

I looked to the room at large. "She's a kid, guys. Since when do we put kids at risk? Isn't that what we're fighting for? To protect the Sabinas of the world?"

Vaughn glanced away, obviously not comfortable with my words, but it was Mandy who eyed me. "What about you?" she said, for once not jabbing me with her tone but simply asking a question.

"I don't know what you mean. Am I going to fight? Hell, yes. But risk Sabina? Doesn't make sense."

"I'm asking what you would do if you were Sabina's age and knew you might be able to help, even in a small way, to stop this Zaradian? Would you fight or be willing to sit on the sidelines?"

That was not fair. "She's not me." I glanced at where Sabina still stood, a small smile playing about her lips. "She has no training as a witch and no training as an agent, and no idea what she's getting herself into. "

"Neither did you at her age." Mandy kept that calm, even, tone and expression I wanted to wipe from her face. Not because she was being unreasonable, for once, but because she had a point. A frustratingly valid point.

"Fudge a bunny," I mumbled, sinking back to my chair.

"Is that anatomically possible?" Kelly asked, earning a few snorts, including one from Van who had to duck his head until he could bring himself back under control.

"Doesn't mean I'm happy with the situation," I said specifically to my dad, Ling Mai and Sabina.

"Then we're back to business as usual," Mandy inserted.

I gave her an I'll-get-you-and-soon glance which she ignored.

When I held my tongue, which I could, every now and then, my dad looked around. "Then we're clear about what we'll be doing?"

He looked at each person and only when they nodded did he slap his hands on his knees and stand. "Good. Then let's get started."

CHAPTER 50

"You sure this is the place?" I asked Van in the early hours the next morning, dawn slowly creeping over the horizon. We, along with Sabina who I was not going to let out of my sight, were hunkered down in a freshly turned bed of dirt beneath mid-sized bushes, sculpted laurel and holly trees. At least that's what Sabina called them. I only knew they weren't lodge pole pines, which is what grew everywhere in southern Idaho. Where trees grew that was.

We were in one of those cul-de-sac streets that seemed to appear by magic in Paris. One step, you're in the twenty-first century, or thereabouts, turn a corner and you step backwards, several centuries.

What might have been a nice-sized estate house sat back from the cobblestone road at the end of a circular drive. A stable or carriage house was to our right while large stonewalls encircled the entire property. While it was still dark, we crept to our present location within the walled area, our backs to the stable.

I'd cast a cloaking spell so the three of us could enter relatively undetected and added an ad hoc binding spell to alter our scents. If a Were inhaled downwind all he would smell was a mulch-like aroma. Neither spell would help if a Were drew too close, which is why we used every tree and brush we could to creep closer to the house.

Since Van hadn't answered my original question I jostled his arm with my elbow.

He gave me a what-now glance, which I answered with a few jerks of my head toward the house. Guess he was used to a different level of military signals from his background. Tough, I wanted some reassurances and as there were no Weres around Van could darn well tell me what I wanted to know.

"Right place? How are you sure?" I whispered, not being a total idiot.

Van waited a few heartbeats, either to try my patience or listen with his shifter hearing for any threats. I was just getting ready to slug him when he leaned closer. "Bran didn't just cover his scent with yours he swapped scents with you."

What the—? I found my tongue at last. "So Padraig ended up at Dad's, thinking I was there because Bran had my scent?"

Van nodded.

"Then what?"

"When you huffed off Dad went after you to make sure no one followed you and I tracked Bran by your scent."

Bran and my family had been hanging around the convoluted Ling Mai way too much. I scratched my head, trying to figure out who smelled like whom.

Van continued, "I lost Bran when they entered a car, but we have someone working with the Weres."

"Willie?" I whispered, knowing of only one Were who'd do such a thing.

"Yeah, he's helping, but there's someone else."

That threw me. "Who?"

"You know him as Frank."

Of course. One of Bran's oldest friends and a MI-6 British agent. I'd met him initially as a gay manager called Franco who made me break out in hives he was so in-your-face-high-maintenance. Last time I'd seen him he was François Dupris, a suave and debonair Frenchman about Paris. It was hard to know who the real Frank was but what I did know is he was a Didi shifter, a rare creature who could change into more than one shape. Unfortunately, Frank's shifter shape was any breed within the dog family. He once shifted into a killer poodle who could flaunt a rhinestone collar like he was born to it.

"You sure he's working with Padraig?" I couldn't see Frank rubbing shoulders with Were thugs. Not without a lifetime supply of Lysol and hand sanitizer.

"He's been undercover for several months. Notified us yesterday where Bran was taken."

Would wonders never cease? Not about the notifying part but about Frank being where you needed him when you needed him.

Good news? I felt much more reassured that we were in the right place. Bad news? We were at the right place with psychotic Padraig, and who knew how many Weres.

Van nudged my shoulder, his gaze steady on mine as I turned to look at him. "What?"

"You know, you could give Dad a little bit of a break. He's not the bad guy here."

"You tell me that after spending a few months in prison because Dad allowed it to happen."

"No, he let human justice take its course. You killed a man. You were paying the price."

Talk about a hard and fast strike.

"He wasn't a man. He was a rogue Were who was trying to kill our brother." I did the finger gesture, linking him to me as if he needed to know whose brother I was talking about. "And technically I didn't kill him, a death demon ripped him apart."

"A death demon you summoned."

"Whose side are you on?" I couldn't believe we were having this conversation right now. "Which of your siblings came looking for your sorry ass? Oh, yeah, that would be me. Who put her life on the line for you less than a week ago? Hello, me again. Who—"

And there I stopped, because we both knew what I was going to say next. Who ended up getting shifter blood and abilities because of him?

"I didn't mean—" he started, but I waved him off.

The timing sucked. He didn't know what he had been doing. Now he'd have to live with the guilt forever and I'd have to live with one more freaky ability that I had no idea how it worked.

I hadn't even started dealing with the ramifications of the shifter blood mingling with mine. Could I change? How would it impact my ability to use magic? To be a shaman? Eventually, to have children as a side effect of any being created to change body shape wreaked havoc on a woman's ability to incubate a child for nine months. Were women could not have children at all. A few shifter women had, but either they, or the baby, had not survived the stress of childbirth.

Too many issues to deal with now. Not with Bran's life on the line and a demon knocking on the door. Then there was this whole trusting Dad's plan issue. Once screwed, twice wary. I might be foolhardy but I wasn't stupid.

"Psst, guys, look." Sabina whispered on the other side of Van. Thank heavens for small witches who knew when to shift the subject.

I followed her jabbing finger to watch a fancy town car turn into the driveway. Since most French cars leaned toward the small and compact, this one looked stretch-limo long, though it was only an average bigger American car.

"The show is beginning," Van murmured, hunkering deeper into the dirt.

I swallowed against the fear rumbling inside of me as the car crept along the drive, tires crunching over the gravel before it slowed, then came to a halt in front of the main entrance. That's when my dad stepped from it, tugging his shirt cuffs down as he gave a casual, assessing glance around. Knowing where the team members were secreted, ready for his part in the mission.

Damn if Van wasn't right, like he usually was. I hadn't given my dad much leeway, acting like the angry, frightened child Dad had to deal with at five when my mother abandoned us and taking out my pain on my remaining parent—him.

Less than a year ago I had a choice. I'd made it and thought I'd accepted the consequences. That's the way Dad raised us. I never expected entitlement because of my father's position, so why had I got my shorts in such a twist now?

What had I expected my dad to do differently? Abandon responsibility and commitment and the right-if-hard road to bail me out? He sat near me every day during the trial and sentencing. He never gave up on me. Never let me hide from my choices. Why had I expected him to do so then?

And what about now?

He was going in alone to face Padraig, to keep the druid occupied or deflected so we could implement the last steps of the plan. And I hadn't told him I loved him.

CHAPTER 51

The Weres and the druid had taken Bran to a small home located near *Montmarte,* but tucked away, all but invisible unless you knew where to find it. It required a lot of financial clout and connections to own such a piece of property in this part of Paris, and he had no doubt the druid held both. Once they arrived, the Weres stepped back as three simin fae flanked Bran on each side, silent and deadly. All fae were known to nurse grudges for centuries, the simin fae even longer. The fact he'd humiliated them earlier by escaping meant they were being extra wary now, going as far as throwing a silver cast chain around his plastic wrist bindings. Since the silver burned as it touched his skin, Bran knew it held a binding spell. No disappearing this time.

They remained eerily silent until the leader inclined his head toward the house. "This way."

Not a lot of options. So Bran followed where they led.

Not through the front door of the home, but around to a back door. A small peek through sculpted trees revealed the horizon had dropped away, and only the tops of bone-white vaults showed along with the pale blue ironwork of the *Rue Caulaincour. La Cimetière de Montmartre,* the Montmartre Cemetery for the famous, infamous and forgotten. Alex would be intrigued.

But now wasn't the time for history lessons, or thinking of Alex, or any thoughts not focused on his survival.

Knowing he was being brought before the Council, and the fact he might not have long to live was a very real possibility.

His silent sentinels didn't pause until they reached a cell deep in the bowels of the building where they left him for long enough he wondered if they'd forgotten him and meant him to rot.

By the time the fae returned Bran figured it was early morning. He was tired, hungry and damn uncomfortable, not able to move his hands unless he wanted his wrists seared with the silver hex. Following behind the fae at least meant a change of scenery which was better until they entered a blood red room, livid with shades of scarlet red and black. Gothic horror run amuck.

Three of the fae veered off and disappeared through one of the far doors while a closer door, just on the other side of a long conference-style table cracked open.

That's where the danger came from. He sensed it before any figures materialized. The pulse of old and powerful magic. Dark magic. The kind Alex feared more than she would ever admit.

So Padraig was not working alone. The menace grew.

Four individuals entered. The first ancient, with the refined skin and prominent bones betraying his age and species. He walked as one much younger, held his carriage straight, his aquiline nose tipped up as if something in the room assaulted his senses.

A vampire. No other being carried arrogance as a second skin so well. In some ways Bran thought of them as the Jesuits of the preternatural world. Born and reared to lead, behind the scenes of course, especially since the human population butted them to the side as myth and folklore.

Behind the vamp came a woman who looked as if she should be standing before a peat-bog fire, stirring a kettle, one filled with human blood and eye of newt. As Celtic as Bran's own da, and ten times as dangerous, though most would only notice her fair skin, curls of red, and eyes of shamrock green. Eyes that if one looked closely screamed of evil and banked anger.

The third individual had to be a demon, though he looked like a London City toff, complete with Saville Row suit and Italian shoes. Someone should have warned him the subtle striping of his cloth did not hide the triple-jointed shifting of his limbs beneath it as he moved. A mistake. Or maybe a threat to the other preternaturals who knew what to look for.

The last person to enter from the door, closing it behind him, looked the most benign, and that alone had Bran stiffening. Hadn't he been raised by a mother so beautiful she'd made grown men weep, a beauty that hid a soul blacker than Hades, and twice as self-serving.

This man looked like a common dockhand, wide of shoulders, stocky of body, with fair hair and an easy smile. Now, he reeked of magic. Old magic, the kind that made Bran's mage forbearers seem like upstarts. Padraig, the Council's druid representative. The one who took Philippe Cheverill's place at the Council table.

The older man had been dead less than a week. The Council acted fast to replace him. Unless the death had been planned to create an opening. A theory that, as long as it remained a vague guess, did no harm, but discovering that the guess was based on a very real possibility, sent an icy chill sliding down Bran's skin.

Cheverill had truly been murdered. What had been a wildfire rumor seemed to be more fact than fiction. Alex's name had been bandied about as his killer because she'd been at the soiree where he'd died. Had even been at his side, holding his hand, though he was a stranger to her.

Then Bran had been targeted as spearheading the killing as an extension of dabbling in designer drugs, which is why he'd been called to the Council in the first place.

Today? It seemed unlikely he'd be brought to trial for drug dealing or murder with only four members present. So what did they want of him? To chastise him for missing his earlier arraignment? One he'd hoped could prove his innocence by producing Vaverek, the person responsible for entrapping Bran's cousin in a plan to distribute a dangerous drug to preternaturals.

Vampire, demon, witch and druid. Were they waiting for the remaining three Council members to join them? Jeb Noziak, as shaman, another as shifter and a fae.

But as the four who arrived moved in a silent processional, each donning livid blue-violet robes, before they sat at the far side of the table, it became clear they were acting alone. And in unison.

So the druid didn't proceed alone, but with powerful allies. Danger increased exponentially.

Bran was directed to stand on the near side of the table. Which he did, keeping his posture rigid and unbowed.

Something the druid seemed to notice as that one cocked his head, a smile playing about his lips.

What did they really want with him? To use him to draw in Alex? Most likely. He'd always heard blood-born witches were more self-serving than self-sacrificing. Alex had proved the exception in a lot of ways. He'd done what he could to protect her. Her father and brother would have to do the rest.

"You were called before us once, but failed to appear," the vampire intoned, his voice roiling with ennui, his gaze focused on his own folded hands. "What do you say to the charge?"

"I came but was stopped by Weres seeking to delay me."

"Says who?" the Celtic witch asked, all sweetness and false-kindness.

Bran looked toward the long arched windows at the side of the room, their silk valances drawn back. "Since the attack occurred in Versailles, within sight of this Council's meeting, who alone knew I was summoned, I am at a loss to identify who arranged the attack."

Risky tactic. Call the Council to task for instigating the events that kept him from appearing while hoping for their understanding and leniency in determining his innocence. Given he doubted any of these four ever experienced either understanding or leniency, his words were not a gauntlet as much as a weak gambit. Buying time.

For what? One of the Noziaks to find him? Not likely. The elder was neither friend nor foe, the son an unknown, and Alex? He only hoped Alex had enough sense to run far and fast. Francois was gone, even if his friend had anything to offer before these beings.

That left words as his weapon. His only weapon.

"You call us killers?" the druid said, his voice ripe with the lyricism of Ireland.

"There is a killer, or killers, somewhere. But it is not I," Bran countered.

"You call yourself victim then?" the druid offered, leaning back in his chair, his fingers steepling. This was all a game to him, one his gaze told Bran he enjoyed playing, as long as he won.

"Nay." Bran rocked forward on the balls of his feet. If they sought to cower him they were wrong. He'd been reared between his da and mother, treated as weapon more than son, a process that honed him more than creating his international business empire. "I would say prosecuted more than victimized."

"Why?" the demon rolled the single word.

"Wrong person in the wrong place."

The witch smiled, an expression lethal sharp. "But you are not just a person, are you? You are a mage master, cousin to a rare Grimple who nearly betrayed all our kind."

"Including myself." Bran spoke the truth, though the words cut deep.

"Tsk, tsk, warlock." The druid shook his head. "For one who pretends his innocence, you have found yourself at the center of too many coincidences."

"You mean my cousin?" Keep the focus away from Alex. That's who this druid really wanted and Bran wasn't going to let him have her. Not while he lived.

"I mean being in the same room as Philippe Cheverill the night he was killed."

Bran held his tongue. It was not a secret, as the building had been full of preternaturals, and rumors had already linked his name with that of the dead man. They seemed very keen to find him at fault, with no proof except proximity. Why?

"Agreed," the vampire nodded, as if something new and profound had been brought to his attention. "His cousin's actions. His nearness to a tragic death. His refusal to appear when called. His escaping the simin fae when they found him again. I think enough has been said."

So they were both jury and judges. He'd always known it could come to this, but like Alex, he was not about to go down without a fight.

The magic rose within him, an automatic response to a death threat, feeling the burn increasing along his hands. He didn't move, except for raising his head and spearing them all with his gaze, letting it land and linger on the druid last.

"You threaten me?" The man rose to his feet, his own mystic powers sweeping around him like an aura, one tainted blood red and black.

Bran braced himself for the wave of magic thrown at him. A tsunami of darkness that hit hard and fast.

But he wasn't without his own resources, including the ability to hold death at bay, for that's what the druid sought. Then seemed to change his mind with a twist to his lips that leeched all the hale-and-hearty appearance from him.

The magic ebbed. Before Bran could breathe, much less counter magic against magic, another assault came. This time not from without but from within.

A sharp glance from the druid to the witch warned Bran who sought his destruction by combining their powers. One would have been formidable but together, there was only one outcome.

A crack of thunder, all the louder for being contained within the small room, a flash of blue heated fire, the echo of a scream. His own. Not with enough time to react. Barely enough time to cast a final mind call. *Alex!*

Warning her. He'd been wrong. Arrogant and wrong, and his actions could cost them both.

Pain ripped through him with the surgical precision of a heated knife. Every nerve ending cried out and then in a blink it stopped.

He froze. Well and truly trapped in an encased shell with no form, though so formidable he couldn't even exhale. Even the pace of his heart stopped. Solidified. Restrained but not dead, for his mind still functioned, his eyes could still see.

Dead but undead.

CHAPTER 52

I gasped, hearing and feeling the slam of Bran's emotions ricochet through me.

Van grabbed my arm. "What's wrong?" he demanded, his voice urgent for all its lethal silence.

All I could manage was a shaking of my head. I felt like a limb had been ripped from me. I could see Sabina over Van's shoulder, her eyes wide and worried. At last I whispered through a dry mouth. "It's Bran. Something's happened to him."

"What?"

I glanced at Van, bracing myself from shaking. "I don't know. I'm not getting a video replay through his eyes."

Sabina actually held Van back. No doubt he wanted to rattle some answers out of me. Fat lot of good it'd do.

"Tell us what happened?" Sabina asked, her voice sounding like she was coaxing a feral cat into submission.

"I don't know," I mumbled, still grappling with the weight of Bran's emotions. "I heard my name."

"And then?" she asked, her voice low and measured, absorbing the parental role.

"And then nothing. As if he … as if he disappeared."

"What—" Van started.

"Nothing else?" Sabina cut off Van. Maybe she wasn't as much of a lightweight as I'd thought.

I looked at Sabina. It was the compassion in her glance that drew me. "He was terrified. But I have no idea what happened."

"Can you tell if he's still alive?" Van demanded.

I swallowed. "I don't know."

"What do you mean? Can't you contact him?"

"No." I all but spat the word. "It's not like I have him on speed dial." *That's right, revert to sarcasm as a weapon.* But it was better than bleeding out in front of them with no clue except knowing Bran needed me.

Van released a heavy sigh but at least he didn't roll his eyes. "Then what is it like?"

What he meant was how can you possibly use this ability if you don't have a clue what it is. Welcome to my world!

"I sometimes hear Bran's voice in my thoughts, that's all."

"When?" Sabina coaxed. "When do you hear him?"

I thought about that for a second, dismissing my first response of whenever I didn't want to hear him. "I don't know." Trust me, I was as frustrated as them. If Bran ... if something happened to Bran our plan on how to contain Padraig was up in smoke. But that wasn't the worst. I couldn't imagine a world without him. Impossible. Dictatorial. Arrogant. All of that but more. Larger than life. Engaged. Making a difference.

Please, Mother Goddess, don't let him be gone.

Van was eyeing me as if a complicated puzzle. Trust me, I wasn't. Straightforward as they came. Except for being witch-born, a shaman and a shifter, but everyone had their quirks.

"Can't you get in touch with him?" Van asked with that I'm-being-patient-here tone.

"No." I almost snorted the word. What part of not-on-speed-dial didn't he understand?

"Have you tried?" Sabina interceded.

"Tried to reach Bran's mind?" Did she realize what she was asking? She couldn't.

She nodded. Very slow and evenly.

"No. He pops into my mind. Usually when it's most inconvenient." Like now. I glanced around, sure a Were or some other nasty wouldn't be ripping around the nearest corner, alerted by the calamity still roiling through me.

"You never contact him? The other way?" she probed.

The words stumbled on my tongue as I slowly shook my head, every atom in my being resisting the implication of her words. "I've never tried intentionally."

"Because?"

I speared both her and then Van with a what-can-you-be-thinking glance. "Are you kidding?" At their blank expressions, I continued, my voice low and urgent. "Do you have any idea what it means to let someone else into your mind? Throw open the doors to your memories, your most personal thoughts and feelings and let a stranger know everything?"

Okay my voice may have risen a little more than I'd intended, which is why I didn't slug Van when he put a finger to his lips. I looked away and not because my eyes started to water. Must be a speck of dirt in them.

Sabina's hushed voiced reach me, though even turned from her. "Wow. I never thought of that. Must take a whole lot of trust." She paused then added, "And even with trust I don't think I could do it."

If it didn't mean I had to crawl over Van to give her a hug I would have and Noziaks are not touchy feely kind of folks.

Van cleared his throat before cupping his finger under my chin and pulling my face towards him. "Look, I know this is hard."

Understatement.

"But if you don't try, if you can't reach Bran and find out what the hell is happening, we'll be going into that house blind."

I glanced at the front door where my dad had disappeared only seconds ago, swallowing a fist-sized lump in my throat.

Was this another of these no-win choices? Mind rape or lose my father?

Van gave no quarter as he pushed. "This is more than Bran's life at stake. It's Dad's. And Kelly's, and your team. We need to know what's happening."

I pulled my head away from his touch, making my choice, though I wasn't happy with it.

"I hate it when you're right," I snarled, taking a deep breath, wondering if I opened this door, this pathway inside me, if I would ever be able to close it again.

CHAPTER 53

I had a plan to find out what was happening to Bran.

Taking a deep, cleansing breath, I wrestled with the nerves and the emotions coursing through me. Worry. Frustration. Fear. Mostly fear.

What was happening to him? Where was he? Could I help? There was a way to find one of these answers and doing something was better than doing nothing.

Being on the squirrel train wasn't helping though so I hunkered low beneath the tree, burrowing my hands into the loamy soil, smelling the scent of bark, of new growth from the leaves, listening to cars humming past somewhere not far away. A robin fluttered by as the sounds of other birds seeped into my awareness.

I'd pulled out my anathema dagger that was against my leg in a sheath. Yes, I know most witches call it an athame, but my mom had always called it an anathema dagger and if it worked for her, it worked for me. Mostly it was used in rituals, but it could be a weapon if needed. I just couldn't combine using an external harming device with any spell casting. They tended to cancel one another out, or backfire, big time, on the witch. If I was going to the other side while chanting a spell I didn't want the dagger to complicate an already complicated situation. So it'd wait here for my return.

If I returned.

Crap, back to focusing and centering myself.

Slower. Quieter. Be in the moment.

Just like spell casting. Bringing oneself to a center point. A quiet grounding before opening up to the universe, to the power around all of us.

Sabina rustled a little then quieted.

Lying flat on my stomach was not the easiest position to summon magic but needs must.

I pitched my voice so low it was more whisper than words. First to acknowledge the spirits watching over us all.

"Light come forth. Clear the darkness. Guide and protect. Light to dark."

I repeated, waiting until the tension between my shoulders eased. It'd be hard enough to open oneself blindly, but it'd be suicidal to make the druid aware of my presence. Nothing like a hear-I-am shout out.

Only when I was sure did I take the next step. Seeking one who I could not find. Not a scrying spell as much as calling back someone.

"Yod He Vau He, king of the east.
Adoni, king of the south.
Eheieh, king of the west.
Agla, king of the north, from whence all warriors abide.
Call back those who belong to you."

A soft breeze kicked up around us, stirring small dust devils with bark, making me squeeze my eyes shut. This next part was the trickiest.

"I seek for one tied to me. Known to me. Bound to me.
By thrice and by syce, I thee call. I thee bind.
By new moon, by old moon. Power I thee call.
My will be thy will. My thoughts be thy thoughts.
Earth and air. Shield harm from me and mine.
Power bound. Light revealed.
I command thee. Be revealed.
There is a reason for being. Journey here to me now.
I seek thee. I call to thee. I command thee.

So mote it be!"

I used my voice to push more power into the last words. The breeze had become a sudden wind, swirling around us. Strands of my hair came loose from my braid and whipped my face. A chill rent the air.

I braced my self. Waiting. Reaching out. Expecting something. Anything.

"Bran?" I whispered, before I realized it.

But it was no good.

Like hitting a hole in space. There was nothing. Not a peep. Just a numb blankness.

My shoulders sagged. My mouth went dry. The wind stilled and then died.

"What is it?" Sabina asked, her voice cracking.

"He's not answering."

As if even the birds waited all sound ceased.

Sabina cleared her throat. "Well that just sucks."

I couldn't agree more.

CHAPTER 54

A roar welled up within Bran, not that it'd do any good, or that he could release it. He was well and truly encased in the prison of his own rigid body. Whatever the druid had done trapped him.

The vampire cast an appraising look toward the smug druid. "Nicely done, Padraig. My compliments."

The one called Padraig bowed his head, but kept his gaze locked with Bran's as if sharing his gloating *mano-a-mano*. There was something in that look that was very personal. Calculated revenge versus an impersonal punishment applied.

"What shall we do with him now?" the Celtic witch asked, licking her lips. "Will he survive long in this state?"

"As long as necessary," the druid answered.

One question down. More pushing at Bran, not that he could do anything about them.

"You are ready for him?" the demon spoke up, looking at his nails as if the answer didn't matter to him in the least.

"Yes."

That's when Bran knew he was well and truly screwed, as an American would have said. Not any American, but Alex, who had a fine talent for putting her finger on the nexus of a problem. Of course, she caused most of them. The woman was born trouble.

He lived but could do nothing. And this totally psychopathic druid meant to use him in some way. But how?

Since panic would do him no good, except to drive him insane, he willed himself to give nothing away, even from his gaze, as the druid seemed to be waiting for the horror, the terror to rip through Bran. There was so little he could control in this situation, except his response. For that, Bran would make the druid wait. Forever.

When Padraig didn't expand on his one word answer, the Celtic witch leaned forward, her glass green eyes bright. "Oh, do something now, Padraig. Don't keep us in suspense."

Padraig glanced in her direction as he smoothed the front of his pressed shirt and returned to his chair. "I'm afraid you shall have to wait, Breena, all in good time."

"You can tell us nothing of the details?" She pouted. A look that might have been attractive on her a few centuries ago but now only served to show her true nature; sharp and calculating.

"Let's say we're one step closer to making our final plans come to fruition. Zaradian is waiting. Behind him, the others."

"I could help. You know that."

He cast her a closed look. "We've discussed this before, Breena. You do not have enough power. It must be the other."

She glanced at Bran, but the look told him she didn't see a man anymore, only a means. "You'll be able to use him to lure the Seekers?"

Padraig nodded as Bran's mind raced. Alex had used the name Seekers before. But who, or what, were they? And what did he have to do with them?

"Patience, Breena, all is in hand."

"You have the witch then? The one in the portents?"

Padraig gave a small shrug.

Bran didn't need a seer to know which witch he meant. There was only one who came to mind. Alex.

His heart, deep within his petrified body, shuddered.

The druid spoke. "This one shall work."

"But I-I thought—" the witch sputtered.

"All is under control, Breena. With him." The druid cast him a disdainful glance. "She will come. Then we shall have two powerful magic wielders."

"And if she doesn't come?" The witch's tone indicated how unlikely she thought another would risk her life for Bran.

"We shall start the process with the mage. He might prove to be just enough to open the portal."

He called out to someone behind Bran's sight. "Bring him to the laboratory."

"Yes, sir."

The sounds of hurried footsteps reached Bran as someone grabbed his legs and levered him to a horizontal position like a ladder, awkward but manageable and ready to be moved. He could smell the sharp scent of Weres. Why had the Weres aligned with the druid and his friends on the Council? Something to figure out and the sooner the better.

"Mr. Byrnes, Mr. Noziak is at the door to have a word with you."

"What does he want?" Breena asked, her voice a little less stable than seconds ago.

"No worries, my dear. I'll take care of him." A pause then the sound of clapping hands. "Hurry now. Remove him. Breena, I'll meet you below."

Bran could say nothing. Do nothing. Not even call out to Jeb Noziak.

But if Noziak senior was about it could mean his daughter was near also.

Why couldn't she use common sense for once and stay clear of trouble instead of running headlong into it?

But that wouldn't be Alex.

CHAPTER 55

"What do you mean you hear nothing from Bran?" Van hissed in my ear as if all this mess was my fault.

"N.O.T.H.I.N.G," I repeated, gritting my teeth as I re-sheathed my dagger. "I can't reach him." Then, before he could ask why I clarified, each word bitten out, "Maybe I don't have the ability. Or he could be blocking." *Or he could be dead.*

Wasn't going there.

"Fine." Van said it like most women used the word, meaning it wasn't fine by a long shot and there'd be hell to pay, later, but right now we were moving on. He was staring at the house as if he could see through walls as he mumbled, "Dad's already gone inside. We'll give him another ten minutes to exit, then snatch him and notify the others there might be a change of plans."

"Meaning?" My turn to glare, at him. "You going to leave Bran in that place?"

"If he's dead, yes."

Gloves were off. Sabina sucked in a deep breath as I held my temper long enough to ask in a slow-measured-slice-and-dice tone. "And if he's not dead? You're guaranteeing that outcome by sitting on our hands out here."

The look my brother gave me could flay skin. Tough.

"Bran came through for you." Two could play contact sports. "Now you're tossing him aside?"

I recognized the tightening of Van's face, the thinning of his lips. I'd scored and neither of us liked that.

"Risking more people on the chance he's still alive can lead to useless deaths." He turned to look me eye-to-eye. "You want those lives on your conscience?"

Of course I didn't. I wasn't an idiot. But neither was I going to assume the worst and by doing so make it a reality. Staring at the house but seeing nothing but Bran trapped and alone, I swallowed the fear leaching through my skin before I asked, "If I can prove he's not dead, will you help then?"

"How——" then he remembered what I was. Shaman born. "You're willing to go to the other side for him?"

"In a heartbeat." I meant it too and I wasn't sure who was more surprised, Van or myself.

My brother nodded before looking away. "You have ten minutes. No more."

"Understood."

"What's she going to do?" Sabina asked, sounding much younger than her almost-fifteen years.

"I'm checking out another realm. See if Bran is there. If not, it's easier to believe he's alive in this realm."

"R-realm?" she stuttered over the single word. "As in you're going to die?"

"Not exactly." I needed every second to focus and travel between realms, not to nursemaid a scared little girl. "Van will explain what's happening."

"She's risking her life on the off chance the warlock still lives," Van muttered.

I was hoping for a little more compassion. Not for me, Van was as much Noziak as I was, but some understanding for Sabina, some reassurances.

"On second thought, don't listen to a word he says." I gave Van a what-the-hell-are-you-thinking look. Which he ignored.

Fine. I could do this myself. Well, except for the need of a heartbeat as a guide to find my way back here.

I butted Van's shoulder with my own. "You going to get that stick out of your butt and help?" He knew what I needed so I didn't have to spell out the details.

He shrugged, then went still, until he could feel the tempo of his own heart beating in his chest. Once in touch he started the chant we'd all learned from standing at my father's knees. Van grabbed two small stones and started tapping them together, his voice tight and low. "A way ah way yah. A way ah way yah. A way ah way yah." It didn't matter what he said as long as he kept the beat steady. Not loud. But the sound of his voice, his beats, would keep me anchored in this world.

I closed my eyes, easing all tenseness coursing through me. It wasn't easy but needed to be done.

I was running out of time.

CHAPTER 56

I hadn't told Van the whole truth. To travel to the spirit realm, I would leave my physical body an empty shell, vulnerable to attack. But with Van here I trusted him to guard me long enough to do what I needed to do.

No, what was going to be tricky was I was crossing over while at the same time as I uttered a soul mate seeking a warlock spell. Think steering a motorcycle on an icy patch of freeway while zooming at seventy miles an hour, blindfolded. To travel between realms took a huge amount of energy. To spell cast also took energy. Combining the two meant the possibility that one or the other wouldn't work. If it was the spell I could still search for Bran, but finding one recently crossed spirit in that other realm made hunting for a needle in a field of haystacks seem easy-peasey.

The big challenge was losing a grip on Van's voice by being distracted. No voice, no navigation back, it was as simple as that.

But I was desperate.

Closing my eyes tight, I inhaled slowly, still in this realm, aware of the scents, the sounds stilling around me. All except Van's guttural singsong voice, creating a slow, melodic cadence, as familiar as a mother's heartbeat. Well, not my mother because she'd bagged me, but my image of what a mother should be.

I framed an image of Bran behind my closed lids. The slash of his rugged cheekbones, the cant of his lips, the flash of those Celtic blue eyes, the protection he spread over those around him. Over me.

Most times. When he wasn't PO'd at me. Or working toward his own agenda, which often was in conflict with mine.

But those other times. When he'd smile, that sexy, warm-the-toes smile that started with his lips and reached his eyes. Or the feel of his touch, sometimes butterfly wing gentle, other times intensely urgent. And his kisses. Oh, Mamma, that man knew how to kiss.

My body warmed, a rush of knowingness. Our relationship was complicated and screwed up, but there was something there. Something that deserved a chance.

I'd told Van the truth. I'd travel between life and death to give Bran that chance. That chance to feel the sun one more time, to laugh again, to find out if what we started together was a fluke or fate.

Only then did I start the whisper chant.

"Light to darkness. Spirit to Earth.
Witch to warlock.
I seek thee. I summon thee.
Bring me to your side."

A flash zigzagged up my leg toward my heart. Not pain, more like a whiplash of heat.

First step done. Now to merge with the other realm.

I uttered a silent prayer to the spirit guardian of my shamanic ancestors that the next breath I took wouldn't be my last, and murmured the first ritual words.

"Come, death, advise me."

I remembered doing this on my last mission in Africa as heat slapped against my skin. Here the Parisian spring disappeared, the scents of tilled earth, the chit-chit of sparrows high in the overhead branches, all becoming a background blur. I closed my eyes tighter and continued.

"Earth be found.
Power be bound.

Stall Nature's course.
Earth, dust, bone.
Bind to me.
Spirits Realm welcome me.
Spirits Realm call me forth."

When I opened my eyes I was there. The Spirits' waiting grounds. The realm between worlds, where the souls of the dead mingled. If only for a brief time.

I braced myself for what was waiting for me. Once darkness, filled with thousands of churning souls, another time an intense heat with a sun so brilliant I could see nothing. This time?

A grayness so thick nothing penetrated. Like stepping into murky fog with no sense of time or space.

How was I going to find Bran if I couldn't see anything? Couldn't feel anything?

I stood still, allowing the wraiths of those in this place to whisper around me. Slashes of chill and whisper-thin sound, like winter storms whistling through an old house. When I was sure my voice would hold steady I continued the chant to find a warlock.

"Bound together, dark and day.
Time forward, meet time reversed.
I seek thee. I summon thee.
Bring me. Bring me to your side.

Voice to heart. Heart to soul.
Show me what I seek.
If thy be here, reveal yourself."

Before I opened my eyes I added a silent, *please*.

Then I looked around. Like a dawn creeping over the skyline, pale pink lightened the gray.

"Bran?" I asked, aware my voice shook, but then so did my hands, and my knees. I took a step forward, cleared my throat and tried again, "Bran? Are you here?"

Nothing.

CHAPTER 57

Van continued to chant, refusing to glance at Alex, not when she looked dead beside him.

Sabina, the kid witch next to him mumbled, "Do you think she's okay?"

Everything in him wanted to give an angry shake of his head. Of all the fool, ill-thought-out, hare-brained ideas, why had he agreed to this?

They had a plan. One that might have worked but it'd gone FUBAR so fast his head spun.

So now his sister was haring off to the spirit realm, which made the hair on the back of his neck stand straight up. His dad had already been inside longer than originally planned, though Van still had four minutes before sounding an alarm, and beside him was a scared, little witch, shaking in her boots as they lay stretched out beneath some sticky leaved trees.

Yup, FUBAR!

He'd run enough missions to know that flexibility was key. That and to keep his focus on the prize. In this case the warlock, Bran. This wasn't just a snatch-and-grab mission though. This was to thwart some bad shit coming down. Shit involving his father, his sister, and now, Bran.

Van knew he owed the mage and it was payback time. So for another four-minutes he'd bite his tongue, keep his chant steady, and refuse to give into the what-ifs.

He glanced at the girl witch and gave a steady nod. He knew if he stopped chanting Alex could be lost on the other side. He wouldn't do that to his worst enemy.

"So you're saying she's okay?" Sabina's voice sounded thin and reedy.

Van offered another nod.

The kid blew a puff of air that made her dark bangs dance as she turned back toward the house. "Good." Then her nerves seemed to get the better of her as she continued to whisper. "I mean you both know what you're doing and I don't, and worry never fixed a thing. My dad used to say that. A lot. Not that it ever helped. But if there was something I could be doing you'd tell me." She glanced at him again.

He nodded.

"Okay. Then I won't panic. Not yet."

He wasn't sure if he should be thankful for small favors or not. Until he noticed Sabina go still, her focus now one hundred percent on the mansion in front of them.

The mansion where two men and what looked like a shaggy huge dog had just exited. The dog looked like a cross between an Otter hound and a Great Dane. Butt ugly but huge and powerful, and if Van's guess was right, a shifter or Were. Most likely shifter because Weres tended to be more predatory animals.

This one was not a happy beast though, barking, and agitated. But why?

His father looked calm enough, his posture a little stiff and formal, but the other man, the druid Van had met this morning, looked like a country squire, his hand gestures expansive, a smile wreathed across his face.

Van brought his Duovid binoculars to his eyes while continuing to chant. Then he increased the magnification until both faces came in sharp and unrestricted.

With greater clarity the subtleties came into range. His father's tight-lipped expression told Van loud and clear not all was well. And the other man's movements through the viewfinder appeared less casual and more a way to defuse nerves. Even the dog's antics looked less benign and more assertive.

If Van dared stop chanting he'd have uttered an oath. As it was he glanced at his watch.

Alex had less than three minutes.

A sharp bark from the dog had him scanning the front door again where the druid seemed to be asking Van's father to return inside the house.

No, demanding. His dad threw off the hand placed on his arm and then froze, as if struck by magic.

A smug expression creased the druids face as his lips moved.

A spell.

Triple FUBAR.

Before Van could move, his dad was walking stiff- legged back into the house, the dog tearing around him, the druid calling orders to whoever was just inside.

Alex had just run out of time.

CHAPTER 58

"Your warlock is not here," a male voice slapped against me. I twisted toward it so fast I almost toppled. But there wasn't a soul around. Just that glowing pinkness, fast becoming my least favorite color.

"Who are you? Where are you?"

"Here." A form shimmered in front of me, more a faint shadow than a body against the glaring light. As if someone was having fun increasing a dimmer switch to bright-holy-hell-Pepto Bismal level. "Does seeing me help you?"

"Not really." Was he kidding? There was something familiar about his voice though, even if all he looked like was a puff of charcoal smoke. I took a stab in the dark. "I know you."

"We've met before."

Like that meant something. Then I remembered. A few weeks back, and my first visit to the shamanistic spirit plane, someone helped me there. Well, technically, I had to twist his insubstantial arm by promising a future favor to get him to find a friend, if that's what I could call Franco. Pain in the patootie was more like it.

"You need my assistance again," Ghost Guy said. He sounded so sure I had to check myself. "And here you're supposed to be so powerful."

"Don't think so." On both counts. I sucked as a witch, with magic burning me more than helping anyone. Then there was the whole ask- for- help thing. Owing a strange spirit one favor was bad enough. No way was I going to sell my soul to him a second time.

He spoke with a snarky get-with-the-program tone, "You can't run from your troubles, Alex Noziak."

Did I look like I was running? No. I was trying my damndest to get some straight answers but who did I get stuck with? Attitude on steroids.

It'd be nice to know where I was and how I could find Bran quickly. As long as a question wasn't seen as a favor, I should be okay.

I started with the easy question first. Sort of warming him up. "Where am I?" I waved my hand and then added, "I mean, I know I'm in the Spirit realm but where exactly?"

"Exactly where you need to be."

I hated zen crap. I didn't have time to play twenty obscure puzzle games.

"Since you can't help me," Or won't. "I'll be moving along."

Not that I had a clue where to look for Bran. The spell to call a warlock seemed like a complete bust.

"You've been sent here to find something," Ghost Guy said, giving me chicken skin.

"You mean other than Bran?" I blurted out before I realized what I'd said. So I scrambled to make clear I wasn't asking for help. "Just curious. No deals."

"Not to worry." He spoke as if he could read the secrets of my mind. Which was downright creepy and raised the hairs along my arms that much more. Maybe he was more ghoul than ghost, which didn't make me feel better. Ghouls made fae look like nice folks. Ghosts being all spirit, I should be able to handle as a shaman. At least in theory.

Then I remembered. Tick tock.

"I don't have a whole lot of time," I said, looking around to see if there might be any other options than Mr. Let's-make-a-deal here, but except for the lightness, the plane was empty.

The ghoul shrugged his shoulders as if it was no concern of his.

"Can you help me find Bran or not?" I demanded, listening to Van's voice start to change. Was something happening in the earthly realm? Were Van and Sabina being attacked?

I turned, fear making my skin clammy, my voice tight. "Never mind. You're no help," I whispered, prepared to return. A failure.

"He's not here," the ghoul said, surprising us both as his form became clearer. Not corporeal but less vague. Now he looked like he might be in his late twenties, early thirties. No way to tell when he might have lived, but if he was able to materialize as he was, it was a darn good clue he'd possessed a body at one time.

"Why should I trust you?" I asked. Yup, that was me. Kick the gift horse in the mouth. But if he lied, and Bran was already dead, we'd fight our way into that house on a fool's errand, and any casualties would be solely my responsibility.

"Because I speak the truth. Your mage is not here. Yet."

"And what does that mean?"

"You've run out of time," he said with what might have been a smile. The smile a snake gave before it struck. "You will return. We shall bargain then."

Not if I could help it.

I swallowed, knowing I didn't have a lot of options. Stay and keep hunting for Bran who might not be here and risk Van and Sabina at the very least. Or trust this ghoul with an agenda and risk us all back on the earthly plane.

I was getting damn tired of hard choices.

You know the old saying? Seek safety in danger. Guess that meant back to the physical realm it was.

I braced myself, closing my eyes at the same time, though I really, really hated to do that so near to Ghoul Guy.

"Till next time," his voice echoed as I followed Van's chant down a long, dark tunnel.

Interesting, before I'd always popped from one realm to the other. What was up with the tunnel?

Wooden beams stacked upright like an underground passage. A coal mine or train tunnel maybe? Row upon row of layered beams, but colored orange and red. Beside and above me. A tunnel of blood-orange color. Like a mineshaft but illuminated by the walls instead of any specific light source. The path looked like gravel with bloodstains saturating each small, sharp rock. And that smell. It intensified, enough to make me want to wrap my sleeve across my nose. What the heck?

Was the blood a nightmare? Could be, but it sure felt real. The pounding of my heart increased even though I'd slowed my pace. My breath chugging in and out. The fear kicking through me as if any minute something horrible was going to jump out at me.

"Get your ass over here," Van snarled, breaking the chant.

I ran. Ran like all the wraiths of hell were chasing me. Ran in the direction I'd last heard his voice.

"Van? Van, are you there?"

Only silence.

If he left me here, in this blood red, endless tunnel, I'd ... I'd ... *oh crap, please don't leave me.*

CHAPTER 59

I was gulping air, my heart pounding, my muscles firing with after burn as I jerked upwards, an arm swinging across me, pressing me into the earth.

"What the—"

"Shhh," Van hissed into my ear. "They'll hear you."

They? Where? Oh, yeah, back in the physical realm. Thank the Great Spirits.

I released a sigh that came from the soles of my feet.

Van whispered in my ear, "Get ready to run."

Run where?

I was shaking, that kind of tremble you get when every muscle in your body has been maxed.

"On the count of three," Van said, mumbling something into his head mic to the rest of the team.

Out of the fire and into an inferno. What was going on?

I raised my head enough to find my own answers. Five Weres fanned out before us, moving toward where we huddled as if they knew exactly where we were.

The protection spell I'd cast earlier?

Oh, peanuts and pistols, I should have had Sabina keep up the chant while I was gone. Now I didn't have enough magic left in me to cast even a How and Why spell.

I could feel Van vibrating next to me, ready to shift. But even in his wolf form, there were too many Weres for him to take on. Unless...

"Sabina, you run to the left. I'll veer to the right. Van, we'll try to divide and conquer."

He snorted. "Tarrington High?"

"You got it, bro. Ready to rock and rumble?"

"You get hurt and Dad'll kill me."

"Pshaw, we're Noziaks. Noziaks don't die."

My stomach was cramping with fear as I rose to my knees. Stealth didn't matter anymore. It was time to play the game.

"One," Van said, crouched. Sabina mimicked him. Smart girl.

"Two." I creaked my neck and hoped like hades I didn't fall in a heap, my legs failing me before I could even get started.

"Three."

We all burst out from under the tree at the same time, yelling like the Sioux or Pawnees, hell bent for leather in three different trajectories.

Weres could be taken by surprise, and bless them, that's exactly what happened, giving us a few vital seconds to gain ground until they split and started charging.

One after Sabina.

Two head-on into Van.

Three after me.

CHAPTER 60

WTF? How'd I get so lucky?

Legs charging, lungs chugging, heart rat-a-tat-tatting a million miles a second. If I'd been just a witch/shaman I couldn't have outrun any of these guys even in their human forms. For the first time since I'd woken up in that crappy laboratory, I was thankful for whatever abilities I now had due to Van's shifter bite. Not that I'd tell him that. We were siblings.

I ran as if the hounds of hell were hot on my tail. Which they were. I heard one shift but didn't dare glance over my shoulder to see what he'd become.

The angle I was blazing across the lawn arrowed me toward the old carriage house. What then?

A stack of crates huddled beneath the far eaves. If I could reach them I might, just might be able to use them to climb on the roof.

Not that the Weres couldn't too, but higher ground usually held the advantage. And I was looking for time. Time for Van to take out his two opponents. Time for the team to arrive. Time to come up with a better plan.

Mostly the last one.

I hit the boxes and scrambled up them the way I'd once seen a kitten clamor up a tree with a badass Doberman nipping at her. Using both hands and knees I clawed my way onto the slate tile roof, thankful it wasn't wet because even dry there wasn't a lot of traction. Before I was fully sprawled across the hard surface I used my foot to kick off the last box. The box and the Were flying up it.

I smacked the Were, right in his open mouth, which was just enough oomph to topple him and the boxes backwards.

But I wasn't home free. Not by a long shot.

Face fully pressed against the slate, I turned my head enough to look behind me.

Thank the Great Spirits, the one Were who had shifted had become a boar. Wicked dangerous on the ground but no climbing boxes for that one, and if he shifted back to human form, it'd take him a bit to recover his strength. One Were down, two to go.

Using fingers, knees, elbows and anything else I could to scurry higher on the roof, I did. I'd give the remaining Weres about two minutes to reassemble those boxes and be after me.

At least I had a chance to catch my breath and see how Van was doing. He was still in his human form but using his speed and strength against his two opponents. Given his military training I wasn't worried about him. He was probably having fun.

But where was Sabina?

Oh, oh, there she was, splayed on her back against the grass, using her legs as battering rams against the Were trying to pin her down.

Teen human against Were? She had seconds at most before the guy broke her legs or simply smothered her by throwing his weight on her.

Where was the rest of the IR team?

As if I'd conjured them, I watched the new girl, what was her name? Nicki. That's right. Nicki came racing from around the back of the house, a bullet on course to do some wup ass on that Were. Of course he was too stupid, or too focused on beating up on a kid to notice what was about to come down on him.

Go, Nicki!

Jaylene and Mandy were close behind Nicki but even as far away as I was, I could hear the snap as she plowed into the Were. Smack. Crackle and pop.

That Were went over like a deflated sandbag as Nicki pummeled him into the ground. He didn't even have a chance to send up a Mayday to his buddies.

Ling Mai had been smart to bring in a shifter to the team.

Jaylene waved Herc forward to help Sabina crawl to her feet before Jaylene headed toward Van.

I threw my arms up and started shouting but already the Weres after me had managed to pull themselves up to the roof's edge. No way could Jaylene or Mandy make it to me, and even if they did, they were no match against angry Weres. And these two were pissed, snarling and raging. I could actually see the face of one already morphing into an elongated snout. Not a canine one but what looked like an ape.

Just great. Something that was even more nimble than I was on the roof.

I started racing to the ridgeline, slipping backwards as much as scrambling forward. Once on top there weren't a lot of options and zip weapons.

Did I have enough magic left in me?

Only one way to know for sure. Bracing myself with my butt on the ridge I faced the Weres, one who had already reached the roof but was finding it as hard to navigate as I did, and the other, the ape already swinging himself from crate to slate. By the time he landed with a loud thud he'd fully changed into a mid-size gorilla.

Not good. Not good at all.

Sucking in a much-needed breath, I raised my hands.

"Air to wind, Earth to dust.
By water and by fire.
Trouble to heed and trouble to find.
Compel. Coerce. Constrain.
I thee call. I thee command.
Threat be gone. Power be bound."

Human Were stopped but Gorilla Guy didn't miss a beat. His long arms swung at his sides, his bulging forehead looking like a battering ram, and then there were his teeth, thirty-two of them, barred in a primordial snarl.

I know in the wild gorillas can be gentle vegetarians, but this one didn't seem to have gotten the memo.

"Hey, monkey, monkey, can we talk?" I whispered, wondering what now? That's when I saw it. A small skylight, halfway down a small hip roof, off to my right.

No idea where it went but it went somewhere and that's all I needed to know.

Throwing myself toward it I half slid, half rolled toward the opening, catching one hand on the metal casing.

I'd nearly ripped my arm off. Holy Goddess, that hurt.

My back was to the window so no time to check out what was beneath it as I rolled on top of it, battering it open with my feet.

Not my smartest move.

CHAPTER 61

I curled myself into as small a ball as possible, protecting my head as I plummeted what felt like miles into a shadowed darkness.

St. Jude, protector of desperate situations, must have been watching over me as I smashed onto the hood of a car, crumpling it, and knocking the wind out of me.

But I was alive. I could work with that.

Rolling off the hood I landed in a crouch by the front wheel of a compact French car, already scrambling for another exit.

Looking up, I could see the gorilla darkening the shattered window. Wouldn't take him long to follow.

I glanced around. A few gardening tools in a corner. Stone walls. Concrete floor.

A doublewide door was closed behind the car. If I could open it fast enough, I could be back outdoors. Where the boar Were waited.

Option number two?

There, just behind me, was a choice. A smaller door.

Leading where?

One way to find out.

I stumbled as I clambered to my feet, pivoting in a less than graceful arc. The hard thud against metal behind me told me at least one Were had breached the window.

I thrust against the door, not trusting that it'd actually be open. But it was.

Thank you, Goddess, for small blessings.

I was through that door faster than a kid aiming for the presents under the tree on Christmas morning.

A hallway. Dark. But the scent was familiar. Too bad I didn't have the time to figure out why as I was too busy running as fast as I could.

At first, the hallway looked like any small, narrow slot leading to a set of other rooms maybe. Or a back door. But it didn't take long for this hallway to start sloping downwards, the width widening, the walls changing from drywall to stone, and the smell. That's what struck me. Musty. Old.

What was this place?

That's when I heard it. Not the thudding behind me but the scream in my head.

"Alex!"

Bran. Bran was somewhere down this hall.

I picked up my pace, ignoring the stitch in my side, how hard it was to catch my next breath. Looked like my amazing shifter stamina was thinning as fast as my magical abilities. At this rate soon all I'd have left was my sarcasm.

I'm coming. Hang on.

I had no idea if he could hear me or not. Or if my team could find me. Or what I'd find if I could locate Bran.

But I kept running. Sliding around the corners. Looking for a way to stop the Weres chasing me.

"Go back," Bran shouted mind to mind. "It's a trap."

Too late.

CHAPTER 62

Now I knew how rats in mazes felt. Each corner I skimmed around led to another short passage and another corner. Whoever made this place must have been paid by the number of angles they could build.

At least Gorilla Guy wasn't adept at the quick burst of speed then adjust and turn school of attack. If we'd been on open ground I'd have been a goner.

Behind the roaring ape I could hear the hard pounding of the human Were's boots meeting concrete floors. He was gaining.

I hadn't seen another door, or window, or even a shadow to hide in. No choice but to keep running.

Next corner, I remembered why the smell struck me. I was back in the corridors Sabina and I had navigated when we escaped the cells.

Talk about coming full circle.

My stomach took a nosedive. If I was right, I was heading straight toward a dead-end where the cells were.

No choice as gorilla gave another roar that rocked off the rock walls.

Not far now. Scramble, slide, flat out burst of speed, another turn and, pow, three cells, two open, one closed, and a dozen people standing in a semi-circle before them.

The welcoming committee.

I skidded to a wobbly stop, huffing breath like a steam engine, wondering if I should grab the open but empty cell and lock myself in before the two Weres caught up with me.

Not enough time as the human Were raced around the last corner and almost ran me over. I sidestepped, which was the only thing saving me as his size and speed kept him rocketing forward until even the folks in the half-circle scattered before being knocked down like bowling balls.

All but three who remained frozen in place. Braver than the rest? I didn't have time to guess as the gorilla ripped around the corner and slammed into the human Were who'd managed to stop.

If I'd had an ounce of breath left I might have snorted. Hadn't I said Weres were not the brightest crayons in the box? Watching these two tangle arms and hairy legs was worth the near-death experience.

Almost.

Should I run back the way I'd come?

By the time I thought through the option one of the three frozen figures in the cell had raised his hand and pointed it in my direction.

Like a laser zap to my nerves I felt his magic from where I stood, suddenly rooted to the ground. Crashing waves of tainted darkness swirled and eddied around me and I stood there. Not a thing I could do to break free.

WTH?

"How nice of you to join us, Miss Noziak," he said and the pennies dropped with a deafening clang.

He'd been in the laboratory. Earlier. When I'd killed the white-coated guy. Colin Farrell voice. That's where I'd heard him before. And the night Philippe Cheverill was murdered. I'd talked to him there, too. Then there was this morning. The druid friend of my father's.

I guess Weres were not the only ones slow on the uptake. Could I really have been so clueless?

"I see you remember me." He sounded so smug, so calmly casual I wanted to lunge for his face and wipe his grin off.

But I couldn't move. Not my legs, or hands, or even my mouth worked. I wasn't even sure I was breathing. All I could do was look straight ahead where I now recognized the other two statue-still figures. Bran and my father. Trapped like I was. Man, this guy had wicked powerful magic if he could keep two magic users and my father ensnared.

Then there were the Weres who'd untangled themselves
and were whipping around, looking for me.

Good news? Fear could still spike an adrenaline rush
through me, enough to make me light headed. Bad news? I
couldn't do a bloody thing about it or the Weres.

"Richard," a woman's voice ordered. She said the name in
the French way. *Reachhard.* Though her accent was pure lilting
Irish. "Do not harm her."

Someday I was going to get an accent that made a command
sound like a sexual act because hot damn if her words didn't
work. On the human Were at least. The gorilla glanced at her
once, drool running down his open mouth, before he turned and
flung himself back toward me.

Two things happened at once.

The spell holding me broke, or was removed, long enough
to fling me sideways, out of the direct line of attack.

Another spell punched the Were full force, stopping him so
fast in his tracks he slammed face forward onto the floor.

Ouch! That had to hurt. Who was I kidding, I knew it hurt
because even landing at an angle pain was ricocheting through
my body.

From where I lay on my side I could see the glare of those
tiny gorilla eyes, so small in comparison to the size of his body,
and raging with hate.

I'd landed with a sprawl on some old hay so I slowly pulled
myself to my knees, bracing myself for another jolt of that dark
magic, keeping my focus split between the druid smiling across
the chamber and the gorilla glaring at me from a few feet away.
Who knew if or when he'd be freed.

"Come, Miss Noziak," the druid said. "You could have
made this much less painful for yourself if you'd hadn't
escaped earlier."

So this was my fault?

Nothing like a cold dousing of anger to give a boost of in-
your-dreams attitude.

I wobbled to my feet, a snarl building inside me. I didn't say
being pissed against a dangerous druid was a good idea, but it
did get me going.

"So next time a psychotic a-hole kidnaps me I should count my blessings?" I asked, my smile so sweet it could sharpen razors.

I saw the druid's brows draw together. "I'm offering you a chance to make history."

Puhleeze. "You offer that same chance to my dad? And Bran?" I pointed to where the two remained so still it backed fear down my throat.

"They are here to insure you would come," was the druid's response.

Man, this guy could sell sand to the Arabs.

"I'm here. What now?"

"Now, together we usher in a new age."

Was he serious?

"I have waited for a long time for you to join me, Miss Noziak. A long time."

"You asking for a date or something else?"

He laughed. A sound that if I didn't know better I'd be attracted to. Did I mention I have lousy taste in men? He wasn't done though. "I'm offering you a chance to change history. We are about to enter a thrilling age, one that the world has never seen the like of before."

"A thrilling age for what?"

"For preternaturals, of course. For all of us." He raised his hands before him in a Moses-on-the-mountain move. "It's time those who possess magic and abilities take our rightful place in the order of things."

"I'm guessing you mean, us on top, humans on bottom."

"The way things once were, Miss Noziak." He was taking that paternal I-know-best tone that gave me the heebiejeebies. "We are set to correct a terrible wrong."

"Sounds like you're wanting to make a new wrong." Note to mouth. Stay shut.

He tsked. The man actually tsked, as if talking to a child. He was so not winning any points in my ledger. But as long as I kept him talking Van and the team stood a better chance of finding us.

I couldn't take out a druid who wielded as much dark magic as this guy did, while being surrounded by Weres and whatever the woman was who'd called to the Were. A witch would be my guess. A black one.

And then there was Bran and my dad to consider. I had no idea how to free them and if, on the off chance I could overcome the druid, would eliminating him leave those two forever encased in stone stillness?

I think my dad's plan had officially tanked and it'd be left to me to pick up the pieces.

I nodded my chin at Bran. "Why don't you release him? A show of good faith and I might consider finding out more about this plan of world domination."

Okay, maybe I could have phrased that a little less snarky. Maybe, but not likely.

"Only a fool would unleash a powerful mage, Miss Noziak, and I am no fool."

It was worth a try. I shrugged my shoulders and asked, "So what's involved in this epic change-the-world plan? Flood? Fire? One of the seven plagues of Egypt?"

"There were ten plagues," the witch woman snarled, her accent echoing the druid's, though obviously not liking all the chitchat going on as she turned to the druid. "Enough of this, Padraig. Ensnare her and call forth Zaradian."

I knew I didn't like this bitch.

Padraig didn't even glance her way as he said, "Patience, my dear Breena. If she helps willingly, she could be a powerful ally in the new order."

Lucky me. I spoke to the druid, cutting out the bitch-witch totally. "I do appreciate the carrot versus the stick approach. It's refreshing."

He smiled. An honest one, which was disconcerting. Much easier to gut a full-fledged bad guy, which I knew he was, but one who could smile made him a little less uber evil. Didn't it?

"I appreciate your wit, Miss Noziak." He turned sober so fast it made my head spin. "But know that there is a stick. I just prefer not to use it."

He flicked his fingers toward Bran, and I didn't need mind-to-mind communication to see the pain flash across his eyes.

"Stop!" I stepped forward.

The druid smiled again, this time it didn't reach his eyes. "Your choice." He looked like he'd scored against me. He had.

"Hurting him doesn't predispose me to want to help you." Oh, look at me, big words when what I wanted to do was bare my teeth and attack.

And who said I hadn't learned some self-restraint.

The druid waited. Guess it was my turn to hold out the olive branch. Or appear to do so.

"Tell me why you need me?" I asked, slightly less caustic than I'd sounded thus far.

"I understand you're able to merge magic with others."

My stomach dropped like an atom bomb. Who'd told him?

My tone held even, regardless of the tap dance of nerves racing through my body. "And if I could?"

"Your power. With mine. We'd be unstoppable."

"Don't, Alex." Bran's voice came through to me. Weak but still dictatorial. It was everything I could do not to shoot my gaze in his direction, which would be a dead give away that I was paying more attention to Bran than the druid.

Not smart.

"So together we'd call the demon Zaradian?"

That frown creased the druid's face again. "Did I say he was a demon?"

Oops. TMI. I ratcheted up an aren't-I-smart smile. "I've done my homework and have read my myths and fairytales."

"She lies." The witch cut me a killing glance. "She seeks to distract you. Don't trust her."

What got her panties six ways to Sunday? Oh, that would be me.

I gave her a glance I'd learned in high school from Terri O'Donnell. Bitch meet bitchier. "And what does your *friend* here have to do with your plans?"

Buy time. Buy time. Buy time.

"I'm not his friend," the woman positively shrieked. Good, throwing her off base would keep the druid from accepting that I was lying and would continue to do so as long as the clock kept ticking. "I'm a full Council member and you'd do well to be wary."

Her voice had slid down a few octaves, which I admit was a whole lot scarier than a screaming fishwife. This time my shrug was not so casual or easy to pull up. "Whatever." I dismissed her, bracing myself for retaliation.

Which came with a roar. Her roar. Followed by a low, breathless chant.

"As I do unto thee.
Smite mine enemy torments of hell.
    Black, black as night. Red, red as blood.
Bring her pains of flesh.

Lesions on skin will glow.
Afflict her with tormented blow.
Sores and pain afflict her now.
Pay her, well endow.

Dukes of darkness, Kings of hell,
Smite mine enemy, bring her hell.
Lessons learned and lessons taught.
Bring her to her knees to rot."

I'd had a kidney stone pass once through me as a child and thought nothing could hurt that bad. I was wrong.

As if a vice was twisted around me, I slapped knees to floor, all breath sucked out, all focus on the blinding pain knife-jacking through me. I couldn't breathe, couldn't beg, couldn't do anything except writhe.

"That shall teach you, puny witch," she hissed.

"Enough, Breena. You undo all I have done."

Stop this pain, druid, and I'll consider doing whatever you ask.

Hang on, Alex. Bran's voice. His timing so sucked.

Light flashed before my eyes. Good. I'd pass out. Surely, that would stop the torment.

Try, harder.

I might have groaned. Or whimpered. I know I bit my lip, could taste the coppery tang of fresh blood.

By the Spirits, make this stop.

I twisted into a pretzel shape, gasping for air, praying for release.

Magic, Alex, use your magic.

Can't.

It was the only word I could think of as the room darkened around me.

"Enough," the druid shouted.

It was too late. I slipped to the floor, welcoming the blackness.

CHAPTER 63

I woke in small, incremental stages. Not trusting my body. My memories. Knowing any second I could slide back into that pain.

Without opening my eyes I took stock. Cool air touched my skin. Hardness beneath me. Machines softly gulping around me.

Where was I? Did I really want to know?

I swallowed, piecing images together. My dad. Bran. Statues. The druid.

I'd been trying to buy time before bad things happened.

The witch.

I'd failed.

Nothing new there. Bitterness joined the wafting breeze surrounding me.

Pity party? Like that had ever solved anything.

I cracked open one eye, refusing to groan when I realized where I was. The lab. The same damn lab where I'd killed the man in white.

"You're back amongst us," Irish Voice spoke. I'd liked that voice a whole lot better when I thought it'd belonged to Colin Farrell, to a person who might have a soul.

The druid had none.

"Where am I?" I asked, already knowing the answer but needing every second I could gather to pull my courage around me. Courage to face the druid. His sucks-for-humans plans. And my role in them.

My fingers felt for the cold lip of the metal gurney I was stretched out on. This too was familiar, and right now it gave me a sense of solidity sorely missing. That and the feel of my anathema dagger against my leg.

Clueless Weres, they hadn't searched me for weapons. Their loss, my gain.

"Miss Noziak ... may I call you Alex?"

Yup, full-fledged nightmare. The boogey man was trying to be nice. Like hiding a suicide bomb in a stuffed teddy bear.

I pulled myself up to my elbows, a distance that was a lot harder to achieve than I'd thought. At least I wasn't flat on my back anymore. A vulnerable position. Too vulnerable.

I ignored the druid's question and threw out my own. "Where is she?"

He didn't have to ask who I meant. "Breena means well."

And if I believed that I deserved all the pain I'd already absorbed. My brow arched. I didn't have to say anything else as I struggled to sit up fully.

"I've sent her away." If I didn't have an idea of what a psychopath he was I might have heard hesitation beneath his words. But he was what he was and I held no doubts what I faced.

Gloves off. I had no idea of what was happening to my team, to Van. No help from Bran or my dad. Only thing I did know is that I was alone, down to the wire and bad things roaring at me.

Not just me. If the druid succeeded—no, I wasn't going down that dark tunnel. That way laid madness.

So it was up to me. Time to get my Noziak on.

I spoke through dry, cracked lips, "What exactly do you expect me to do?"

A fleeting smile sparked his expression but he wasn't a fool. He stood half way across the room as if wary of being caged with a witch/shaman/shifter.

Smart because I was feeling my shifter self rising to the fore, waiting, just waiting to rip me some heads off and I had my eye on one right now.

"You'll see you've made the right choice ... Alex."

I just bet. But I held my tongue.

I also held his gaze, knowing he expected me to turn away, lower my eyes, quake. I might but it'd be a frozen day in the Sahara before I showed him.

He was messing with the wrong Noziak.

"I expect you to pull magic from your warlock. Between your power amplified, and mine, we'll open a seam between worlds."

"A doorway for your demon?"

"He's not my demon. He is the salvation of this world."

Dream on.

Obviously the druid couldn't read my expression. Either that or I was getting damn good at hiding my thoughts.

"Come," he said, beckoning with one hand. "I'll show you the power. The possibilities."

I was pretty sure his vision was different than mine. Yet I slid from the metal gurney, swallowing bile, knowing no miracle was going to save me now.

Unless I made one.

Once I was steady on my feet, or as steady as I was going to get I asked, "Where's Bran?"

He glanced at a door so seamless I'd never noticed it before.

"You know I can't ..." *Can't do this.* "Can't tap into his power as long as he remains in whatever state you put him in earlier."

"Can't or won't?" he asked, just enough of a sneer to make it easier for me to tighten my spine.

"Does it matter which?" I glanced around and offered a rock hard shrug. "You want my help, you have to play some things my way."

He angled his head. "As long as you are very clear who's in charge here, Miss Noziak."

So we were no longer BFFs. Lucky me.

"I have no doubts." About what I planned to do. No idea how I was going to accomplish my primary goal, to stop him, and a demon who was buddies with the second son of Christ, and avoid a psycho Celtic witch who had me in her sights. Good thing my daddy and brothers raised me to fight back. Because that's all I knew how to do.

But I still had some questions. "Why this particular demon? Why Zaradian?"

"He will lead the others."

Oh, this was getting better and better. I swallowed the bile building in my throat. "Others? As in more demons?"

"The Seekers." He looked perplexed for a flash. *Welcome to my world.* "But I thought you knew."

I shook my head, treading the fine line between being in-the-know-enough-to-be-taken-seriously and totally lost in the dark. Hard to act hard-core when I was the latter. "I've been hearing a lot about the Seekers." None of it concrete. "But I'm a little vague on why this first demon, who is so powerful and dangerous, isn't a Seeker himself."

"The Seekers expect him to prove that this world is worth subjugating."

"So Zaradian is to show these other guys that humans can be destroyed? Or at least beat down enough to make it worthwhile to what?"

"Humans are food, Alex. Nothing more. They live beneath abilities, breed incessantly and destroy whatever they touch."

"And yet preternaturals hide from them." I tried to keep my voice casual. Wasn't doing too good a job of it based on his expression.

"Like cockroaches, humans have proven hard to exterminate."

"So bad-guy demon number one is supposed to wipe out enough to make it easier for these Seekers to do what? Invade? Are they coming from where Zaradian is?"

"They are not demons, Alex," he sounded like a stick-up-his-butt professor talking down to the slow-witted witch. "They will make Zaradian's rule seem benign."

I nodded. Easier than spewing the contents of an empty stomach. "So what about the preternaturals currently in this world? Do they all agree that they want Zaradian lording over them and then these Seekers doing the same?"

"Do not be naïve, Alex. Those who are wise will relish the chance for some, how do you Americans say, some payback."

"And the rest?"

"They do not matter."

And that about summed up the druid. With him and you'd get the leftovers after a demon was finished and then, lucky you, some bigger, badder creepos would be coming making things worse. Against him and you'd be annihilated sooner rather than later.

If I had any doubts that stopping him was not the best idea I'd ever had, he'd just clarified for me why I had no choice. He was bad news. For every living being. For every innocent child, for all of the young lovers, caring elders who inhabited the planet. Someone had to stand up for them and right now, it looked like I was the only one who could.

So be it.

"This way then." He waved one hand before him in a gesture that should have been more gallant and less threat, but it wasn't.

Now I knew how innocents felt heading to the gallows, or the guillotine, judged guilty simply for who they were, not what they'd done.

One step in front of the other. I ignored the sweat beading on my skin, the roiling of my stomach, the stiffness in my muscles. One step at a time.

The secret door whisked open, surprising me because so much of this dungeon area was ancient and felt more medieval than modern.

I ducked my head, though the frame wasn't low. It was more a primordial instinctual response to expecting an attack without any idea from which direction.

All of them would be my guess.

The room I'd stepped into was empty though. Except for Bran, lashed to a wall with chains so thick I didn't know how he could stand.

But he did. Stand and glare with the force of retribution so strong in those laser blue eyes I paused. Now I know why they painted those images of the ancient prophets as they did. The ones that made me quake as a small child in Sunday school. The ones you knew, down in your bones, would show no mercy, no forgiveness and no choices. Except one. Annihilation.

Finally Bran and I had common ground.

He looked exhausted though. His tailored clothes, torn and dirt smeared. Dark shadows beneath his eyes. One eye swelling shut. But he still looked ready to take on the druid and win.

And I was supposed to harness Bran's magic, against his will, and use it to unleash blackness onto Earth.

Why'd I get all the easy jobs?

My dad's plan, in shambles as it was, still might work, or bits and pieces of it. That would have to be enough.

I glanced over my shoulder at the druid. "So where's this seam or portal or whatever you're calling it?"

"When the time comes you'll know."

Yeah, like that was going to work for me. Not.

"Either I'm helping you or I'm not." Yes, there was a snarl in my voice, not because I liked facing scary megalomaniacs but because my only chance to save Bran was to have the druid thinking I really was working with him. Not as a servant, I figured he had enough of those types pussyfooting around him, but as an equal.

Talk about biting off a lot to chew.

"Don't, Alex." Bran's voice sounded raw and hoarse.

I didn't even look in his direction though it took everything I had not to give him even one quick glance of reassurance. Instead I ignored him. Him and the shaking of my legs. "Well, Padraig." It was all I could do not to spit his name out. "Are we in this together?" The, 'or not', was implied.

I didn't start breathing again until the druid gave a sharp shake of his head and stepped past me, deeper into the room.

Point to Alex.

Until he said something so low I almost didn't hear his words. "Bring her in."

Her?

I twisted around as I heard scuffles, and oaths ringing off the stone walls, coming closer and closer.

My blood froze even before I saw Sabina being dragged down that shadowed hallway, struggling between two Weres who looked like they enjoyed pulling her arms out of her sockets. This was not how my revised plan was supposed to work.

I stepped forward. An automatic reflex before I whirled on the druid. "Is this the way you treat your allies?"

He had the gall to smile. "Yes, as a matter of fact, I do."

Point to Padraig.

"What the hell—" Sabina snarled before the Were on her left backhanded her so hard her head snapped back.

"Do that again, bruiser, and you'll get to deal with me," I growled low in my throat, sending a pulse of magic toward him. Not enough to rile him, more like a current of air strong enough to ruffle the two lank braids he wore hanging down his chest.

He raised his mouth to show teeth and attitude.

"Try it, doggie breath," I dared him. It was a bluff, pure bluff, but I doubted the druid would risk losing his amplifying witch. At least I hoped he didn't want to lose me. Not until I'd proved useful.

The Were rocked forward on his feet, crouching to lunge, when he glanced over my shoulder and must have caught his boss's gaze.

My, my, how quickly one could be cowed.

Though I didn't say anything out loud both Weres got the message. Confusion flashed across the second Were's face as if wondering why he didn't get to play his petty and punitive Were games. Sort of like a cat who didn't know why its master wasn't happy when he brought him half-alive small rodents and wanted to continue to torment them.

Maybe it was the cat word, or something else, but suddenly a huge, ungainly, and butt ugly dog came loping down the hallway hell bent for leather. Actually the beast made a beeline for Bran, skittering to sniff me once or twice before smacking into Bran with a full doggie greeting. His front paws were on Bran's shoulders, making me want to cringe at the pressure and pain they must be causing, as his tongue and tail wagged a million times a second, his woofs loud enough to bring the rock ceiling down around us.

"Who?" the druid growled.

What? was my first thought, followed by a suspicious second glance. Just about that time, the monster left Bran and raced toward me, his head butting into my stomach, and toppling me backwards. I staggered, avoiding that squeegee tongue. If I didn't know better, I'd say he assumed we were BFFs separated for far too long.

On the other hand, his antics did break the tension and gave me an excuse to slide sideways, grab Sabina's arm and tug her away from the clueless Weres. The dog bounding between them and us made it hard for the Weres to snatch her back.

Maybe we were BFFs. If I could have reached the dog's head I'd have patted it.

"Sorry, boss," a winded Were called, popping in behind the two nasty Weres. "He got away from me."

For the first time since I'd woken up on that gurney, a glimmer of hope sputtered through me. Sure Bran and I were still way outnumbered, especially with the druid's freaky abilities. But with the arrival of this last Were, who was either Willie the recovering Were or his twin brother, meant that the monster dog stood a good chance of being Frank or Franco or whatever he was calling himself this week.

It wasn't an ideal cavalry to be saved by but it wasn't like we had a lot of options.

I kept my gaze averted from Willie, afraid I might give myself away with a big grin, but eyed the dog very closely. Franco, as that's what he was called first time I'd met him, was a Didi shifter, which meant he could morph into multiple types of the same creature. His creature was *canis lupus familiaris*, the common dog. But since there was nothing common about Franco in his human form, it came as no surprise there was nothing common about the dog forms he chose.

If he wanted to be hound of the Baskervilles I wouldn't stop him. Especially if it meant we might walk out of here alive.

"You imbecilic moron," the druid snarled, though I wanted to point out his comment was a little redundant. "Take that beast away. Now."

Willie cleared his throat. "There's a bit of a mess upstairs." He glanced at me as if to say it was all my fault and it was all I could do not to give a fist pump in response. "Thought it might be best to keep him down here. If you need him."

The scorching glance Padraig shot Willie's way was enough to singe the hair off even a Were, but I bit back saying anything, slowly edging Sabina away from all the Weres and closer to Bran's cell.

If I had to I would toss her inside and clang the door shut. She and Bran would then be safe from Were attack, but no iron bars could keep out Padraig's magic.

I was working on that though.

Padraig seemed to consider Willie's comment for a moment before chopping his hand through the air. "So be it. You." He pointed at Willie. "Stand guard there. You two, over there and there."

Basically, the hallway was being blocked against further advances.

Padraig wasn't finished though. "And, idiot, keep the dog beside you."

Franco gave a doggy whine and slinked to Willie's side when the Were whistled for him. Good doggy.

Not.

I wondered how Franco could hide what he was from Padraig, unless Padraig knew he was a shifter but wasn't worried about the monster-sized animal being a threat to anything except other targets.

So the druid wasn't as smart as he thought he was.

I assumed the mess upstairs meant my team was making inroads. I was absolutely positive about it when the druid barked a new set of orders, "We're losing time. The ritual must begin now."

His eyes lighted on me as I shoved Sabina behind me as much as possible.

But not enough as Padraig's eyes narrowed and his mouth thinned. "Move out of the way, Alex," he said, his tone so cold it made me shiver.

"No." My brothers would have recognized the rock-solid determination behind my single word. It was clear the druid could not freeze, or whatever he did with his dark magic, as long as I kept Sabina so close to me that he could not separate us. If the vestiges of my father's plan were to work, I needed to protect her.

"Do not push me, witch," he said. Druids have always been known for their arrogance. They even gave warlocks a run for the title of biggest PIAs and that was saying something.

I cast Bran a quick glance, catching his Celtic gaze while finding his frown. Of course. But his look said he was trusting me to know what I was doing, even if he didn't like it.

I just hoped he could keep that trust long enough to get us both through what was about to happen.

"Are we going to get this party rockin' or stand around all day?" I eyed the druid but caught two of the Weres looking over their shoulders, probably anticipating blood. Willie didn't look any different but I heard a suspicious snort from him covered by a quick cough. The dog started barking. Doggy speak for way-to-go, Alex!

That was my translation anyway.

If this a-hole wanted a battle, I was ready.

I thought.

CHAPTER 64

The druid cast one hard glance between Bran and me before inhaling a deep breath and raising his hands. He closed his eyes, stilling himself, and even from here, I could feel the power he called up. No fieldstones, no oak and mistletoe, no marking of a sacred space. And yet already the magic rose, like an untapped dam waiting to be unleashed, as he started his chant.

"Ageless wisdom, I seek thee now.
Unknown to Seekers' clouded eyes.
Come Ancestors, spirits of the unjust dead.
Ancient truths are strange to all who hold the lie."

The shadows grew thicker around us all, the chill deeper as the druid's voice, like angry waves slamming a rocky shore, rolled through the enclosed space. I could smell underground places of age and dampness, the copper penny smell of fresh blood, the fecundity of moist earth.

"Those who follow the path, the Old Way.
I summon and stir thee!
Come and manifest in this sacred place.
I summon. I implore thee!
Follow me as I have followed thee."

Sabina shook against me, burying her head against my shoulder. I didn't blame her. I had the same urge. But she had to be ready. Since there'd always been an off chance she'd be

close enough my father had created a Plan A and a Plan B. It's
where I got that gene. Only challenge was we were on about
Plan S by this time. Plan Stay alive.

"Be ready," I whispered to her, keeping my voice low
enough the druid's chanting covered it.

"I don't know if I can—"

"You can and you will." I wasn't the nurturing one. She
should know that by now. "If I say go, or push you away, then
run."

"But—"

"No *buts*. It's the plan. Follow it and you'll live. Take
Willie and the dog away."

"What about you?"

"Worry about yourself." Yeah, I sounded like a bitch but no
need for both of us to die.

"Spirits of the ancient dead show me the path.
Spirits of the Earth, call back thy ancient son.
Shining Ones I implore thee.
Power called and Power sought."

Bran started rattling his chain, attempting to break the curl
of black magic encircling all of us. Franco caught on and added
some high-pitched barks.

The druid opened one eye and pointed a single finger
toward Franco who yelped then sank to the floor.

If that bastard killed Franco?

I moved toward the dog but Sabina held me back. She was
right. Willie was there. He'd do what could be done. The druid
closed both eyes again and began anew, even as out of the
corner of my eye I saw Willie hefting Franco and moving him
away.

"I call dark energy to weave a circle of power.
I call on that which has been hidden for too long.
Belial. Zamiel. Samael. Ahriman, I call thee all.
Brothers and sons and followers of darkness.
Open to me."

I didn't know if it was me, or Sabina who was shaking more. It didn't matter. When Padraig opened his eyes and looked at me the man who'd inhabited the body was gone. Milky white eyes stared out. Ancient eyes. Crazy eyes. "Come, witch," he whispered, crooking his finger toward me.

Show time.

If this plan didn't work my dad would hear about it. From me. On the other side, fat lot of good it'd do.

I had no choice. My feet started shuffling forward even as I dragged my boots against the concrete floor. Like a zombie acting on autopilot, I edged closer to the druid, Sabina acting as my shadow.

Fear rampaged through me. I wanted her far, far away from here. But if I pushed her away too soon she could become an easy target for the druid.

I glanced toward Bran. An automatic response.

He was shaking his head. His voice murmuring through me. "It's a trap, Alex. Don't!"

This was one choice I did have. If I ran he lost, Sabina lost, the world lost.

I simply shook my head and kept inching forward until I stood not more than a hand's length from the druid. Here I could smell a difference. He now reeked of fire, the acrid taint of brimstone and age, the kind of age one found in ancient tombs and burial sites.

"Join with me, witch." He extended his hand and every cell in my body screamed against touching him.

But I did it. My arm trembled, my fingers curled as if to pull back, but I did it, stretched out my hand until his paw curled around mine.

With my free left hand I reached back to push Sabina. Not to run but to start inching away. When she didn't move at first I shoved harder.

She had to keep to the plan. It was the only chance any of us had.

And I needed one hand free.

Like an electrical shock from a too-strong power source the druid's magic arced through me. Dark swallowing light. Energy clashing against energy.

The druid's lips curled in a thin line. A triumphant cant to it. What had I gotten myself into?

CHAPTER 65

"I call to the Dark and the Power of Satanail.
I call to the four corners of the Earth,
Strengthen this circle and let the power flow.
Power begets and power sustains.
Darkness hear my command and obey."

The druid's voice tightened around me, smothering, pressing, squeezing.

"Now, Alex," he commanded.

Sabina was no longer pressed against my back, which I hoped meant she was scooting away. I couldn't focus on the druid, Bran, and her all at the same time. Triage. Biggest threats first.

If I'd been smart I'd have warded myself with a protection spell. If I'd thought ahead I'd have cast a banishing spell over Sabina and removed her from this place. If I was any kind of a good and decent witch I'd have never found myself here.

Regrets would not get me through the next minutes, nor protect the people I cared for, even the ones I didn't know.

The only thing that would help now was grit, determination, and a hell of a lot of luck. A typical Noziak approach.

Swallowing deeply I stood taller and started pulling from Bran's magic. Not asking his permission or forgiveness. Making it my own.

"*Adeo. Adeo. Agero. Adepto.*
Come. Come. Increase. Acquire."

I could hear the rattle of Bran's chains as he realized what was happening. I expected resistance, instead I heard his voice begging, "Don't. It's too dangerous."

That nearly brought me to my knees. Powerful, arrogant warlocks did not beg.

Trust me. I spoke to his mind, now, before the druid could enter mine.

Bran's response should have soothed me, "I'm here with you. You're not alone."

But he was wrong. I'd do everything within my power to protect him. I knew that. But the timing had to be right. If I acted too soon against the druid he could destroy us all and find another way to bring forth Zaradian. If I acted too late ... well, then it wouldn't matter anyway. We'd all lose.

I strengthened my voice, tamping down the nerves and the doubt and the fears coursing through me. I could do this. *Please Great Spirits, help me do this.*

"Suscipio. Solvo.
Receive. Break free."

I wove the words I'd promised my father I'd never use and each time I broke that promise there had been consequences. *Sorry, Dad.*

"Singluaris. Praesentia presencia.
Free the power."

Bran's chains rattled as I heard his breathing increase, felt the pounding of his heart, the pulsing of his blood. His own magic rose to my call.

"I thee seek. I thee command. I thee bind."

A heady rush of magic washed against me so strong that I braced myself against it.

I remembered this. This exhilaration. This nirvana.

Sabina gasped beside me and moved farther away as if I burned.

I did. Like an energy vacuum I sucked from not only Bran but all the other non-human abilities around us, the Weres, Franco, even Sabina.

Which is why she had to get out of here, grab Willie and Franco and beat feet down the hallway. Last time I'd pulled magic from preternaturals most of them died. I didn't want that happening to my friends, but once the magic began calling to other magic I could only ride the swells. I didn't control a damn thing.

I was the nexus of a freaking power vortex. Again.

The druid smiled at me. Understanding. Celebrating. He knew. Of all in this room he comprehended what power really meant.

"Yes, Alex, now is the time."

He raised his gaze upwards. The room heated, degree by degree growing so hot sweat dripped from my face. I could taste the salt on my lips.

I followed his gaze, expecting to see the stone vaulted arch overhead. Instead, a funnel of wind whirled in colors of angry red and gray.

"Unleash the power, Alex. We need it now."

I hesitated, fear locking my muscles, roaring through me.

"No, Alex." Bran's voice.

"Now." The druid's arms shook, lightning flashing from his fingertips, threading through the churning clouds.

I didn't notice when he moved, reaching behind him with his free hand and pulling out a dagger, like mine only older, crafted from meteorite and molten materials. Fashioned from fire, cooled with incantations, aged in sacrifices and blood.

A cry erupted from my lips as he grabbed my left palm and turned it toward him. The slash of his dagger was swift and deep, blooding pooling until it trickled and dripped from hand to floor.

"Now, Alex," he whispered. "Be who you are meant to be."

A siren song for someone riding a power vortex. I reveled in the potency. Dangerous to everyone around. But not me.

"This is what you're meant to do."

Another voice had said that to me once. My mother's. Now the druid's.

Maybe they were right. Maybe now was the chance. One I'd avoided my whole life, playing by the rules, my father's rules. To protect you, he'd say, to keep you from harm.

Or to keep me from this? My true nature.

I heard the plop, plop, plop of the blood, my blood. Black magic I'd avoided my whole life. Yet here I wielded it as if born to it.

I raised my right hand to mirror the druid's and zeroed in. Thrice called, thrice to contain.

"As thou be, so now change.
Thought to image.
Image to bind.
Bind to blood let."

I raised my head skyward, aware of the swirl of grit and the widening of a rent overhead. The seam. We'd opened a seam.

Stop, Alex. You're going too far.

Bran's voice again. I could feel him resisting, pulling back but like the psychic vampire I was I tapped deeper into his power. Feeding off it. Craving more.

"Come, Zaradian. We beseech you!" the druid shouted. "We are here to do your will."

The rent widened, like looking deeper into a powerful waterfall, layer upon layer of mist mingling with darkness.

"Continere. Continere. Continere," I shouted, feeling free, truly free.

A crack of thunder answered me. A flash of white gold light. I heard the thud of the Weres crashing against the floor, their energies sucked dry while I felt I could go on for hours.

The druid spared me a quick glance. A grin of excitement making him look for an instant, just an instant, like the young man I'd first met.

Which made it even harder to do what I needed to do next. It all came down to choices. Not easy ones, or pleasant ones, but ones that had to be made.

An angry voice roared from the overhead void. "At last."

It was prayer and threat and gripped me like an incensed hand around my throat.

"Hemma, hanna, druia." The old words I spoke, hearing their echo through me. *"Hemma, druia, sanctum."*

I pulled forth more of Bran's magic and made it my own, amplifying and expanding, hearing his heart slow as I taxed everything within him. Still I pulled.

Time slammed to a halt. My head roared, blood pounded behind my eyes, nerve endings jangled. The seam became a door, beckoning to the demon waiting on the other side. His impatience pulsed toward me. Demanding. A greedy nature already wanting more.

"No," Bran's voice came as a whisper, a good bye and I knew it was time.

I couldn't reach my anathema. Not with the druid clasping my hand the way he was. What now?

Only one choice.

Dad, I hope you're right, that this is the only way.

Grabbing the druid's hand still holding his dagger I twisted his wrist and plunged the dagger into my chest.

CHAPTER 66

All Hallow's Hell broke loose as I crumpled to my knees.

The druid screamed, his oath ricocheting through my skull. Above me another called. A deep, dark base roaring in a language I didn't know but felt, whirling deep and black in my body. The only voice I listened to was Bran's, shouting my name, over and over.

"Trust me," I whispered even as I felt the shuddering of my heart, the slowing of its beat, the gurgle of blood pumping out of my organs and drenching my clothes.

The floor came up to meet me. The concrete rough and cool.

The druid grabbed my shirt, hauling me up, but it was too late. The link between Bran and I was broken. The power source the druid needed had winked out. For all the dominion he possessed he didn't have enough to finish the ritual. He couldn't tap into Bran's magic, or what was left of his abilities; only a witch amplifier could do that.

I'd ruined his plans.

Like a vacuum-packed sealed jar unleashing a loud *whish,* the pop exploded through the room and the seam closed.

"No. No, it can't." Padraig was reaching upwards, as if his need alone could reopen the seam, dangling me like a ragdoll, which is all I was.

My heart slowed more. The air around me stilled. Quiet washed against me.

Then my eyes closed.

No choice this time, just an easy, inevitable letting go.

CHAPTER 67

Arriving in the other realm this time was different. Even though I'd been here only a few hours ago, everything felt and looked unfamiliar.

For one thing, the light was bright white, diffused around the edges, not the murky shadows I was used to. I wore the clothes I'd been in but there were no longer any bloodstains, and I was walking upright, as if I'd been walking down the street and just turned the corner. It felt like home. Welcoming.

I wasn't expecting that. Or the sounds of birdsong somewhere in the distance. It was neither hot nor cold but a perfect temp and I felt more alive being dead than I had being alive.

Which freaked me out. Dead should feel dead.

That and the absence of a heartbeat. No sound, except for the birds, tethered me to where I'd been.

"Dad?" I called out, my voice expanding into the emptiness like a long, slow echo. "You here?"

That had been part of his plan. He, as a shaman, could cross over and meet me, but like other elements of this scheme it wasn't happening exactly as we'd discussed.

I stood there, looking around, expecting, I didn't know what. Not the wraiths, which was a good thing, but something else. Maybe I expected to feel sadness, or anguish, or even some fear. After all this was it. I wasn't visiting. The dagger I'd used to stab myself was real. My death was real. But nothing felt real.

"You have returned," a voice spoke so close to me I jumped.

Yup, let me face a demon sneaking back to Earth no
problem. Surprise me by talking over my shoulder and I fell
apart.

I twirled so fast I expected to be dizzy, but I guess you
didn't get bad side effects in this place. Good to know.

It was the Ghoul Guy, the one I'd met on other visits, only
now I could see him, just as if we'd met on a sunny street. He
was taller than I expected, maybe five ten or five eleven, with
light brown hair that held a bit of a stubborn curl. He looked
younger than me now by a couple of years but older at the
same time, as if he'd seen too much in the time he'd had before
he'd arrived here. His face was lean, hollows in his cheeks, a
stillness in his dark brown gaze, as if waiting for something
bad to happen.

Which is when I noticed what he was wearing. Khaki. A
uniform. "World War II?" I blurted out.

He nodded, a wry smile touching his lips. "1st Infantry
Division." He tapped a red badge on his shoulder. "The
Fighting First."

"What happened?" I knew I had other things to do. Finding
my dad being the first but it seemed important to know.

"Operation Torch. North Africa." His smile turned down.
"El Guettar, Béja, and Mateur. Saw them all."

"And then?"

"Battle of Gela. Sicily." The way he said it made my heart
crack. Such pain, layered with regret, wrapped in a longing so
strong it felt palpable.

"Alex?" It was my dad's voice.

At last. Relief softened my shoulders as I turned to see if I
could spot him but couldn't.

"You have to help me," Ghoul Guy said, the sound
rebreaking my heart. "You promised."

"I know. I did and I will. Just not now."

"Alex, where are you?"

"Over here, Dad," I called out, waving one hand in case he
could see me. A hand that no longer dripped blood but did have
a wicked looking scar across my palm.

Ghoul Guy reached out and tapped me. I hadn't expected
that. Before everyone on this side had been spirits, not able to

touch. His hand rested on my arm as if he too had been surprised. Or had forgotten how to touch.

A shiver ran through me as he repeated, "Remember, you promised."

"I will." I pulled away, knowing I didn't have all that much time to reach Dad, yet reluctant to simply abandon this boy man.

"Alex!" My dad who was the soul of calm and collected, raced out of the lightness and swept me into his arms. His hug was so tight I feared ribs cracking, but I didn't want to release him either. When he set me on my feet at last he was already moving. "Come. Your body is in danger."

Why wasn't I surprised?

I turned around to say good-bye to Ghoul Guy but he had disappeared.

"Hurry, Alex." My dad was holding my hand as he had when I was a child, only now he was running, racing into the light and it was all I could do to keep up with him.

The luminosity swirled around us, so clean after what I'd seen back where I'd been in the cells. "Bran?" I asked, a catch in my breath.

"Waiting." My dad shook his head. "And very angry."

"Then all's normal," I sighed, forgetting about my dad's phenomenal shifter hearing.

"I can't blame him," Dad said over his shoulder, his pace just now slowing, though how he could tell where we were was beyond me. "Seems he thinks you are too rash, foolish and what was the third? Oh, yes, take too many unnecessary risks."

"You did tell him this was your plan?" I asked. "Even with a few ad-libbed modifications."

"I'm not a fool," came his quick response as he pulled up short and turned toward me. "You ready?"

Not really. It was kind of nice to be pain free for a bit, but I knew that couldn't last. I nodded. "Yeah, go ahead."

My father stood straighter, his two hands wrapped around my shoulders, his concentration so intense I could feel him vibrating.

He began a chant in the Shoshone language, that much I recognized. I squeezed my own eyes shut, listening, hearing his words hum through me, the sound of his heart, the small beat of my own growing louder second by second.

The air around us chilled, bone-deep cold. For the space of a breath I wanted to scream, No, leave me here.

Instead I swallowed the words as I heard another voice. "Come back, Alex. Come back to me."

I opened my eyes to pain and chaos. Why had I expected anything different?

My head was cradled in Bran's lap. That was nice. No, better than nice, but like surfacing after a wave knocks you for a loop, I was trying to process too much at one time.

The smells: fresh blood and a sour, acrid taint. The sounds; fighting and shouting, and thuds of fists hitting flesh. Bran's expression, looking more strained than I'd ever seen him, his blue, blue eyes so dark and drained they looked like obsidian daggers.

"I almost lost you," he whispered, brushing one hand across my forehead, the other gripping my hand as if afraid to let go.

I tried to sit up.

Bad idea. Really bad.

Bran pressed me down, getting that what-am-I-going-to-do-with-you frown on his face. "Not yet. If I lose you again I don't have enough magic to call you back."

Pieces started clicking into place as Sabina's face came into view over Bran's shoulder.

"I told you to leave," I said through dry lips. It was meant to be a growl but came out more like a whimper.

"I did." She smiled, a grin that stretched from ear to ear, as if she was having the time of her life. Silly witch. "The Were and I and that adorable dog ran as far as we could down the hall until we heard fighting on the other end. Then we headed back this way but only came close when the druid started cursing and screaming at you for dying. Thought that was my cue."

It was but I was having a hard time getting around Franco as an adorable dog. That'd really go to his head, especially since in the version I saw him in he was butt ugly and that was being nice.

"And then," Sabina was almost breathless with excitement. "I got you. Saw you all gross and bloody, but I still grabbed your shirt and flew you over here."

Thanks, I needed that visual.

"And Bran looked nearly dead."

I glanced at him, seeing from the exhaustion on his face how close he had been.

"Sorry," I whispered, not able to do much else. What I wanted to shout was sorry for getting you into this, for sucking your magic from you, for nearly killing you.

His lips quirked as he shook his head. "Never a dull moment around you."

Sabina was obviously insensitive to the vibes and continued head long into her recap of events, "So there you were. A bloody heap next to the druid but ..." she paused as if facing her fear all over again.

I reached up to brush my hand against hers. "It's alright. The fear, I mean. He was a mega scary guy."

She nodded, the whites of her eyes quieting a bit as she glanced at Bran. "I flew you in here, though it wasn't easy—"

"Get on with it, kid," I ground, knowing dead weight was heavy but sheesh!

"Bran said to kick the cell door closed. So I did." She looked beyond the metal bars. "Once I got the chains off him enough he could move he started his magic." She glanced at him again, this time in awe. "I've so got to learn me some of that magic."

"Mage magic, kiddo. Not witch magic," I said, trying to ease Bran off the hook.

"You mean as a witch I can't do that?"

I shook my head. "Nope."

"Well that just sucks."

A laugh welled up in me. Hurt like the dickens but it was good to know one still existed inside. It winked out the second I asked, "What about the others? The team?"

"Herc's all right except his woo-woo spidey weapon got used up right away. He's not happy about that, which is why I had to run ahead and get caught. I mean they were fighting the Weres and there were a boatload of them and I couldn't wait."

Good to know where her priorities were. "And the others?"

"The bad-ass instructor dude got hurt." She must have seen my expression as she quickly followed with, "Not bad. A broken collarbone I think. Sounded painful but he'll live."

I wouldn't be telling Stone about her concern, or lack thereof, about him. "And the team?"

"The shifter one is a real ass-kicker. She tore into those Weres like she'd been waiting forever to beat the crap out of them. Did you know she was some kind of big cat? Not like a tiger but big, like a female lion only not a lion."

"No." She was exhausting me. "Didn't know."

"And Van? He's sexy as a wolf. No wonder Kelly has only eyes for him."

What? That had me squirming. No way was I going to let Kelly become one of Van's love-'em-and-leave-'em conquests. Even if she didn't mind. No way.

"Shhh," Bran soothed, actually laughing at me. He didn't know my brother. That side of my brother and I sure as hell wasn't going to let Kelly know that side either.

"I think Alex needs to know if the other members of the team are safe and where they might be now?" Bran spoke to Sabina who hung on every word.

"Oh." She shook her head. "Isn't that what I've been saying?"

Before I could groan out loud she shrugged and added, "Far as I know, they were okay. When I left them." She glanced over her shoulder toward the hallway. "I haven't seen them for a while, but as Franco and Willie and I were running back this way I heard them still fighting, only in the hallways, not outside."

"Franco got a bad gash on one paw but Willie took care of it. Then beat feet saying he was allergic to too much blood."

"Recovering Were side effects," I said. "I bet Franco will think we kept him from all the fun."

At least it sounded like they'd made it through okay, which made it easier for me to do what I needed to do next.

I squirmed in Bran's lap, which might have been very distracting in any other situation, but now all I wanted was to see what had happened to the druid.

I wished I hadn't looked. The last place I'd seen him standing there was what looked like a dried-up lump of clothes. "That him?" I didn't realize I'd spoken out loud until Bran's arms tightened around me.

"After you—after you left," what a euphemism for *killed myself* if I ever heard one, "he went crazy."

Crazy didn't leave one looking like dirty laundry. "And then?"

"I think he'd drained himself to the point there was nothing left." He glanced where I was still looking. "Closest I can describe, it was as if all the magic bled him dry, leaving his body a husk that imploded."

I might have cringed a little, but not very much in spite of what sounded like a painful way to die. But Padraig had no qualms about unleashing a demon on innocents, master minding the deaths of hundreds of thousands if not more. Payback was a bitch he deserved.

"And the demon?" I asked, turning back to look at Bran, even finding a smile for him.

"Wasn't able to pass through the portal." He brushed the back of his fingers down my face, making me want to purr. "Seems one determined witch slammed the door shut just at the right time."

I was basking in the moment, but Bran seemed to have his own agenda. Why wasn't I surprised?

"Explain how your dad was able to cross over and find you?" Bran said, his voice low and husky. "I know firsthand that I could barely think, I was locked so solid. So how did your father escape?" I waved the fingers of one hand, which was about all I could move without pain.

"Old shaman trick. Before he met with the druid, he used a pipe to smudge himself as a protection. An ancient Native American shamanistic practice that had been used a lot more than it is now, which is why dad was hoping Padraig forgot the custom."

"You mean like a peace pipe?" Sabina asked, her voice incredulous.

"That's a white man's term. Any shaman worth his salt knows the combination of herbs and tobacco needed to create protection before any startling information is shared. Whites didn't bother to learn; it isn't just some quaint ritual but a way to provide immunity from an enchantment spell."

"Which is exactly what the druid cast." Bran whistled.

I nodded and closed my eyes for a moment, accepting that my body was still healing, in micro bits by the aches and the pain twanging through me. But I was alive and that wasn't anything to sneeze about.

"What now?" I murmured, feeling all vague and fuzzy.

"Seems we wait for your team to finish routing the bad guys, find us, and hope someone has a key for the cell door," Bran said, practical and forward thinking as always.

Only one of the reasons he made me happy. Very, very happy.

CHAPTER 68

It was sunset three days later as I stood in an open balcony doorway looking out over the red and cream rooftops of Paris, my wounds mostly recovering. A few Technicolor bruises across most of my body, the spot where I'd plunged a knife into my chest still sore and a clean, deep scar on my palm healing into a white ridge. Not bad for being all the way dead not that long ago.

"You look pensive," Bran said from the sole bed in the room. I glanced in his direction because he looked good, damn good, rumpled and sexy among the white sheets. For a second I forgot about what was tumbling through my mind. Which was good and sorely needed.

"Just thinking." I shrugged and turned back as if to memorize the skyline. "You know, this is how I thought of Paris," I admitted, running one hand along the crisp cotton curtains bracketing the doorway, inhaling deeply of the cooling spring breeze. Not cold enough to shut the door just yet, but enough to have me rubbing my bare arms. The ecru silk nightgown Bran had given me was not meant for warmth. Well, not the kind of stand-alone kind of warmth.

Without my hearing him, Bran was suddenly beside me, pulling my back against his naked chest and long, lean legs, wrapping his arms around me, resting his head against the top of mine. Warlock blanket. I liked it and knew I could so easily get used to this.

"Want to share what's putting a crease between your eyes?"

Mages could see way too much. "Is that a nice way to tell me I'm looking haggard?" I asked, trying to go for light, though I failed miserably.

"What is it?" he asked, all seriousness in his voice. "Your father and Van are well. Your team came through mostly unscathed."

"Except for Stone and Mandy." Sabina had been right. Stone earned a broken collarbone, several cracked ribs, and brain lash while fighting a particularly nasty Were. Mandy had reinjured her arm, the one broken when I'd called an echo demon during early days of training. A time that seemed years ago, yet was less than a month or two. Amazing how fighting preternaturals made time fly.

"Your comrades were hurt but they will recover," Bran said.

"This time." The words slipped out unbidden.

"Is that's what's bothering you?" He turned me in his arms, no doubt trying to distract me with the breadth of his very solid, and very yummy shoulders. Ones I'd been admiring since we'd arrived here, to recuperate he'd said. Ha! No one told me recuperating could be so fun, and inventive.

Bran had been gentle, and insisting we take things slow physically between us. I think he just wanted to torture me or drive me crazy. Kisses and touches were divine but not when my body craved more. More of him. More of us. More reassurance that we were both alive and alive was good.

Have I mentioned patience is not one of my strong suits?

"Alex, talk to me," he murmured, grabbing both my hands in his so I couldn't continue rubbing my fingers along his skin in ever widening swirls. And I had been having such fun.

"Fine." Yes, I said it in that way that meant there was nothing fine about any of the situation. So I stepped back, just enough to be able to breathe instead of swimming on the scent of Bran's skin just inches from me.

"Talk to me," he said again in that CEO voice that said he wasn't going to stop until I did. Didn't he get the male handbook that said all talking was inherently dangerous? I was so going to have to get him together with my brothers for some serious clarification.

On second thought, nix that.

I was avoiding. I do that when I'm just not ready to bare my soul. As in all the time. So go with the easy issue first. "Sure, we stopped Padraig, but what about the demon? There were more Council members who were working with Padraig to release that demon and that doesn't count the Seekers. How are we going to stop them?"

Bran scrubbed his hand over his face. "One problem at a time. Your father now has some leverage over the remaining three known Council members who supported the druid. That might help keep them in line, and your father is not without his own allies on the Council."

Council politics made me itch. I raised my gaze to Bran. "And the Seekers?"

"I don't know, Alex, I seriously don't know."

That's not what I wanted to hear. Bran was the focused one, the one who made decisions and took action. On the other hand he was right. He was a dress designer, not a trained, or somewhat trained agent sent to fight the preternatural bad guys. Which is what my real problem was.

I turned away from him totally, stepping farther out on the balcony, watching the sun inch closer to the horizon, wondering why stopping one very bad guy and saving the world just wasn't enough some days. Like today.

"You're thinking about us, aren't you?" he laughed behind me. Laughed?

I twisted to face him so fast my hair flew in a curtain of black behind me. "You think this is funny? There is nothing funny about any of this."

He went to step closer, then thought better of it and paused, struggling to wedge his lips into a serious cant. "You make me happy," he said, stealing all the air out of my blustery sails. "That's why I'm smiling."

He took that last step, that put him close enough he could cup my shoulders, not holding me as much as reassuring himself that I was really there.

"If you didn't care too, you wouldn't be so agitated."

Oh, for being so dam sexy the man had a few things to learn. One did not call one's lover agitated. No matter how true it was. "I'm not—"

He placed his fingers across my lips. "You care, that's what matters and so do I."

There, he did it again, that melting my heart thing. So not fair.

"But is this real?" I asked in a wimpy-assed voice that did not sound at all like me.

"You mean what's happening between us?"

I couldn't speak around the solid lump in my throat so I nodded, keeping my eyes focused on his chest again, not trusting myself to meet his gaze.

"Are you thinking of the prophecy?" His voice at least had turned serious, though his fingers were playing with my hair. An action I don't think he was even aware of.

"Yes." He'd nailed it. "I don't want to be here, with you, simply because of some silly announcement made by a coven and witches and warlocks who knows how long ago."

He nodded, then repeated the words he'd used to describe the prophecy the first time he'd told me about it. "Acies, acendo, adamo. Lost in the mists of time, the meeting has been foretold between a powerful warlock and the even more powerful witch who would bring him to his knees and start the time of change."

"Change, no problem, before you said something more."

"The time of loss," he finished, shadows in his gaze.

"That's the part that gives me the heebie-jeebies. As if fighting wicked powerful uber bad guys isn't enough, now I have to deal with bringing loss. To who? Us? Me? The world?" I shook my head, the aches through my body punctuating my resistance. "I can only handle so much," I said. My voice low, almost cracking. "I have barely tapped being a witch, not to mention developing as a shaman." And fulfilling my promise to a ghost on the other side. "And now with this shifter blood ... I can't—"

This time he silenced me with a kiss. His lips firm and coaxing, covering mine, teasing me to join him, to release the frustration and fear and yes, the agitation rocketing through me. When he finally raised his head I swore my knees were weak and his body was telling me loud and clear where it wanted that kiss to lead.

"That's not fair," I murmured.

He smiled again, that sexy, all-male, hot warlock smile. He so did not play by Noziak rules. Yet he was serious as he whispered, his hands once again in my hair. "I don't have all the answers," he said, his voice low and husky. "But I'm here. I'll be here until you push me away and together—"

He rushed the last word when I squeaked at the thought of pushing him away. Not just yet, it'd taken us both too much to get together.

"And together," he continued, taking my hand and leading me back to the bed, "we'll find answers."

"To what the prophecy means?" Have I mentioned that I don't do the trust thing real well either?

"Yes, to the prophecy."

"And my being a shaman?"

"I'm sure your father will help there." He raised his free hand to stop my jumping into the whole we're-not-where-we-once-were-relationship-wise issue with my dad. We were doing better but shadows still remained. Bran continued, "We don't have to solve that issue this week, this month or anytime soon. But he will help, you know that?"

We paused by the bed, my feeling like a sulky kid as I nodded. "Yeah, I know that."

"Good. And the shifter issue we'll tackle, too."

He'd said the "we" word. Hard to feel alone and overwhelmed when someone you cared about made it clear they weren't going away, in fact, they were staying close, to help.

"So we're together?" I asked, looking at him, no doubt my heart was in my eyes because it sure damn well was making it hard to breathe.

"Yes. We're together." He gathered me in his arms then, which is the one place I wanted to be. Then he almost messed everything up by adding, "Sometimes I want to hate you—"

My gaze locked with his.

But he wasn't finished. "Because you have touched me like no other woman has ever touched me and I am changed until the day I die."

Those were not tears in my eyes. So not.

Leave it to a warlock to break down my barriers.

"I know you're scared, Alex, about what's between us, but so am I. You hold my happiness, my sanity in your hands."

When I could speak again I cleared my throat. "Damn, and here all I wanted was some hot, sweaty sex."

He started laughing, throwing back his head in one of those deep chested it's-good-to-be-alive chuckles as he scooped me up off my feet and tossed me on the bed. "Good! That works for me."

Then he went on to prove it. Several times.

What aches and pains?

CHAPTER 69

Stone sat on the arm of the chair in Ling Mai's hotel room once again. Vaughn at his side this time. Only a week since the last time he'd met with Ling Mai alone. A lot had happened in one week. Alex was alive. A new member had joined who proved her mettle in a fight, though would take some time to settle in with the other women. Two younger recruits who looked like they'd become the nucleus of an Invisible Recruit Academy for young and gifted teens. Plus, the team had managed to stop a three-thousand-year-old demon from returning and annihilating mankind. The Council of Seven wasn't so happy with them, being down to six members and their nasty factions exposed to outsiders.

Tough, they could deal with it. His team was still alive, though hurting, even more than last week, with the bandages around his shoulder and ribs chaffing on a lot of levels.

Ling Mai walked in looking as she always did, calm, collected and totally enigmatic. "You are feeling well?" she asked of him.

"Well enough."

Vaughn gave him a small nudge to his hip, probably one of the only places on his body not damaged. What? Was he supposed to moan and groan?

"Good." Ling Mai cut short the glare Vaughn was giving him. "I have been considering what you said not long ago. About the need for further training and more recruits."

"And?"

"Your concerns have merit."

Stone bit back a snort. Damn right they had merit. Every fight they'd gone into so far they'd walked away from by the skin of their teeth. That was a crapshoot waiting for casualties.

But Ling Mai obviously had an agenda. Nothing new there. She gave a soft cough as if to refocus him. "I think it would behoove us to accept a small job, one where all the team is not needed to participate."

Stone didn't say anything, though the skin along his neck told him there was no such thing as a small job. Not in their line of business. It was Vaughn who was left to ask, "Meaning?"

"There is an item. A rare one which is called an *orkheos*."

"An orchid?" Vaughn asked. Leave it to her to understand Latin or Greek or whatever language the word was in.

"The word orchid derives from *orkheos* but it does have other meanings." She and Vaughn exchanged a funny smile.

"I'll explain later," Vaughn said to him as if there was a private joke.

They were going flower collecting now? He asked, "What's so special about this orchid?"

"I have information which indicates this *orkeos* is a key which can lead us to more intelligence regarding the Seekers."

"The ones Alex spoke about?" Vaughn asked, stifling a shudder that Stone caught in spite of her best attempt.

"Yes."

"Do we have any other intel about who they are or what they want?" Stone

asked.

"Not enough to create an effective defense against them," Ling Mai said,

her voice sounding determined. "I have the Librarian working on seeing what she

can find."

Ah, the all-knowing librarian. This mysterious figure who kept track of preternaurals, to figure out who bred with whom to see if their offspring were human or non-human. She also appeared to keep a tab on all things preternatural and then sold that intel to those willing to pay.

"So we do what?" Stone asked, zeroing in on business. "Send a small group in to collect this orchid, or *orkheos*?"

"That was my idea. We don't need more than three or four agents at the most."

It was sounding too easy again. Then Vaughn spoke up, "If it's a straight snatch and grab undertaking I think it's time Kelly led an assignment."

Both Stone and Ling Mai looked at her, waiting for the punch line.

Vaughn offered her palms up, classic body langue for giving. "I'm not ready to be much help and neither are Mandy or Stone."

Nice way to massage his ego, which they both knew she was doing.

She continued, "Nicki isn't ready in spite of her shifter abilities. Alex needs some recovery time so why not let Kelly take the lead, and Jaylene and Nicki back her up with Mandy acting as control central in a stationary location."

"She has a point," Stone conceded, earning another poke at his hip. At this rate it was going to be as bruised as the rest of his body. "If it is a straightforward operation." His tone indicated that he was still concerned. Still, he continued, "Running an op will give her some more self-confidence. Make her a stronger team member."

Vaughn was nodding even as Ling Mai cleared her throat again. "There might be one small problem."

He knew it. He absolutely fucking knew it. It was never easy, especially with Ling Mai. He found himself bracing as he asked, "Because?"

"Because the orchid is blooming near the area of Africa where Kelly's sister was killed."

That was it? He glanced at Vaughn before saying out loud what they were both thinking. "That shouldn't be an insurmountable issue."

"I don't know." Vaughn was pursing her lips and not in the good let's-kiss way. More let-me-throw-a-kink-in-the-works kind of way. "That could be very emotional for her."

"Agents can't afford emotions," Stone snapped, wondering, and not for the first time, what he was doing leading a team of all women. Talk about a touchy-feely quagmire.

"Don't be stupid," Vaughn shot back, then turned toward Ling Mai. "I'm still sure Kelly can do an excellent job. Not—"she cut a sharp glance at Stone.

"Not because she can not handle her emotions but because she knows there's a job to do and she's qualified to see it through."

Whatever.

Ling Mai looked to Stone. "Do you agree?"

"Yeah. The part about letting Kelly lead. She'll have back up. Vaughn and I can give feedback via headquarters in Maryland. Those who need some healing time can get it. Let Kelly go in, find this *orkheos,* and get out."

Ling Mai's smile told him he'd said the right thing. The absence of Vaughn poking at him also let him know he had her support, maybe not for the reasons she wanted, but it wouldn't be the first time he said tomahto and she said tomato. So why was his gut telling him even easy missions could backfire?

THE END

Did You Like INVISIBLE FATE?

Let the world know by posting a review on Goodreads or Shelfari. Write a Customer Review. You = Awesome. Me = Grateful.
I also love hearing from readers! Find me on Goodreads or Facebook or Twitter!

Questions? Comments?

Help make the next edition of this book even better. If you've found a pesky typo in this book, here's your chance to let me know. Have a writing craft issue you'd like me to cover in the next books in this series, let me know. Email suggestions to:
Assistant@MaryBuckham.com

PRAISE FOR MARY BUCKHAM'S BOOKS

"Not since Kate Daniels and Mercy Thompson have I fallen in love with a female character like I have with Alex Noziak." ~Urban Girl Reader.

"This is a definite must read for anyone who enjoys a bit of a thrill, a good laugh, and great characters with attitude." ~Parchment Place

"I. . .encourage those of you who like action, magic and sassy heroines to snatch up this series." ~Romancing the Genres

Want to read more about Alex Noziak and the Invisible Recruit team? Check out:

INVISIBLE PRISON (novella)
On her first days with the Invisible Recruit Agency, Alex Noziak learns she's not the only recruit with secrets to hide. But hers could get her kicked off the Team even before she begins Or they could get her killed.

INVISIBLE MAGIC
(full length novel)

On her first official mission for the Invisible Recruit Agency Alex Noziak discovers that to save the innocent she must call upon her untested abilities. But at what cost? She has nothing to lose, except her life.

INVISIBLE DUTY (novella)

The mission sounded easy for Alex Noziak, part witch/part shaman. And easy is what she needed. But in the heart of Africa, she finds something so deadly it will test her in ways she never expected.

INVISIBLE POWER (full-length novel)

When Alex has a chance to save her brother and expose the Weres who held him hostage, she must make a hard choice with lives at risk, including her own.

**Be the First to Find Out When the next books in the
INVISIBLE RECRUITS series come out.**
Sign up for my newsletter on
MaryBuckham.com

KELLY MCALLISTER BOOKS
COMING IN 2014

INVISIBLE FEARS
(novel – coming Spring 2014)

She's a human fighting for the preternaturals.
He's a preternatural fighting for the humans.
Kelly McAllister's Invisible Recruit mission is to destroy a threat to preternaturals. Van Noziak's military mission is to retrieve and deliver a botanical bio-weapon. In deepest Africa the race against a deadly bloom reveals secrets, exposes fears and forces unlikely alliances.

INVISIBLE SECRETS
(novel – coming Fall 2014)

INVISIBLE EMBRACE
(novel – coming Winter 2014)

ABOUT THE AUTHOR

 A USA Today bestselling author I started my career writing romantic suspense novels. Nothing like bombs and gunfire making a relationship more complicated. Between publication dates I was also fortunate to become a writing craft instructor, offering live workshops around the US and Canada as well as online workshops to writers throughout the world. As fun as the travel, and getting to know so many writers of all genres was, my first love has always been fiction. Thus the Invisible Recruit series was born and took off running!

I love conflict. On the page. The conflict between dark magic and white. The conflict between beings created with different needs and wants. Witches. Mage warlocks. Shifters, Weres, and demons all trying to co-exist against their natures. Bring it on!

I'm a huge paranormal and fantasy lover. Especially Urban Fantasy and any paranormal fantasy series that allows me to throw myself into magic and mystery page after page, book after book.

The paranormal world of the Invisible Recruits is built on women who must learn to embrace their preternatural talents to fight good and evil. Talents that they've hidden from the human population for fear of being different.

But because I love conflict I've dropped these women into a world where magic and fantasy exist side by side with humans intentionally kept in the dark about Shifters, Weres, warlocks, witches, and especially about magic.

Throw in a strong dose of romantic suspense, emotional relationships to add more conflict, and paranormal beings you've never heard of before, and you'll know why readers can't get enough of this fast-paced paranormal thriller series.

www.MaryBuckham.com
www.InvisibleRecruits.com